"You should be in bed," Shea said when her heartbeat settled down. "You've been shot, remember?"

She tried her hardest not to stare at Nick's bare chest. A man shouldn't look so good in nothing but a pair of jeans, she thought.

"So should you," he said.

"*I* haven't been shot," she countered.

But she might have been, she remembered. "Would you really have shot me back there?" she asked in a soft voice.

He hesitated, then said, "Probably." Something smoldered in his eyes, and she realized he could see right through her nightgown. His eyes were riveted below her waist.

"But I'm glad I didn't have to," he added huskily. "It would be a shame to scar those legs of yours." He very slowly lifted his eyes to her face, taking his time, and gave her a crooked smile that set her heart to pounding again. "A *real* shame…"

Dear Reader,

As always, Intimate Moments offers you six terrific books to fill your reading time, starting with Terese Ramin's *Her Guardian Agent*. For FBI agent Hazel Youvella, the case that took her back to revisit her Native American roots was a very personal one. For not only did she find the hero of her heart in Native American tracker Guy Levoie, she discovered the truth about the missing child she was seeking. This wasn't just any child—this was *her* child.

If you enjoyed last month's introduction to our FIRSTBORN SONS in-line continuity, you won't want to miss the second installment. Carla Cassidy's *Born of Passion* will grip you from the first page and leave you longing for the rest of these wonderful linked books. Valerie Parv takes a side trip from Silhouette Romance to debut in Intimate Moments with a stunner of a reunion romance called *Interrupted Lullaby*. Karen Templeton begins a new miniseries called HOW TO MARRY A MONARCH with *Plain-Jane Princess,* and Linda Winstead Jones returns with *Hot on His Trail,* a book you should be hot on the trail of yourself. Finally, welcome Sharon Mignerey back and take a look at her newest, *Too Close for Comfort.*

And don't forget to look in the back of this book to see how Silhouette can make you a star.

Enjoy them all, and come back next month for more of the best and most exciting romance reading around.

Yours,

Leslie J. Wainger
Executive Senior Editor

Please address questions and book requests to:
Silhouette Reader Service
U.S.: 3010 Walden Ave., P.O. Box 1325, Buffalo, NY 14269
Canadian: P.O. Box 609, Fort Erie, Ont. L2A 5X3

Hot on His Trail
LINDA WINSTEAD JONES

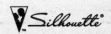

INTIMATE MOMENTS™

Published by Silhouette Books

America's Publisher of Contemporary Romance

With many thanks to my good friend Sabrah Agee, and to all the good people of Marion, Alabama.

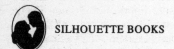 SILHOUETTE BOOKS

ISBN 0-373-27167-0

HOT ON HIS TRAIL

Copyright © 2001 by Linda Winstead Jones

This edition published by arrangement with Harlequin Books S.A.

® and TM are trademarks of Harlequin Books S.A., used under license. Trademarks indicated with ® are registered in the United States Patent and Trademark Office, the Canadian Trade Marks Office and in other countries.

Visit Silhouette at www.eHarlequin.com

Printed in U.S.A.

Books by Linda Winstead Jones

Silhouette Intimate Moments

Bridger's Last Stand #924
Every Little Thing #1007
Madigan's Wife #1068
Hot on His Trail #1097

LINDA WINSTEAD JONES

has loved books of all kinds for as long as she can remember, spending her leisure hours with Nancy Drew and Miss Marple, or lost in worlds created by writers like Margaret Mitchell and Robert Heinlein. After years as an avid reader she decided to try her hand at writing her own stories. Since 1994 she's been publishing historical and fantasy romance, winning the Colorado Romance Writers' Award of Excellence for her 1996 time-travel story *Desperado's Gold*. With the publication of *Bridger's Last Stand,* her first book for Silhouette Intimate Moments, Linda stepped into the exciting arena of contemporary romance.

At home in Alabama, she divides her time between her husband, three sons, two dogs, reading whatever she can get her hands on and writing romance.

SILHOUETTE MAKES YOU A STAR!
Feel like a star with Silhouette.
Look for the exciting details of our new contest
inside all of these fabulous Silhouette novels:

Prologue

No one would look at him. Five men and seven women filed gravely into their seats, their eyes on the floor or their shoes or the back of the juror before them. One woman dabbed at her red eyes. Tears. That couldn't possibly be a good sign. Nick's heart felt like it was about to burst through his chest.

The judge didn't look at Nick, either, nor did the aide who remained close by the judge's side. The assistant district attorney appeared to be supremely bored. His steely gaze wandered the room in an aimless way.

Nick's own lawyer didn't look at him, either. Norman's solemn eyes were on a blank sheet of paper on the table. His fingers worked restlessly.

From beyond this very small part of the world, in the seats beyond the jury box, eyes were trained on Nick. He knew that. But in the past two weeks he had learned to ignore those onlookers so completely they ceased to exist. His mind had remained on the witnesses against him, the evidence the D.A. had presented so competently, the defense Norman had put together.

His defense was simple, but it was enough. It had to be. Innocent men didn't go to prison for the rest of their lives. They didn't go to the electric chair.

At the judge's direction, he and Norman rose to their feet. Still, no one looked his way. Not the judge, not the D.A., not the members of the jury. Everything was so…quiet. Nick wondered if they could all hear the beat of his pounding heart and the way the blood rushed through his veins, so loudly he could hear the roar in his ears.

He waited to hear the words *"Not guilty."* He waited for Norman to smile, to clap him on the back, for relieved eyes to turn his way at last.

Guilty. At first he wasn't sure he'd heard correctly. The noise that followed the verdict was deafening. The crowd murmured loudly, with individual voices raised. A few men and women hurried from the room: reporters, damn them all to hell. The judge banged his gavel, and the sheriff's deputies came to take Nick away. They didn't look at him, either. Norman said something low and indistinct, something Nick couldn't hear for the roar in his ears.

Numbly, he allowed the two sheriff's deputies to lead him away. Through the side door, through the small office, into the hall by way of a doorway near the elevator that would take him back to jail. Back to jail.

His heart beat much too hard now, threatening to burst through his chest. He couldn't breathe. His vision dimmed. *Guilty?*

One of the deputies reached for his handcuffs. In a move more instinctive than deliberate, Nick lunged for the man's weapon.

Chapter 1

Shea ran up two courthouse steps, spun around quickly and lifted a hand to her hair. She smoothed one dark strand, which barely brushed her shoulder. "Do I look okay?"

Mark, in his usual ratty T-shirt and a backwards ball cap that covered most of his bright red hair, cocked his head and glanced from behind his video camera to smile at her. He was the same age as Shea, twenty-five, but could easily pass for sixteen years old. Since he didn't stand much more than five foot six he looked like a kid lugging around that big camera. "You're beautiful, sweetheart."

She didn't feel beautiful. The August heat was suffocating, humid and almost overwhelming. Her hair was going to fall, her makeup was going to melt...and she had to look her best.

If she'd had more time she might have chosen the royal-blue suit instead of the red one, but it was too late to worry about that now. The call from the station had been unexpected, and she'd had less than fifteen minutes to put on her makeup and change clothes. Fortunately, she was getting good at this. Concessions had to be made, though, in the name of expediency. Her legs were bare and she was wearing a pair of running shoes instead of the red pumps that matched this suit.

It didn't matter; she'd only be on camera from the waist up.

"So," Mark said casually, the heavy camera that was resting on his shoulder leaning precariously to one side. "What did you give Astrid to make her sick?" He wagged his pale eyebrows and gave her a devilish smile.

Shea restrained the childish impulse to stick out her tongue. "Nothing, I swear." She grasped the microphone nervously; her palms were sweating. Oh, she never got nervous filing a story!

But then, she'd never covered a story like this one. Astrid Stanton had been with Channel 43 for nearly seven years, and the Nicholas Taggert murder trial was *her* story. She'd even gotten a few seconds of play on the network. *The network!* If not for a nasty bout of the stomach flu— which Shea had absolutely nothing to do with—it would be Astrid standing here; six foot tall, blond-haired, blue-eyed, ratings-go-through-the-roof-when-she-smiles Astrid.

"Weird case," Mark said, sensing Shea's nervousness and trying to make conversation. "I mean, Taggert actually killed his neighbor because the guy was painting his house the color of Kermit the Frog?"

"Chartreuse," Shea said. "The color was chartreuse."

"Whatever," Mark answered with a grin.

"And there has to be more to it than that," she mumbled, as much to herself as to Mark. "People don't kill over something so inconsequential." At least, she hoped they didn't. The very possibility was depressing.

This was Shea's chance, and she knew it. Reporting the

news was what she wanted to do more than anything else in the world, and she was tired of filling in for the weatherman on the weekends, sick of smiling inanely through stories on how pets looked like their owners or how a bunch of schoolkids had celebrated spring with kite day. She was in this business to cover real news, and murder was as real as it got.

The jury was coming in; they had that much. No one had much doubt as to what the verdict would be. Even though Nicholas Taggert had maintained his innocence throughout the trial, the evidence was overwhelming. The state had DNA—a couple of stray hairs on a blood-and-paint-stained Taggert Construction T-shirt. A small amount of the same blood and paint had been found in Taggert's kitchen. They had the murder weapon, a baseball bat with Taggert's fingerprints on it, and several neighbors had witnessed a heated argument between Taggert and his neighbor, the late Gary Winkler.

Still, Taggert had been convincing on the stand as he'd professed his innocence, and these days when you put twelve people together and called them a jury, anything was possible.

Nicholas Taggert had been residing in the jail on the ninth floor of the Madison County Courthouse for the past ten months, as there had been no bond set for this bizarre and grisly case. Today a jury would decide if he'd remain imprisoned until his sentence—either life without parole or death by electric chair—was passed, or if he'd go free.

Shea's producer, Kimberly Lane, came bursting through the courthouse doors. ''Guilty,'' she said, breathless from her run from the second floor.

A deep breath calmed Shea. Suddenly her palms were dry, her heartbeat slowed and she was no longer nervous. *I can do this. It's who I am, it's what I want.* Her shoulders squared as Mark nodded to her, and she lifted the microphone to her mouth.

"This is Shea Sinclair reporting for Channel 43 live from the Madison County Courthouse, where Nicholas Taggert has just been found guilty of murder. Ten months ago the successful building contractor was accused of killing his neighbor, Gary Winkler. Mr. Winkler—"

An unexpected bursting noise, like a firecracker, broke her concentration, and Shea snapped her head around so she could see the glass courthouse doors. "That was a gunshot," she said softly into the microphone. Muffled shouts followed, and then another sharp report of gunfire from within the building.

She climbed a step, her eyes on the doors.

"Get back here!" Mark growled at her. She looked at him once, just to make sure he was following her, and ignored his advice.

"There seems to be something happening in the courthouse," she said softly and clearly. "Whether or not it's related to the Taggert trial, I can't say at this time."

A man with a gun in his hand pushed through the doors and onto the covered walkway that encircled the courthouse. Shea recognized Taggert right away, with his neat black hair and expensive gray suit.

That face was unforgettable, even if it hadn't been plastered regularly on the evening news and in the newspapers for the past ten months. It was handsome, with intelligent eyes and distinct, sharp lines. More than one woman who'd glanced at Taggert's picture had proclaimed it a crying shame that he'd gone bad. "What a waste," Astrid had said on several occasions.

Mark yelled this time. "Shea, get down here right now!"

She glanced over her shoulder to see that he had his camera on the escaped murderer, but she ignored his order and took another step toward Taggert. Maybe she could catch a word from the convicted murderer with her microphone. Oh, this was too good.

Taggert limped, she noticed, dragging his right leg with every lurching step he took. As he came closer she saw that there was a nasty hole in his pant leg, and he was bleeding badly. He left a thin trail of blood on the white concrete pathway as he headed for the steps.

The courthouse doors burst open again, and five law enforcement officers rushed out, weapons drawn. Two Madison County deputies came through the doors first, and three Huntsville City uniformed policemen were right behind them. No one fired; there were too many civilians on the street and the sidewalk.

"Are you getting this?" she asked softly, her eyes never leaving the drama that was taking place just a few feet away.

"Yeah baby, I got it, I got it," Mark whispered.

There were other camera crews in the area, but she and Mark were closest. No one else would have a shot like this one on the five o'clock news. No one. Shea smiled.

Taggert jogged in her direction, and he locked the coldest, bluest eyes she'd ever seen onto her face. Suddenly she realized that the pictures in the newspapers and the clips on the evening news had not done justice to his size. The man was tall—over six feet, surely; wide in the shoulders and long legged. Shea's smile faded, and she shivered from the top of her head to the tips of her toes. Taggert was pale, and frantic, and dangerous...and staggering straight at her.

She waited too late to take Mark's advice and retreat from the situation. Taggert grabbed her microphone and tossed it away, and in a swift, sure move he wrapped one arm around her waist and spun her about with a jerk, so that she faced the advancing officers. Her heart leaped into her throat as she stared down the barrels of several guns.

Taggert backed down the steps, the hand that held his weapon snaking past her waist as he took aim at the officers.

"Put 'em down," he said hoarsely. His hot breath touched her neck, and she could feel his irregular breathing against her skin. The officers didn't immediately do as he asked, so he wedged the gun he held into Shea's side. The oddly warm black metal pressed sharply against a rib.

The advancing armed men came to an immediate halt and lowered their weapons.

"Now, Taggert," a gray-haired deputy in a khaki uniform said calmly. His Southern drawl was like molasses, thick and sweet and dark. "Let the girl go and come on back in. We can write this off as a moment of poor judgment on your part, get you to a hospital and get that leg fixed up, and then we'll just forget it ever happened."

"Yeah, right," Taggert said into her ear, his hoarse voice so low Shea was sure no one but she could hear.

A tall, thin man in a dark suit skirted around the lawmen. Shea recognized him, from numerous news reports, as Taggert's lawyer, Norman Burgess. "Come on, Nick," he said calmly. "Let the lady go, give me the weapon and let's go back inside." Absurdly, his voice was almost sweet, serene and musical. "It's not over. We can appeal."

"They don't believe me," Taggert whispered again. Shea didn't know if the statement was meant to be heard or if the injured man was talking to himself. His arm tightened around her, and he dragged her down another step.

One cop raised his gun. *I can take him.* Shea read his lips as he whispered. She didn't have to read the lips of the deputy who reached out to make him lower the weapon again, drawling a loud curse as he tried to avoid more bloodshed.

"You might hit the girl," he added in a calmer voice.

As if she wasn't panicked enough with the muzzle of a gun stuck to her ribs! That one hothead would take the chance without a second thought, if he believed he'd get Taggert. She was expendable…but not as long as Mark had the camera on her and Taggert. No law enforcement agency could afford that kind of bad press.

"A car," Taggert whispered breathlessly into her ear again, and he jerked around so they were half facing the street. "Is one of these yours?"

She made a split second decision, an easy one when she weighed all her options. "The red Saturn," she said, nodding her head in the direction of the car that was parked at the curb. "The keys are in my pocket, and you can have them. Just let me go."

The idea of getting into the car with Taggert terrified her. He was desperate, he had a weapon and she remembered too well the stories Astrid had filed on him. A former military man, he'd spent several years in Special Forces. Before that he'd been a teenage troublemaker. The state had made part of their case the fact that Taggert was capable of anything.

He dragged her toward the car, holding her in a viselike grip and keeping her body between him and the officers. He kept the gun pressed tightly to her ribs.

Burgess ran down the steps. "Nick, you're making a terrible mistake. This is kidnapping!"

"The keys," Taggert said, the whispered words an unquestionable order.

Shea reached into the pocket of her red jacket and pulled out a small silver key chain with the initials S.L.S. engraved in the center in a delicate script. Two keys hung from the chain— one to the car, the other to her apartment. She considered trying to remove her house key, then decided against it. Her trembling hands would make the task too difficult, and besides, she could have the locks changed this afternoon.

"Here," she said. "Take the car and let me go."

Taggert ignored her request for freedom, but he did take the keys from her hand. His hold on her faltered for a fraction of a second as he made the transfer. "If anyone follows, I'll shoot her," he rasped, tightening his grip as he made the threat. "Let me get away clean, and in two hours I'll release her. You have my word."

"Nick, don't," Burgess whispered.

The door to her Saturn was unlocked, and Taggert reached behind him and threw it open. He sat down hard and brought Shea with him. She dropped back and down, and ended up sitting in his lap and practically falling to the front passenger seat. Warm blood touched the back of her calf. He was bleeding pretty badly; maybe he'd pass out....

With the hand that held the weapon he threatened her with, Taggert slammed the passenger-side door shut, and for the first time Shea actively tried to get away. The slamming of the door was so final, so terrifying. Gun or no gun, she refused to willingly ride off with a murderer.

She used her elbows first, lashing back into his ribs with all her might. One elbow connected solidly and Taggert grunted, but he didn't loosen his grip. She used her feet, kicking back blindly. Taggert let out a howl when the heel of one running shoe connected solidly with his injured leg. While he yelled she snapped her head back and bashed his nose. He let out a string of low curses and grabbed her hair, twisting her head and forcing her to look at him. He held her so tightly she couldn't move, not even to look away.

Her short struggle gave the officers an opportunity to move closer to the car, but with Taggert in control there was nothing they could do. The escaped murderer glanced

at them and made sure they saw the gun he had pointed
at her head.

His face hovered close to hers, so close she could see
the dark stubble on his chin and the beads of sweat on his
brow. A thin trickle of blood seeped from one nostril. Shea
shivered. The ice-blue eyes he locked on her were colder,
more menacing, than anything she'd ever seen.

"I don't want to hurt you," he whispered.

"Then let me go." She struggled against his grasp as
he slowly maneuvered over the console and into the
driver's seat. His hold on her never slackened. His moves
smooth and sure and amazingly quick, he placed the
weapon between his legs and jammed the key into the
ignition.

Instinctively, she reached for the gun. She was fast, but
not fast enough. The engine started, and Taggert snagged
the gun before she could. He pointed it at her chest.
"Don't make me hurt you."

He released his hold on her, slammed the car into drive
and took off. The weapon he pointed at her never wavered.
When they were well down the street he glanced at her,
and those icy eyes softened a little. "I'm really not going
to hurt you," he said. "In two hours I'll let you go. I
promise."

Shea settled warily back against the seat, her eyes on
the weapon Taggert lowered slowly. She was terrified; she
was angry. And for some odd reason, she believed him.

He didn't have much time. They'd have news helicopters in the air in a matter of minutes, and while they might
not attack while he had a hostage, they would definitely
be looking for him. In order to make this work, he had to
disappear.

Nick glanced in the rearview mirror. An unmarked car
followed, at a distance of course. Since he had a hostage,

they were playing it safe, being cautious, but if they could stop him now they would. That wouldn't do.

He turned right, and then quickly turned right again, and before the car that was following turned onto the residential street, he made a sharp turn into a narrow alley that ran between two old houses. The car lurched as it hit a pothole.

His heart pounded so hard he could feel it, and in his head he could still hear the guilty verdict and the roar of the courtroom that had followed. His leg was bleeding badly and the girl sitting in the passenger seat looked like she was thinking of opening the door and jumping out, taking her chances that the fall would be less dangerous than he was. He cast a quick, warning glance in her direction to change her mind. And then he returned his attention to his driving. He concentrated on getting out of here in one piece, and tried to dismiss the nagging certainty that he'd just made a bad situation worse. He had nowhere to go from here.

He knew these downtown neighborhoods well; he'd renovated several of the historic homes here, when he'd first started his business. Years ago, a lifetime ago. Another sharp turn put him in a backyard, where he was hidden from view for a few moments. The car bounced over a short stretch of rough terrain until he found another dirt lane, one that led to another quiet street.

With one hand on the steering wheel, Nick drove the car down a series of tree-lined roadways. The major roads would be covered; there was no way he'd be able to drive straight out of town. News helicopters were probably already overhead, but the heavy canopy of trees in this old neighborhood would keep the car out of sight. For now.

He wasn't a hundred percent, mentally or physically, right now—not even close—so two hands on the wheel would have been better…but he didn't dare set the pistol down again.

The adrenaline pumped through his veins, adrenaline and fear and rage. The rage kept him going, kept him from pulling the car over and collapsing. He'd been so sure the verdict would be not guilty. He was innocent, and if the system worked, if there was any justice…

But there wasn't any justice. If a man could be convicted of a murder he didn't commit, if everyone was so damn quick to convict an innocent man, then there wasn't any justice at all.

His leg throbbed. It had been blessedly numb until the girl had kicked it, and before too much longer it would hurt like hell. It continued to bleed, but the flow had slowed some. He'd have to bandage it…soon.

Nick again glanced sideways at the girl he'd grabbed from the courthouse steps. She'd fought for a while, but now she was quiet and she no longer gripped the door handle as if she was thinking of jumping. He half expected to see tears, fear, anger, anxiety—but she remained relatively calm. Her hazel-green eyes were fixed on him, clear and unafraid, and at that moment she looked very familiar, like an old friend whose face you recall but whose name escapes you. She was a reporter, he knew. Hell, he'd grabbed the microphone from her hand and tossed it down. But still he couldn't place her. He just couldn't quite remember…

"How'd you get away?" she asked softly, just a hint of the South in her voice.

"What difference does it make?" He returned his attention to the empty, tree-lined road that headed up Monte Sano Mountain.

"I want to know, that's all."

He hadn't planned it. Up until the moment the jury foreman said "guilty," Nick had been so sure he'd be walking out of that courtroom a free man. "A deputy was taking me upstairs to the jail, but before he could put the cuffs back on I grabbed his pistol right out of the holster and clipped him under the chin. He went down like a stone. Another one came at me." *Out of nowhere, with a shout and a hand on his weapon.* "I brought him down with a swift kick and headed for the stairs."

"You make it sound easy."

Easy. "It is, if you're fast enough and strong enough." And desperate enough. God knows he was desperate enough, and since he'd been such a model prisoner for the past ten months he'd had the element of surprise on his side, as well.

A thick overhang of trees shaded the road they traveled, allowing no more than a few small dapples of sunlight here and there on the road. If he was lucky the patrol cars and helicopters that were searching for him right now would be focused on the major roads out of town. After all, he'd be a fool to stay in an area where everyone knew his face and his name, and believed him to be a killer.

Of course, thanks to the press, everyone in the country knew his face and his name. He hated the reporters. They'd grabbed on to every detail of his life, had hounded everyone he'd ever known in the months since his arrest. They'd made his life hell and done their best to convict him long before the trial. He glanced at the girl again. Reporters like *her,* though in truth he couldn't remember ever seeing her cover the story of Winkler's murder or the trial. Until today. That didn't mean anything. Lately he'd tried *not* to watch.

He pulled off the mountain road and onto the dirt trail he'd been heading for, a winding, narrow path barely wide enough for her car. A sharp turn took the car into a copse of thick trees and low-lying bushes. No one would see them here, unless they knew exactly where to look.

"Who shot you?" the girl asked in a soft, controlled voice.

"The deputy I knocked down." He braked to slow the car as the trail got rougher. "Son of a bitch," he mumbled. If he'd been thinking he would have taken that weapon, too, or at least taken the time to knock the second deputy out...but no. His only objective had been to get out, and he'd forgotten his training. It had cost him.

The path grew narrower, and green-leafed branches brushed against the sides of the car. The girl flinched with every grinding scrape, but she said nothing. When the winding trail came to an end he put the car in park and shut off the engine.

He needed time to think, time to plan, and time was one of the many things he didn't have. He had no time, no money, no ally...no chance.

"How did I end up here?" he muttered, laying his head against the steering wheel and closing his eyes. Less than a year ago he'd had a successful contracting firm, a woman in his life he'd foolishly thought had potential for a long-term relationship, and a nice house he'd built himself. Ten months later the business was history. Lauren had not turned out to be the woman he'd thought she was, and even if she had been, twice-monthly conversations through scratched Plexiglass was no way to keep a relationship alive. The house was empty, up for sale so he could pay his legal fees.

Once again, he literally had nothing.

He should've known the reporter he'd snatched would try to take off once the car was stopped, but she startled him when she threw open her door and scrambled out. He tried to reach out to snag her before she got away, but she was too fast...or he was too slow.

Nick opened his own door, scraping it against the branches of the bush he'd parked alongside. Even here in the shade the warmth was oppressive, thick with strength-sapping summer heat. It threatened to drag him down, to finish him, once and for all. He shook it off.

The pistol fit comfortably in his right hand, and as he fought his way through the bushes his eyes found the hostage and stayed on her as she made her way slowly through the same dense growth he fought. Her dark hair danced with every step she took. The red she wore made her an easy target.

When he rounded the front of the car, his leg gave out from under him, buckling so that he fell to his knees. He righted himself quickly, but found he could not stand. All of a sudden he had nothing left to give. Well, almost nothing.

"Stop!" he shouted once with surprising strength, and then, almost without conscious thought, he raised the pistol and fired.

Chapter 2

The blast took Shea by surprise, and she waited for the impact of a bullet in her back. *Oh God, I'm going to die.* She stopped running, and still she fought for every breath she took, her heart pumping so hard she could feel it pounding in her chest.

But she wasn't dead. He'd missed!

"Stop!" he shouted again. "Hold it right there or the next one goes in your leg, not a tree."

Shea cut her eyes to the right and saw where a bullet had exploded, embedding itself in a tree not two feet away. The shot had been a warning; he hadn't missed at all. She looked at the splintered bullet hole in the center of the tree trunk and knew Taggert had hit exactly what he'd been aiming for.

She slowly turned around. Taggert was on his knees in front of the car, the weapon he held pointed steadily at her.

"You said you wouldn't hurt me," she said.

"I said I didn't *want* to hurt you." Taggert had gone deathly pale, and a strand of thick black hair fell over his forehead. His suit was rumpled, the tie loosened slightly, and it seemed to Shea that he swayed ever so slightly, there on his knees in front of her car. Through all that, she saw his unwavering tenacity. He was inflexible. In spite of his wound and his weakness, he was damned and determined to have his way.

Part of her job was to read people when she had to. She had to be able to smile and nod through an interview, all the while knowing in her heart who was lying and who was telling the truth. It was an instinct some people had and others didn't.

In this instant Shea saw something she'd rather not. Nicholas Taggert really didn't want to hurt her, but he would.

"If I shoot you in the leg you won't die," he said passionlessly. "Unless you go into shock, which is always a possibility. Won't we make a pair." A humorless smile barely touched his lips. "You can try to hobble away and I'll hobble after you."

"What do you want from me?" Shea asked. "You got away from the courthouse. You don't need me anymore."

"I need time," he said softly as he lowered the weapon. "We're too close to houses, roads. If I let you go now I won't have time to get away."

"What if I promise not to tell them where you are?" Shea took a step back and Taggert raised his gun quickly, snapping it up and training the sight low on her body. The leg, he'd said. He was pallid and weak—growing weaker with every second that passed—but the hand that held the gun remained steady.

"No good," he said. "Even if you keep your mouth shut, and I doubt that's possible, simply by showing up on this mountain you'll tell the cops where to search."

Shea took a single step forward, and Taggert dropped the gun again. He looked relieved, and that evident relief told her, as much as any instinct, that he was willing to carry out his threat. He didn't *want* to, but he would.

She returned to the car, shaking and angry. On her run she'd ignored the branches that snagged her clothing and scratched her bare legs, but on the return trip she felt every scratch, every gentle brush of a leaf, as if it were an added indignity.

"I'm going to watch you fry for this," she said bravely when she was no more than five feet from Taggert.

He struggled to his feet, but all the while he kept a steadfast hand on his weapon. "Yeah, well, you're going to have to stand in line," he muttered. "Right now everybody wants to see me fry." He motioned with the gun toward the car. "Sit down."

She had to fight branches to return to the parked car, pushing angrily past thin, flexible limbs that made way for her and then snapped back. Stepping in a small hole she'd managed to miss in her failed escape attempt, she lurched forward, grabbing on to the opened door for support. But she obeyed Taggert's surly order and lowered herself into the passenger seat again.

He slammed the car door when she was seated, and she winced at the sound of the branches scraping against the Saturn. This car wasn't even a year old, and it was her first *new* car. It would be a mess when this was over, between the bloodstains and the scratched paint.

Taggert limped around the front of the car, leaning on the hood occasionally for much-needed support, stumbling twice before he fought his way to the driver's-side door and plopped down beside her. He waved the gun in her direction. "Put on your seat belt."

"What?"

He locked those cold blue eyes on her again. They were

chips of ice in a pallid face, hard and uncompromising. Those extraordinary eyes showed no mercy, not even a hint of apology for what he'd done to her. "Do it."

She fastened her seat belt, muttering every curse word her brothers had ever unwittingly used in her presence. If she did decide to run again, she'd have to stop to unfasten the seat belt, warning Taggert of her intentions.

She waited for him to start the car, but he didn't. Instead he shifted his body so he leaned against his door, and he very carefully lifted his wounded leg and placed it in her lap. The weight was more than she'd expected, and warm blood seeped through his pant leg onto her skirt. Suddenly he seemed too big for her compact car, the leg in her lap too long and heavy. A surge of panic raced through her own blood. This was all too much, and Taggert was too close.

"You're going to have to help me with this," he said softly.

Shea stared at the leg in her lap, at the blood-soaked gray fabric and the hole...two holes and a *lot* of blood, she saw from this angle. If possible, she felt more terrified than when he'd fired the gun and she'd thought she was dead. "I can't," she whispered.

"You have to."

Taggert jammed the gun into the waistband of his trousers and shrugged out of his jacket, moving cautiously, as if every small movement hurt him. "Wrap this around the leg," he said as he tossed it to her.

"You're kidding, right?"

Taggert shook his head and began loosening his tie.

Shea took a deep breath. She positively hated the sight of blood, and there was too much of it here. Taggert should be passed out, or going into shock, or at least getting woozy. She quickly glanced at him as he whipped the tie from his neck. He could die from this wound to the leg, if he lost too much blood, if he went into shock.

She wrapped the jacket around his injured calf, taking great care not to move the leg any more than was necessary. Still, when she very easily lifted Taggert's leg to shift the jacket around the calf, he winced. She tried to place the thickest part of the makeshift bandage over his wound, to staunch the bleeding, and she wrapped the jacket arms around crosswise, making a relatively neat bandage, given what she had to work with.

When the jacket was swathed around his calf, he handed her the necktie. "Wrap this around a couple of times and bind it tight."

"Like a tourniquet?"

"Not that tight. Just tight enough to hold the jacket snugly in place."

She did as he instructed, crisscrossing the tie several times around his leg. He didn't flinch again; she wondered if he could feel anything at all. "You need a doctor," she mumbled as she brought the ends of the navy blue tie together and fastened them in a knot.

"I'm sure you're right," he muttered darkly, "but I'm not likely to run across one anytime soon." He took a deep breath. "You'll have to do."

When she finished the unpleasant task, Taggert very cautiously removed his leg from her lap, leaving behind a nasty stain on her skirt. That dark stain was a reminder of how very serious the wound was. He could easily die. Even though he'd kidnapped and threatened her, she didn't want that to happen.

"Why are you doing this?" she asked as he swung his body around to face forward, resting against the wheel as if he wanted nothing more than to lay his head there and go to sleep. "You have to know they'll catch you, eventually."

"I know," he whispered. "But I can't just sit back and accept what's happened. I have to do something. No one else can prove my innocence, so I have to do it myself. When I have the proof I need I'll turn myself in."

Taggert slowly rotated his head until he faced her again, and Shea saw something that startled her. Eyes that had been like ice just a few minutes ago had softened. She didn't know if the ache she saw in his eyes was there because of the wound in his leg or for some other reason. Like it or not, his ache touched her. Goodness, that pain went deep; seeing it made her shiver.

"I thought the system worked," he said, and his voice wasn't simply soft now, it was weak. "I thought the truth was sacred. But you know what? No one cares about the truth. The police want a conviction, the D.A. wants a win. Why bother to look for the truth when you have a convenient patsy sitting right in front of you?"

Shea's instincts were in perfect working order, in spite of the trying events of the afternoon. She'd never been so scared; she didn't scare easily, but Taggert had terrified her. For revealing that weakness, she should hate him, and she did. She did. But heaven help her, she believed him. Nicholas Taggert was innocent.

He slowly propelled himself away from the steering wheel until his dark head fell against headrest. His eyes fluttered and then closed, but all the while one hand rested over the gun that was tucked into his waistband.

"What are we waiting for?" Shea asked.

Taggert's eyes drifted open. "Dark," he whispered. "We're waiting for dark."

Nick wanted, more than anything, to sleep. He fought the urge to close his eyes again, knowing that if he did he'd likely never wake up. The girl would take off, and this time he didn't have the energy—or the will—to chase after her. He'd either wake up surrounded by cops, or he'd never wake up at all.

"It's supposed to rain tonight," she said in an absurdly conversational tone of voice. "Visibility should be poor, and the cops will be busy with fender benders all over town. Maybe that will help you some, keep some of them busy elsewhere. And maybe the rain will cool some of this heat," she added, her voice low, as if she were talking to herself.

Nick turned his head but didn't lift it. The girl watched him, her eyes wide, her lips slightly parted. For the first time he really looked at her. She was pretty. Not gorgeous, maybe, but striking and yes…very, very pretty. Her warm brown hair looked soft and thick. It fell straight and smooth, like a dark waterfall, but the ends curled under just a little. Her eyes tilted up slightly at the corners, but not enough to give her an exotic look. She had too much of the girl-next-door in her to ever be exotic. And if a woman could have a perfect mouth…

Rain. "I know who you are," he muttered. "You're the weathergirl."

The sunlight was slowly dying, and an oddly grayish light washed across her face. Yes, the light was fading, but it was enough to show Nick her displeasure at his recognition. Her lips came together and thinned, and her eyes narrowed.

"I am *not* a weathergirl," she insisted frostily.

He began to feel a dullness within, as if the light inside him was fading as surely as the light of day. He lifted his head in an effort to clear it. "Yes you are," he said. "I recognize you. You're a real favorite in the TV room at the Madison County Jail, almost as popular as that big blonde."

"Astrid," the weathergirl muttered.

"Yeah."

"Astrid should be here, you know," she said angrily. "You're her story and I was just filling in." When she got really angry she did things with her mouth. Her lips pursed; something twitched. "If she hadn't come down with the stomach flu she'd be sitting here right now, not me."

Nick shook his head gently, unable to make a more vigorous move. "No, she wouldn't."

"And why not?"

He leaned slightly toward her and whispered. "I never would've grabbed the big blonde. She scares me."

The statement obviously took the weathergirl by surprise. Her eyes widened, and finely shaped dark brows lifted. "She *scares* you?"

"A little. I think it's that big silly grin on an Amazon that does it. It's not natural." He was losing it, could actually *feel* himself losing control. His heartbeat was thready, his vision less than clear and his head swam uneasily. "You don't have a silly grin," he added. "You have a nice, real smile. 'This is Shea Sinclair with the weekend weather.'" He smiled himself, for some reason. "Shea Sinclair," he said again, "weathergirl."

She looked like she wanted to hit him. Senseless girl. He had the pistol, he'd kidnapped her, everyone in the world believed he was a cold-blooded killer, and she looked like she wanted nothing more than to reach out and smack him a good one.

"I am *not* a weathergirl. I do the weekend weather, at the moment, but I also file stories. I'm a reporter, Mr. Taggert."

For some reason he fixated on the memory of her smile. It really was a nice smile, relaxed and genuine, as if the cold or the heat or the rain that was coming didn't bother her at all. She'd smiled, he remembered, as he'd run from the courthouse.

''Why were you smiling as I came out of the courthouse this afternoon?'' he asked.

Her anger dulled; she even looked a little embarrassed. ''I didn't mean to, but I got excited about the possibility that we might actually catch a word or get a really great picture no one else would have.''

Ah, Shea Sinclair really was a reporter. He'd become familiar with the breed in the past few months. They were wolves after a piece of meat, and he was the sirloin. No, that was too kind, much too generous. Wolves were majestic, if deadly. Reporters were little yapping dogs, eagerly fighting over a scrap of meat, and he was hamburger.

Nick had been angry at the world for months, and right now he experienced a flash of blinding fury at his hostage for turning out to be another annoying, ambitious reporter who'd found reason to smile at his desperate escape. ''Well, come tomorrow you're going to have a real exclusive, aren't you, weathergirl?''

She didn't correct him this time, but pursed her lips together in apparent disapproval and turned away to stare out the passenger-side window. Her shoulders were squared, her spine too straight. Evidently the silent treatment was punishment for his last offense. Good.

When darkness fell he started the engine and backed slowly down the path. The trail was bumpy, the branches and leaves that brushed against the car invisible but noisy. He made the turn almost blind, leaving the route and lurching through a low spot before getting the tires on the trail again. The weathergirl continued to silently stare out of her window, even though there was nothing to see. Just darkness and shadows and the gray-green bushes and trees that had shielded them.

At the two-lane road, he switched on the headlights and continued the journey he'd started in the daylight, heading for the other side of the mountain. He didn't think there would be a roadblock on this little country road, but every time the car rounded a blind corner Nick held his breath until he saw a length of clear road stretching ahead.

She'd been right about the rain. It started, a light sprinkle, as he steered the Saturn across a level stretch of road at the top of the mountain. When they passed one car on the winding downward slope his heart beat a little bit faster, but the vehicle didn't so much as slow down. They were just another pair of headlights on a rarely used road.

When the mountain road was behind them and the terrain was level again, Nick pulled off the pavement and onto a rutted dirt path, rounded a bend and stopped the car with a lurch. For the first time since he'd made the mistake of calling her "weathergirl" once too often, Shea Sinclair turned her head to look at him. The headlights lit the dirt path before them, their reflection illuminating her stoic face in shades of gray. The light-headedness that wouldn't go away made her face look like ivory—ivory with soft, black velvet shadows.

He waited for her to throw open her door and take off, but she just stared at him.

"You really didn't do it?" she whispered.

Nick shook his head.

"Then who did?"

"I don't know, but I'm going to find out."

She didn't make a move, so Nick reached over and unfastened her seat belt. "Go."

Shea turned her head away again, to glance out at the deserted field. "Here?" Her head snapped around, and she stared at him wide-eyed. "You're just going to dump me in the middle of nowhere, in the dark, in the *rain?*"

"That's the plan," he mumbled.

Instead of jumping from the car and making her escape, Shea Sinclair stared him down. "No," she whispered.

Surely he misunderstood. "What did you say?"

"I said no."

Nick cursed beneath his breath as he reached out and snagged Shea's wrist and dragged her toward him, easing himself from the car and hauling the uncooperative weathergirl with him, over the console, across the driver's seat. A soft, cool drizzle struck his face, and droplets soaked through the white dress shirt he wore. The cool water cleared his head slightly, as he pulled on Shea Sinclair's arm. He was making progress until she grabbed the steering wheel and refused to let go. It hit him, as surely as the gentle rain, that right now he didn't have the strength to forcibly remove her from the car.

"Are you nuts?" he yelled, poking his head into the car and placing his face close to hers. They were practically nose-to-nose, and in the semidarkness he locked his eyes to hers. She didn't flinch, didn't show any sign of backing down. "I'm trying to let you go!" Yelling was not such a good idea. His head swam and his knees went weak. Damn.

"You can't let me go," she argued. "You need me, Taggert."

"I'm not a..." He swayed slightly. "I'm not a kidnapper."

Shea smiled, and Nick's knees wobbled uncertainly. The smile was all wrong; wrong time, wrong place. There had been a time when a smile like this one would've given him hope, would've made him list easily forward to kiss her...but not now. She should be running scared right now, and he should be well down the road, running to God knows where.

"Actually," she said softly, "you are. And since I don't think there's a different charge for long-term versus short-term kidnappings, you might as well make the best of what you've got."

He clamped his hand more snugly around her warm,

slender wrist. If she knew how long it had been since a pretty girl had smiled at him, she wouldn't do this. The smile made his insides tighten and his mind spin. The gentle upturn at the corners of her mouth, the sparkle in her eyes promised so many things. Shea Sinclair had no idea what she was doing to him.

Then again, maybe she did. She let go of the steering wheel and slowly reached out for him, that delicate hand uncertain and enticing, those long, pale fingers as promising as her smile and her eyes. She was going to touch him. For a second Nick was frozen at the very idea. More than anything he wanted this woman to lay her hands on him. He craved the warmth of a woman's delicate fingers, a tender caress.

It had been a very long time since anyone had touched him; a fat deputy clapping on handcuffs didn't count.

Without warning, her motion changed from slow to lightning fast, and she grabbed the pistol from his waistband and pointed it at his midsection.

His head spun dangerously and still he laughed. It was the perfect ending to the worst day of his life. He'd been found guilty of a murder he didn't commit, had been shot in the leg, and now he stood in the rain with a pistol pointed at his gut. "Caught by a weathergirl," he said unsteadily. "Won't this make a fine story on the ten o'clock news?"

"You're hysterical," Shea said as she scooted into the passenger seat, taking the pistol with her. "Sit down before you fall down."

He dropped into the driver's seat, clearheaded long enough to notice that she held the weapon like a woman who was used to handling one. At least if she shot him it wouldn't be an accident. He let his head fall back and closed his eyes. Maybe it would be better if she did shoot him here and now. All he wanted was for this to be over, and it would make a helluva story for the weathergirl.

All he had to do was lunge for her and this would be over and done with. He couldn't move.

"Now what?" he whispered.

"You tell me." He turned his head to see Shea slowly lower the pistol. "Do you have a plan?"

"No."

"Well, you need one, but first you need to rest." She placed the pistol on the floor at her feet. "Until the wound in your leg heals I'm afraid you won't be able to do much of anything. You really should let me drive."

He had to be dreaming. "Yeah, that would be real smart," he muttered.

"You're in no condition to drive," she said sensibly. "And you're going to have to heal before we can begin the investigation. We need to dump this car pretty quick," she added as a mumbled afterthought. "Everyone will be looking for it by now."

"I know."

She pursed her lips thoughtfully. "Do you know how to hot-wire a car?"

He stared at her, hard. "No."

She wasn't leaving, and he didn't have the strength to force her from the car. The rain picked up and the light sprinkle turned into a downpour, obscuring everything outside the windows.

Shea Sinclair had said he needed her, and maybe she was right. But could he trust her? It had been such a long time since he'd trusted anyone.

"I know where I can get a truck," he said softly, "not too far from here."

"That's a start."

He wished she had touched him, just once, something easy—a hand on his face, maybe. Her hands were soft; he could tell just by looking at them. Soft and warm. Her wrist had been temptingly warm and wonderful in his grip, but what he wanted, what he needed was for *her* to touch *him.*

"Why are you doing this?"

In the distance a flash of lightning arced across the sky, lighting the interior of the car for a split second. A rumble of thunder followed.

"If I can help you find the real killer it'll make one hell of a story." She grinned. "And they can find someone else to do the weekend weather."

Nick didn't want to look at her anymore. He stared instead at a windshield so washed in heavy rain he could see nothing beyond it. "So I'm a good story."

"The best."

It was better than nothing, he supposed. He sure wasn't going to get far on his own in this condition. "Okay," he whispered. "You can stay."

Rain pounded against the car. "I have just one question," Shea said softly, and something about the tone of her voice forced Nick to turn his head to look at her again. This was the first time he'd heard trepidation. She wasn't smiling now.

"Ask it," he prodded when she didn't continue.

She pursed her lips and hesitated, and then she took a deep breath. "Back there, on the mountain, would you really have shot me in the leg if I hadn't stopped?"

The weathergirl had to know what she was getting into. He had to make sure she knew, so that she had a chance to back out while she still could. As the car rolled across the bumpy, muddy road, he turned his head to stare at her.

"Yes."

Chapter 3

Taggert wouldn't make it much longer, but he absolutely refused to pull over and let her drive. He braced himself over the steering wheel, his eyes trained straight ahead. They hadn't spoken for the past fifteen minutes; Shea suspected he didn't have the energy to talk.

He stuck to back roads that took them into Marshall County, and except for the occasional car or truck they passed, blurred by the rain, they had the wet roads to themselves.

Dean would have her hide for this, but her oldest brother was the least of her problems right now. Boone would understand, and so would Clint, though Boone would likely lay the blame for her decision to stay with Taggert on her early influences of Nancy Drew and Agatha Christie.

Shea strengthened her resolve with the selfless notion that if she didn't help Taggert he didn't have a chance. He'd die, either alone from his wound or when the cops caught up with him. And they *would* catch up with him, soon. He wasn't thinking clearly, and he didn't have the strength to run and hide for long. Not without her help.

If he died the truth died with him. A murderer would go free, and the courts would be satisfied that Nick Taggert was, indeed, a killer. That wasn't right; it wasn't justice. Together she and Taggert would search for the truth. And wow, this was going to be a great story.

Taggert turned her battered Saturn onto a long, gravel driveway. Sitting at the end, visible through the rain, sat a small house that looked very much like a log cabin. It waited for them, simple and square and solid. Welcoming lights burned, harsh on the front porch and muted through the windows.

"Who lives here?" she asked, keeping her voice low as they neared the house. Taggert didn't answer, and her heart skipped a beat. She believed he was innocent; he'd declared it so indignantly, so righteously, and she had seen the truth in his eyes. But he *had* kidnapped her. What did he have planned now?

The drive circled around the house; the crunching noise the tires made on the gravel was sure to be heard by whoever waited inside. At a window near the back door a pale blue curtain fluttered. They'd been seen.

"You're not thinking of doing anything drastic, are you?" she asked as Taggert stopped the car and put it in park. Finally, he turned his eyes to her.

He listed forward slightly with his arms resting on the steering wheel, shoulders slumped and those normally piercing eyes half-closed. "Drastic?" he repeated.

It was a rather ridiculous question, she supposed, considering what had transpired so far today. He'd escaped from the courthouse, been shot and kidnapped her. Everything had been drastic. But still… "There's no reason to involve anyone else in this," she said sensibly. "We can steal a car. Well, we can *borrow* one without asking, and leave a note or something. My purse is in the trunk, and I have a little cash, so there's no reason—''

''You think I'm going to rob the man who lives here?'' Taggert interrupted.

You heard about it on the news all the time. A convict escapes from prison and storms into someone's home— preferably an isolated house, like this one—for hostages and money and food.

''Aren't you?''

He managed to shake his head once, and the expression on his face changed subtly to one of disgust and maybe even disappointment. ''Why don't you take off right here, weathergirl?'' he whispered. ''Start walking.''

''No,'' she answered just as softly.

The back door opened and bright light spilled onto the yard and the long gravel drive. An older, heavyset man stood there, squinting out into the night and waiting patiently.

Taggert threw open his door and stepped into the rain. Shea scooted across the seat, making the awkward move over the console and placing herself quickly right behind him, knowing, even if he didn't, that he wouldn't make it to the house under his own power. She was there to catch him when he practically fell back into the driver's seat. Slipping an arm around his waist, she allowed him to lean on her as she stood beside him. He hesitated, and then his arm circled her lightly. Taggert was tall and hard and muscled, and in normal circumstances he would have overpowered her. But at the moment he needed her help to stay on his feet.

''He's a friend?'' she asked, and Taggert nodded once.

Relief washed through her. She should've known that he wouldn't break into someone's home like a common thief. Even in his weakened condition, Nicholas Taggert was anything but common.

He leaned on her heavily as they approached the open back door, moving slowly in spite of the rain. Her arm around his waist, and his around hers, provided unsteady but effective support. Taggert was too big; if he fell she'd never be able to get him up. After they'd taken several tottering steps the old man made his way to them and added his strength at Taggert's other side. Shea supposed she could let go and allow Taggert's friend to lead him inside, but she didn't. Nick seemed to lean into her, still, so she kept her arm around his waist and canted in his direction, bracing his heavy body as best she could.

The back door opened onto a brightly lit kitchen. An oak table and four chairs sat there, and Taggert's faltering path took him and those who were assisting him directly toward those chairs.

"Boy, can you make it to the den?" the old man asked.

"Sure," Taggert answered weakly, and they bypassed the oak chairs and went through a wide doorway into a square, rustic room. The old man steered them toward a long, mustard-colored couch, where they deposited Taggert in a slightly awkward maneuver.

When his arm slipped from her back, the palm of his hand skimmed down her spine and across her hip, as if he needed support, still. As if he didn't want to let her go.

Once Taggert was deposited on the couch, the old man started cussing—long, inventive, loudly delivered profanity as he removed thick, rain-splattered glasses and cleaned them on his shirttail. Taggert leaned his head back and closed his eyes until the tirade ended.

The old man took a deep breath and visibly calmed himself as he placed the glasses on his nose. "What the blue blazes were you thinking, boy? You could've gotten yourself killed. And kidnapping this poor lady." He turned his head her way and squinted at her through thick lenses, even though they stood close. "Now, that was stupid."

"I know," Taggert said weakly, without so much as opening one eye.

"We'll talk about it in the morning," the old man said softly. "Right now we'll see to that leg and get you to bed. In the morning—"

"No." This time Taggert's eyes did open. "We can't stay here, Lenny. I just…I need your truck."

"It's yours," Lenny said without hesitation. "And I tell you what, you leave the little lady here and I'll see that she doesn't call anyone or go anywhere until you've had a chance to get on down the road a ways."

"Sounds good to me," Taggert muttered.

"No." Shea directed her denial to the man Taggert called Lenny. "I'm going with him."

The man drew his bushy eyebrows together. "What for?"

"I'm a helluva story," Taggert said caustically before Shea could answer. He locked his eyes on her, and in spite of his weakened condition they were cold and strong. Piercing, as if he had never known weakness. "But this is one part of the story no one ever hears, you understand me? As far as the cops are concerned we're stealing Lenny's truck. He didn't see anything, we didn't talk to him, he is *not* involved in this. Is that clear?"

Shea nodded, and Taggert closed his eyes once again.

Lenny looked Shea up and down once, squinting as he brought his gaze to her face. He even leaned forward slightly. "Name's Leonard Caudel," he said.

"Shea Sinclair," she answered, offering her hand.

Caudel took her hand and shook it gently. "I know." A smile bloomed on his face. "You've been all over the news today, young lady. I can't see real good, but if I get close to the television I can see well enough. You've been on the television before. You're the weathergirl, right?''

Before Shea could correct Caudel, Taggert laughed. It was a weak, nearly silent chuckle, and he didn't even bother to open his eyes. "You've done it now, Lenny," he whispered, and then he fell silent once again.

Shea was annoyed, but decided it wasn't worth the effort of an argument. "Do you have a place where I can clean up? I've been out in the rain, and the man bled on me, and..." She felt dizzy for just a moment, light-headed. "It has been the longest day," she finished.

"Come this way," Caudel said, taking her arm and leading her into a long hallway. "You could use a change of clothes, I reckon."

She looked him up and down. He was as tall as Taggert and twice as big around. No way was there anything in this house that would fit her, even in a pinch. "Well..."

"My late wife, Judith, she was about your size. I guess I shoulda gotten rid of her things years ago, but I never could bring myself to do it." He grinned. "But I wouldn't mind at all if you could find something in her closet that would suit this occasion."

In a small, sparsely furnished bedroom at the end of the hallway, he threw open a closet. "You'll have to do the choosing. Like I said, I can't see so well no more, so there's no telling what I'd pick out. You just take what you want. There's a bathroom down the hall if you want to clean up a bit. I'll see to Nick's leg."

The contents of the very full closet were brightly colored and years out of fashion. Orange, bright pink, a shade of green so garish it hurt her eyes. A glimpse of tie-dye and a pair of orange bell-bottom pants said "sixties" as surely as if a neon sign hung there. "I'm sure I'll find something that will do," she said optimistically.

Caudel was leaving the room when she stopped him with a question. "You know him well?"

He turned in the doorway, a smile on his face. "I gave Nick his first job out of the military, taught him everything I know about the construction business before my eyesight started to fail." The smile disappeared. "He's a good man, and he didn't kill nobody."

She didn't believe he had, either, but still... "He shot at me."

The smile came back. "Ma'am, if he didn't hit you, he didn't shoot *at* you. Nick could shoot the flies off a pile of, uhhh..." He cleared his throat. "Off a pile of sugar," he said, "and never disturb a single grain."

For some reason that was a comforting reassurance. Shea turned to the closetful of old clothes and listened to Caudel's retreating footsteps.

"I shoulda been there."

Nick opened his eyes at Lenny's mumbled self-censure. "I told you a thousand times I didn't want you in the courtroom," he said. It was the truth. Lenny was more like a father to him than the man he'd called Daddy for the first eleven years of his life. Nick didn't want Lenny to sit in that courthouse and watch the trial; it would have been an unnecessarily harsh ordeal for the old man. "Besides," he added, "you can't drive anymore."

"I can, too," Lenny mumbled.

"You're blind as a bat, you've got no business... dammit!" He came up off the couch like a shot when Lenny's removal of the makeshift bandage proved to be too painful. "Just leave it alone," he said as Lenny unwrapped his bloodstained jacket and tie.

Lenny ignored the order and took a pair of scissors to his pant leg, cutting the fabric away with an easy touch. "No. It's going to be cleaned and bandaged properly, and then we're going to get you out of these filthy clothes and into a warm bed.''

Nick shook his head as he lay back down. The lumpy couch felt as good as any soft bed he'd ever slept in. ''They'll look for me here sooner or later, probably sooner, so I can't stay. I won't risk involving you.''

''They won't think to look here for a while, I reckon,'' Lenny insisted.

''Can't risk it,'' Nick whispered.

The roar of water from the bathroom reminded him of Shea's presence in this house. She should be gone by now; another chance had come and still she didn't run. He wouldn't chase after her if she took off now, and neither would Lenny. Nick was crippled and Lenny was half-blind; Shea could walk out of this house and they wouldn't be able to stop her.

Nick closed his eyes and tried to relax as Lenny very carefully tended to his wounded leg. Nick couldn't think straight, and that wasn't good. In fact, it was damn bad. All he could think of with any clarity was one fact: Shea Sinclair smelled great.

When he'd hovered close in the confines of the car, when she'd wrapped her arm around his waist and steadied him, there had been moments when her scent had almost overpowered him. He wanted to bury his nose against her neck and breathe deep, to sleep with that scent in his nostrils.

Nick wondered if he was running a fever; God knows he was delirious.

He should leave right now, while Shea was getting cleaned up and prepared for her grand adventure of a story. Unfortunately, she was right: he needed her. He wouldn't get far without Shea Sinclair's help.

As Lenny tended the leg, Nick drifted off. He didn't wake until he heard Shea's voice. That voice was already so familiar that it struck a chord somewhere deep inside, like the voice of an old, dear friend.

"How is it?" she whispered.

"Not too bad, considering," Lenny answered just as softly. They thought he was asleep, and didn't want to wake him, he supposed. If he had the strength he'd say something and prove them wrong...but he didn't. "He's doggone lucky, if you ask me. The bullet grazed his calf. Made a deep furrow, but there doesn't seem to be any muscle damage to speak of. He lost a lot of blood, though, and he'll have to watch for infection."

"I know. I wish we had some antibiotics." Her voice was a little bit closer now; he could almost feel that voice, as if it vibrated deep inside him. How odd.

"I've got part of a prescription I didn't finish," Lenny said, a bright note in his voice. "Just a few days' worth, but it's better than nothing."

"Yes, it is," Shea said, sounding relieved. "He'll need a change of clothes, too."

"I rounded up some old clothes I outgrew years ago. They're on the chair by the fireplace," Lenny said, groaning as he stood. "I'll get those pills and a glass of water."

Nick half opened his eyes. Lenny entered the kitchen, and Shea stood over the recliner by the cold stone fireplace. She wore a pair of tight white pants that ended just below her knees, and a pale blue blouse that was cropped so that the hem hung just at her waist. The severe red suit had disguised her figure, but this outfit enhanced it, hugging every curve. Her dark hair had been pulled back into a thick ponytail.

She turned around, the pile of clothing in her hands, and Nick let his eyes drift closed again.

"I can't believe I'm doing this," she muttered as she kneeled on the floor beside him. "If I had a lick of sense I'd run like hell and not look back."

Yes, you would.

"Dean will kill me," she said.

Boyfriend? Husband? Lover?

"Well, maybe Clint and Boone will protect me."

More boyfriends?

"Goodness knows they've saved me often enough." Shea sighed, and then Nick felt the warmth of her hands on his chest. She flicked one button of his shirt and then another. The tips of her fingers grazed his skin as his shirt came open, and his eyes fluttered open.

"What are you doing?" he whispered harshly.

She wasn't at all startled that he was awake; she should be. "I'm getting you dressed so we can get out of here."

"I can dress myself."

She smiled. "Yes, I'm sure you can." She'd washed the makeup off her face, revealing smooth skin with just a few pale freckles sprinkled across the nose. Even without lipstick, her lips were rosy, pink and full.

He should push her hand away and finish the job himself, but he didn't. He liked the occasional brush of her fingers against his skin, and she was so close he could smell her again. He liked it; he liked it too much.

"Can you sit?" She flattened her hand on his back and helped him raise up, and then she slipped the damp white dress shirt off his shoulders.

"Why are you doing this?" he asked as she took a blue-and-green-plaid cotton shirt and helped him into it. Her hands were easy, gentle and sure. He had to remind himself that she wasn't his friend, she wasn't his ally, it didn't matter how good she smelled or how enticing the simple brush of her fingers felt on his skin. "It's the story, right?"

"Yes," she said without hesitation. "The story."

All of a sudden he knew he couldn't do this. Somehow he had to get rid of the weathergirl. With all the strength he could muster, Nick reached out and took Shea Sinclair's chin in his hand and made her look him in the eye. He didn't have the strength to force her to do anything, but he damn well knew how to send her packing.

"I haven't had a woman in ten months," he whispered. "I haven't so much as *touched* a woman in ten months."

Her face went pale; her hazel-green eyes widened. But she didn't back away.

"You want a thrill, weathergirl?" he asked, his voice so soft it was little more than a breath of air. "You think this is fun? Some kind of adventure?" He leaned down, placing his face close to hers. Damn if he couldn't smell her, feel her breath and the warmth of her skin. Her lips were so close, right there before him and tempting as hell. "I promise you this. You stick around, and as soon as I get my strength back I'll show you a thrill or two."

She didn't back away. "I know what you're doing, Taggert," she whispered. "And it's not going to work. You can't scare me."

"Yes, I can." He reached out with his free hand and touched the base of her throat, let the back of his fingers trail down to the valley of her breasts. She was warm and soft, as he'd known she would be. He watched the movement of his roughened hand on her pale skin, marveled at the way the sight teased his insides and made his head spin more than it had before.

He didn't want to scare the weathergirl anymore, he wanted to hold her. Hard and fast. He wanted to sleep with her in his arms, that's all. His mouth drifted closer to her. No, that was *not* all. He wanted everything; he wanted all of her.

Shea moved her head back and gently grabbed his wrists, moving his wandering hands to his knees. "You're not well, Mr. Taggert," she said as she stood. "So I'm going to forgive you for behaving in an inappropriate manner."

"Oh, thank you," he muttered dryly. Hell, he'd even failed in frightening her off. Apparently he wasn't a very imposing figure, at the moment.

Lenny came back into the room with a glass of water and a small plastic bottle of pills. "It's just four days' worth, I'm afraid."

"That's better than nothing," Shea said as she leaned forward and began to button the plaid shirt she'd slipped onto Nick before he'd foolishly tried to scare her off.

He brushed her hand away. "Dammit, I can dress myself."

She backed off and allowed him to finish buttoning the shirt. It was more of an effort than he'd ever let on. When that chore was done, Lenny handed him a pill, which he dutifully took with a swig of water, and Shea tossed a pair of faded jeans onto the couch beside him.

"Do you have the makings for sandwiches?" She directed the question to Lenny, who slowly nodded his head.

"Help yourself. I've got plenty of bread, peanut butter and jelly, ham and cheese, and there's some leftover tuna salad in the refrigerator."

"I'll make us something to take in the truck while Taggert finishes getting dressed."

Nick let his head fall back against the couch. He felt less light-headed with the support, a little sturdier. The sensation of strength was an illusion, he knew. He was about to pass out.

It would be so easy to drift away, to close his eyes and fall asleep and give up. He wasn't a man to give up easily. He'd fought long and hard for everything he'd had. He'd worked his way up from nothing. Literally *nothing*. After all those years of hard work he was back to nothing again. He should fight, as he always did; he should defy the odds. But right now—right now he considered giving up, giving in. It would be the easy thing to do.

Hell, he hadn't taken the easy way very often in his life. Why should he start now?

"Now what?" he whispered, "Dammit, I don't even know where I'm going yet."

Shea walked confidently toward the kitchen, a lively spring in her step. Watching the sway of her hips and the bounce of that ponytail made him a bit dizzy. She'd been so afraid just a few hours ago, but she didn't look like a hostage anymore. And there wasn't even a hint of worry in her eyes. There should be, dammit, there should be.

But he was the one sitting here remembering what she felt like, what she smelled like. He'd been so close to a kiss, and he'd wanted it. For a moment he'd wanted it as much as he wanted freedom, the truth, his life back. So who was the hostage now?

"I don't have a clue where to go from here," he said again, his voice so low he figured no one would hear.

"That's okay," Shea said without so much as a glance back. "I know exactly where we're going."

Chapter 4

Every now and then, quite frequently, actually, Shea glanced at the sleeping man in the passenger seat of the rumbling old pickup truck. Shea didn't know what year Lenny's two-tone, pale blue and white Ford was, but it was definitely old. They just didn't use chrome like this anymore. Taggert had not wanted her to drive, but he hadn't put up too much of a fuss. He had to know that he was in no shape to drive.

Taggert didn't completely trust her, but he didn't have anyone else to turn to. And he needed help.

Sleeping, he looked much less menacing than he had when he'd threatened her with a gun and tried to send her packing in the rain. Lips soft, ice-chip eyes closed, features relatively relaxed, he was simply beautiful. Not a pretty beautiful, but a *manly* beautiful. The kind that made women's hearts thud and their eyes go misty while they sighed in wonder. He had a real man's face, with a long straight nose and a sharp jawline and a dusting of five o'clock shadow. And that beautiful face was resting atop a nearly perfect body.

She smiled crookedly. Leave it to her to finally find a man she was insanely attracted to *now,* at the most inopportune time and place in the most unsuitable of circumstances. She'd been so focused on her career lately that she brushed off most men who asked her for a date, and the few dates she'd suffered through hadn't been much fun.

She'd let Grace talk her into a blind date with a homicide detective a few months back. Luther Malone. Goodlooking guy, smart, and as anxious for the blind date as she'd been, which meant the evening had gotten off to a very bad start. She hadn't found him to be much fun, and he'd gotten quickly annoyed with her nosy questions. He'd taken her home early and there hadn't been a second date.

Shea took a quick glance at the gas gauge and whistled low and sharp. Almost empty. Like it or not, she would have to stop soon. Better here on a country road than on the interstate, she imagined, spotting the solitary sign straight ahead.

Placing an Atlanta Braves cap, one of Lenny's contributions, on Taggert's head, she left him sleeping while she pumped gas into the guzzler of a truck. She didn't think she looked too strange, even though the outfit she'd scrounged from Lenny's late wife's closet came directly from the sixties. Capri pants were making a comeback, and the blouse was fairly simple, so she didn't think her attire would raise any eyebrows. She'd steered clear of the tiedye T-shirts and the neon-green bell-bottom pants.

When the tank was full she went inside to pay, heading for the back of the store to grab a couple of soft drinks and two banana Moon Pies. Taggert hadn't eaten nearly enough of his sandwich, and he'd need his strength. Maybe a sugar boost would do it. She could use a sugar boost herself, truth be told.

She was at the counter counting out bills when the state trooper walked in. Her heart nearly stopped.

"Hi, Billy," the clerk said with a wide smile. This was apparently a regular stop for Billy, the tall, thin trooper.

"Toby," the officer said with a professional nod. "How's it going?"

"Slow," Toby said as Shea very carefully counted out her change. "You know how it is."

Her first instinct was to turn and run like hell, but she didn't. She took her drinks and Moon Pies and declined a bag, and glanced through the window to see that Taggert still slept. Thank goodness she'd thought to put the ball cap on his head!

"Where you headed, little lady? That your truck outside?"

Shea's heart stopped. The trooper was talking to her! She took a deep breath and turned to face him, hoping the change of clothes and the fact that her hair was pulled severely back and her face scrubbed clean of makeup made enough of a difference in her appearance that he wouldn't immediately recognize her.

She looked at him closely before speaking, to see if he made the connection. Apparently he didn't. "My husband and I are headed to Florida to see my mama," she said, putting on her best, deepest Southern accent. She sounded a lot like her cousin Susan, she decided as the words left her mouth. "Hate to get that old truck on the interstate, since it won't do more than forty-five, and besides—" she gave the trooper a bright smile "—I like the drive better this way."

He nodded. "I know what you mean. You be careful, though. When I came on duty I heard a murderer from

Huntsville escaped this afternoon.'' Billy shook his head, a quite large head on a long, narrow neck, she noticed.

''Really?''

''I hear it was all over the news, but since I'm on night shift I slept right through it.'' He gave her a crooked smile. ''Didn't you see nothing about it?''

''Nope. I guess I was busy packing for the trip when the news was on.''

The trooper looked through the window to the truck, where Taggert stirred. Just a little.

''I'd better get moving. In a couple of hours it'll be my turn to sleep and Pookie will have to do the driving.'' *Pookie?* What was she thinking! ''He'll expect to find us a ways down the road when that happens.''

Shea shuffled the drinks and Moon Pies to make sure they were secure in her hands, said good-night to the clerk and the trooper, and escaped into the muggy night air with a sigh of relief. He hadn't recognized her! Would he later, when he saw her picture on television or in the newspaper? Maybe. Maybe not.

She climbed into the truck and placed her purchases on the seat between her and Taggert. He opened his eyes, just slightly, and reached up to remove the ball cap.

And the trooper left the store with a cup of coffee in his hand.

Taggert leaned forward, moving slowly toward her, his lips parted to speak. The trooper was just about to pass in front of the truck, and his head rotated in their direction. After her heart leaped into her throat, Shea drew a deep breath and followed her instincts.

She took Taggert's face in her hands and pulled his mouth to hers, kissing him to hide his face from the trooper. Out of the corner of her eye she saw Billy smile as he passed. She watched the trooper turn his attention to his patrol car, his smile still in place, and all the while her lips were glued to Taggert's.

Feeling the danger was past when Billy stepped into his car, she started to pull away, but Taggert grabbed the back of her head with tender fingers and held her in place. His mouth moved over hers, soft and tender, as his tongue tasted her lower lip. Heavens, he was warm, softly arousing, close and intimate. There was no searing demand in the kiss, in fact it was quite sweet, but as it continued, she instinctively kissed him back, and something deep within her stirred. Something that didn't *need* stirring, thank you very much.

Taggert's hand slipped down and settled at the back of her neck, and a low growl escaped from deep in his throat as he continued to kiss her quite thoroughly. He didn't touch her anywhere else, but Shea felt that kiss all through her body. Her nipples hardened, her knees shook, she felt her heart rate increase.

The trooper pulled away, and Shea turned her head to remove her lips from Taggert's. He didn't fight, but instead let his head fall heavily onto her shoulder. ''Did I tell you how good you smell?'' he whispered. ''Fresh and clean and feminine. I didn't know I would miss the way a woman smells,'' he said in a low, groggy voice.

''Go back to sleep, Taggert,'' Shea said, placing her hands on his shoulders and forcing him gently into his corner of the truck. ''With any luck, you won't even remember this.''

''Nick,'' he said as he settled back with his eyes drifting closed. ''Any woman who kisses like you do should call me Nick.''

''Nick,'' she said softly, placing the baseball cap on his head. He immediately removed it and tossed it to the floor, where it landed on a small stack of T-shirts Lenny had contributed to the cause.

She sighed heavily and started the rumbling engine, pulling away from the pumps and onto the two-lane road. Heavens. If that trooper ever did recognize her and realize who the man in the truck was, she would be in deep. Way too deep.

About a mile down the road, she took the cell phone from her purse and switched it on. Mark was on speed dial. This would be her last chance to use the phone. Once they got where they were going it wouldn't be safe. The cellular company could trace them to this area, but right now they were on the move. From here they could go anywhere. Georgia, Florida. South Alabama.

"Mark," she said, when her cameraman answered the phone. "It's me."

"Shea?" he shouted. "Oh my, are you all right? Did he hurt you? Where are you? I'll come—"

"Mark, I just have a minute," she interrupted. "Listen carefully."

She heard him breathing, but he said nothing. "First of all, call Boone in Birmingham and tell him to call my folks and Clint and Dean and tell them I'm all right."

"Are you?" Mark asked softly.

"Yes, I'm fine," Shea assured him. "Ask Boone to check into the Taggert trial and the Winkler murder and see if he finds anything odd."

"Done," Mark said, all-business.

"Then call my friend Grace Madigan and see if she'll do the same. She and Boone will take different tacks, so they might come up with different results." Grace's husband was a private investigator in Huntsville, and she'd been working for him for months. Mark and Boone and Grace. Shea didn't trust anyone else.

"Okay. Shea? What's going on?"

"Just…trust me, Mark."

She heard his uncertain sigh over the crackling line.

"Do you have caller ID yet?" she asked.

"Nope."

"Don't get it," she said. "I'll call you in a few days and this will only work if you don't know where I am."

"Jeez, Shea," he said in a low voice. "This sounds dangerous."

She glanced at the man sleeping beside her. "It is," she said softly.

Tara, Nick thought dizzily as he opened his eyes. A gravel driveway crunched beneath the slow-moving truck tires, and the moonlight shone brightly on…Tara.

"You're awake," the weathergirl said in a low voice. "That's good. I was afraid I wouldn't be able to rouse you, and I really do not want to spend the night in this truck."

He'd been out for hours. Plenty of time for Shea Sinclair to reconsider her foolish plan and drive him directly to the nearest police station.

But she hadn't. "Where are we?"

"Marion," she said with a smile. "My aunt's house. They're on vacation. My cousin Susan lives in California, and her first baby is due in a couple of days. Aunt Irene and Uncle Henry won't be home for weeks."

The gravel drive circled the house, and Shea stopped before the back door. *Not Tara,* Nick thought as he looked at the peeling white paint and overgrown garden. *But not a police station, either.* It was such a relief to know that someone, anyone, believed in his innocence. He might be a good story to the weathergirl, but she had to believe…. She wouldn't bring him here if she thought he was guilty. She wouldn't stay with him if she thought he was a cold-blooded killer.

She didn't kill the engine, but jumped out of the driver's seat to circle the truck and open his door. She offered an arm in assistance, and he took it and stepped down.

"You wait here," she said softly, "while I hide the truck in the barn."

"There's a barn?" He leaned on her and remembered...something. The way she smelled, the way she tasted. The way she *tasted?*

"It's pretty far back on the property and hidden from the road, so I don't think anyone will even think to look for the truck there. It's too far for you to walk, though." She left him leaning against the kitchen door and hurried back to the truck. As it rumbled away, he watched the tail lights. When he couldn't see them anymore, he closed his eyes and slumped to the ground. How did he know what she tasted like?

The next thing he knew Shea was there again, and he was sitting on the porch with his back against the door. He'd fallen asleep, or passed out, while she'd been taking care of hiding the truck. She lifted a potted plant and reached beneath it, pulling out a key. What kind of a town was this?

"The kind of town where people trust their neighbors," Shea said as she assisted him to his feet and placed an arm around his waist, propping him up while she slipped the key into the lock.

"Did I ask that out loud?" he whispered.

"You mumbled," she said, opening the door to a dark kitchen.

"No lights," she said. "I don't expect any of the neighbors are up this late, and most of the house is shielded by trees anyway, but I don't want to take any chances. We haven't come this far just to get caught because we turned on a light."

We, she said.

"The moonlight will do," she said sensibly. "For now."

He let her lead him through the kitchen, through a huge dining room, to the foot of the stairway.

"Can you make it up the stairs?" she asked, uncertainty in her voice.

"Of course I can," he snapped, angry at his weakness, at his inability to think straight. Tomorrow morning everything would be better. Tomorrow he would know what to do.

Moving up the stairs was slow going, with Shea on one side, the banister on the other and his body being completely uncooperative. He was breathless when they reached the first landing, near to passing out again when they reached the second floor.

"Carol's room is the closest," Shea said, turning him to the right. "I hope you like purple."

Nothing had any color in the moonlight, but oh, the double bed looked soft, and warm, and if he could just make it that far...

At the edge of the bed he tumbled, falling to the soft mattress, pulling Shea with him. She squealed a little, in surprise, just before they landed with a gentle bounce.

He held on tight to still the spinning in his head. Shea Sinclair could make the spinning stop. She could ground him. He drew her close, testing her softness and warmth. Feeling the wonderful way her curves settled against the length of his body.

"You can let me up now," she whispered.

"Not yet." He buried his face against her hair, reached out and removed the rubber band that contained the dark strands, so her locks spilled down and around. "You smell so good."

"So I've been told," she muttered unhappily.

"You smell like sunshine and soap and...sex."

"I do not," she insisted, pushing against his chest.

He didn't let go. He hadn't slept in a real bed in ten months, had forgotten what a soft mattress felt like. He'd forgotten what a woman felt like, but Shea brought it all back. The feminine shape. The gentle suppleness.

"How do I know how good you taste?" he asked, pulling her close and resting his head against her shoulder as he laid one leg, the uninjured one, over both of hers.

"You don't," she snapped. "You're delusional."

He pressed his lips against her neck, very briefly. "No," he said. "I'm not." He used what little strength he had against her, holding her down gently, locking his leg around hers, laying an arm over her chest.

"Let me go."

"I just want to sleep," he said, feeling himself drift away. "And I want to hold you while I sleep. Smell you. Taste you."

"Taggert…" she said, her voice distant and uncertain.

"I won't hurt you, I swear," he whispered. "I would never…"

As he drifted away he heard her whisper, "I know."

Taggert was heavy, warm and massive, and sound asleep. It might've been possible to slip out from under him and make her way to Susan's room for the night, but Shea allowed herself to remain beneath him as her own exhaustion washed over her.

Besides, maybe he really did need to hold her as he slept. She liked that idea, that someone needed her in such a simple way. She didn't have to worry about him trying anything funny. He was in no shape, physically, to be a threat to her.

Stretched out beside and over her exhausted body, touching and holding her, Taggert seemed massive and overwhelming. He fixed her to the mattress with his muscled arm and one long leg. He leaned into her, too, in a way that pinned her down without crushing her beneath his weight.

Still at last, safe in the dark, she finally had time to ask herself the big question. What had she done? Taggert had given her the chance to escape, and other chances had come and gone. Yes, this was a big story, but it was more than that.

The same sense of right and wrong that had driven Dean to the U.S. Marshals Service and Boone to the Birmingham Police Department and then into his own P.I. practice lurked within her, too. She couldn't stand by while an innocent man went to prison, and maybe even to the electric chair. It went against everything her parents had taught her. Justice. Honor. Moral integrity. Okay, they were old-fashioned ideals in a technical world, but they were what she knew and believed in.

She sank into the mattress, Taggert's heavily muscled leg over hers, his arm across her midsection, his breath against her neck. She had to admit, as her eyes drifted closed, that it felt good, after an endless, crazy day, to sleep entangled with a long, warm man. It was a sensation she'd never experienced before, one she was surprised to like so much.

Shea didn't drift toward sleep, but fell. Hard and fast.

Chapter 5

She remembered this large old kitchen well. Summers spent in this house had been magical for Shea. For a few weeks she had the sisters she'd never known, a mother who danced in the kitchen and a father who told gross jokes to make the girls laugh.

Not that she didn't love her own family. She adored her brothers, each and every one of them, and her parents had been wonderful to her. They just weren't much fun. Her mother was reserved and her father was solemn. The only time she'd seen them display any real emotion was when Clint had run off to join the rodeo. Her mother had almost fainted, and her father had turned quite pale and said words she'd not heard from his mouth before or since.

They would be livid when they learned that she'd passed up a chance at escape to remain with Nick Taggert. And they would find out. When this was all over, she couldn't let anyone think he'd kept her captive this long! She'd tell anyone who would listen that he'd tried to let her go a couple of hours after the initial kidnapping.

She'd awakened this morning to find herself still trapped in his arms, but extricating herself had not been difficult. He'd been dead to the world. His breathing had been deep but normal, and he hadn't felt hot to her, so she decided to believe that he was simply sleeping deeply. Not unconscious. If he got worse, she would have to call in a doctor. Nick wouldn't like that, and if *anyone* knew where they were hiding they wouldn't have time to find the real murderer. But what good would the truth be if Taggert was dead?

Shea rearranged the sizzling bacon in the pan and sang along with the cassette that played in the boom box on the windowsill. With two female cousins to hang out with and Aunt Irene's all-time-favorite music playing most of the day, they had formed their own girl group every summer. They hadn't sung and lip-synched to the popular stuff of the day, but to good old sixties Motown. The Supremes. Martha Reeves and the Vandellas. Oh, Shea had so wanted to be a Vandella, a doo-wop singer in a slinky green sequined gown and a voice that made people stop in the streets.

Well, she had a voice that made people stop in the streets, but not for the right reason. Still, she wanted to be able to doo-wop, and when she'd stayed with her cousins and her Aunt Irene, she had. They never threatened to gag her the way Boone always did when he caught her singing.

"Heat Wave" came on, and Shea couldn't help but sing along; very softly, of course, to keep from disturbing the man who slept upstairs. She turned the bacon again and then threw in one of the old moves she and Susan and Carol had practiced. A step to the right, a swing of the hips, a twirl…and she found herself facing the tall, dark man who leaned against the kitchen doorjamb. In spite of herself, she squealed.

A wry smile crept across his face. "Good morning. I smelled the bacon."

In the jeans he'd slept in and a very wrinkled plaid shirt, his short dark hair only slightly mussed, Nick Taggert still was temptingly handsome. That stubbled chin made him look rough and untamed.

Shea quickly gathered her composure. "I found a package in the freezer, and a half-dozen eggs in the fridge. What are you doing out of bed? I was going to bring you breakfast when it's finished. You should be resting."

His smile didn't last long. Too bad. It was rather nice. "Where's the pistol?" he asked in a low voice.

She prepared to do battle. "Sitting in the front seat of my car, along with what's left of our clothes."

"At Lenny's," he said, his nostrils flaring slightly.

"At Lenny's." She wasn't going to allow him to intimidate her. They had too much to do, no time to waste. Besides, with three older brothers to harass her all her life, she'd never intimidated easily. "What's the matter, did you plan to shoot someone this morning?"

"No."

"Neither do I." She flashed him a grin. "So you see, we don't need that pistol at all."

He sighed, long and slowly, before speaking again. "Why are you still here? Didn't you wake up this morning and come to your senses?"

"Apparently not," she answered softly, aware that no matter how she tried to pretend otherwise, the mere presence of this man kindled something inside her. Cool was impossible, calm was unlikely. She, who was always so together, felt jumpy when he rested those blue eyes on her this way.

Shea dismissed her inappropriate attraction for a dozen different reasons. She'd never slept with a man before. That alone might give her these tingly, jumpy sensations.

They were surviving a crisis together. She'd probably be attracted to any halfway decent looking man in these dire circumstances. And Nick Taggert was much more than halfway decent looking.

Then there was a woman's habit of being drawn to exactly the wrong kind of man. Shea had never let herself fall into that trap before, but Taggert was definitely the most wrong kind of man a woman could imagine.

He limped to the kitchen table and took the nearest chair, moving cautiously, stretching his wounded leg carefully before him. "Now that my head is clear, I want you to explain to me exactly why you're still here and what you're planning to do."

"You're a great—" Shea began.

"A great story, I know," he snapped. "Honey, I'm already a great story. I kidnapped you on camera. You could leave here right now and be interviewed by all the major networks. Every morning show in the country will want you to be a guest, every—"

"But you're innocent," she interrupted.

He locked his ice-blue eyes to hers. "You still believe me?"

"I do."

"Why?"

Shea took the bacon off the stove and set it aside, and grabbed the chair across the table from Taggert's. She sat, perching on the edge of her seat. "Instinct," she said softly. "Common sense."

"Your nose for news?" he asked sarcastically.

"I want to get at the truth," she said, not letting his anger or her unsuitable fascination deter her. "If I let an innocent man go to prison, then I'm just as guilty as the ones who falsely convicted you."

She caught the softening of his eyes, the spark of hope there. It only made him more attractive to her. Vulnerable and all too real. Not a story at all, but a person who needed her.

"I didn't think anyone cared about the truth anymore," he said quietly.

"I do."

He nodded his head once, and she jumped up and left him sitting there, grateful to return to the stove.

"So," she said brightly, feeling better with her back to him. "How do you like your eggs?"

"Who's Boone?" Nick asked as Shea leaned over his leg and very tenderly cleaned the wound.

She lifted her head sharply and met his gaze. "My brother," she said. "How did you know about Boone?"

He gave her a small smile. *Brother!* "You mentioned him last night, at Lenny's. What about Dean?"

"Also a brother."

"Clint?"

"The youngest of the Sinclair boys," she said, returning her attention to his leg. "He's just a year and a half older than me."

Nick would never forget walking toward the kitchen, drawn by the smell of food, and catching sight of Shea as she danced into his line of vision, singing off-key to "Heat Wave" and twitching her hips in time to the music.

She had found more clothes, a pair of khaki shorts suited to an old house with no air-conditioning, and a white tank top. No bra, he noticed, though he tried not to allow his eyes to wander there too often. Her dark hair had been pulled back and up again, off her slender neck. Just a touch of sweat made her skin take on the sheen of summer. Shea Sinclair was sleek and fresh, an all-American girl with a pretty face and an unusual sense of justice.

And she was modest, too. She'd turned her back while he removed the old jeans Lenny had given him, waiting until he was in the bed with the covers strategically placed over his midsection before turning around to examine and tend to his wound.

He hurt like hell, he was on the run, and at the moment all he could think of was the feel of her hands on his leg, the way her fingers were so tender, the way she smelled, the way she'd slept beneath him last night.

"All brothers," he said after a delay that lasted too long. "What about a husband? A boyfriend?"

"No," she said nonchalantly. "I don't have time for a love life, thank you very much."

Maybe she looked so good because he'd been in jail for almost a year, or maybe it was because she was helping him that he felt...affection.

No, he corrected himself. Not affection. Lust. And if she didn't have time for a love life, maybe she wouldn't be averse to a little casual sex, something hot to blow off steam. A heat wave of their own, when he was stronger and could give her the time and attention she deserved.

He didn't think it would be long now.

But he had to keep her talking, at the moment. It was too soon, for her and for him, to take this conversation where he wanted it to go.

"Tell me about them," he said as she began to rebandage his leg.

"My brothers?" she asked, obviously surprised.

"Yep."

She finished wrapping the length of gauze around his leg and sat on the side of the bed, one protective hand on his knee. "Dean is the oldest. He's seven years older than me, which makes him thirty-two. He was always the serious one." She smiled affectionately. "Determined to keep Boone and Clint out of trouble, taking responsibility for...for everything. He's a Deputy U.S. Marshal now."

Nick swallowed hard. "A Deputy U.S. Marshal?"

"Yeah," Shea said, grinning widely as she looked down at him. "Boone was next, two years younger than Dean."

"What's he, FBI?" Nick snapped.

"No," Shea said with a shake of her head. "Growing up, Boone was always in trouble, and Dean was always trying to help Boone when he didn't want any help, thank you very much. He drove my parents crazy, and the girls...well, let's just say no one got near the phone for a few years."

"Where is he now?"

"Birmingham. He used to be on the police force there, but he had some problems. Boone has never been very good at following the rules." She lifted her eyebrows meaningfully. "A couple of years ago he quit the police department to open his own P.I. business. He specializes in finding lost children."

Nick sighed deeply. "I am afraid to ask about the youngest brother."

Shea's smile turned brilliant. "Clint is a rodeo clown. We all thought Boone would be the black sheep of the family, until Clint ran off to join the rodeo. It was quite a scandal," she teased.

"I can imagine," Nick drawled.

"He rode bulls for a while, but he got bored with that and became a clown."

Nick sat up straight, his back resting against the pillows at the headboard. "So, of all the women available for kidnapping, I had to choose the one who has a brother who's a federal agent, another who's a bad-ass ex-cop, and another who'd rather play with bulls than ride them."

Oh, her smile was brilliant. "That's about it."

He reached out and snagged her wrist. Her reaction was to flinch, not because she was afraid, but because she felt what he did. He didn't let her go.

"Okay, is there anything else you're not telling me?

Any other vital information I should have?'' He pulled on her arm and she scooted along the bed, coming closer. Her hazel eyes flashed; her cheeks flushed pink. And he wanted, more than anything, to pull her down beside him and kiss her. That's all he wanted, for now. Just a kiss.

"Well," she said finally, "my Uncle Henry? The one who owns this house?" She was close now, close enough for him to pull her down for that kiss. He tugged on her arm, just slightly, and she didn't protest as her face came close to his.

She bit her lower lip, then licked. "He's a district judge."

Nick forgot about the kiss and laughed bitterly. He was so screwed.

Thank goodness the summer days were long. There was no need for lights, even at this time of night. She didn't want to rouse the suspicions of anyone passing by who knew the Hunters were out of town.

Shea stepped into Nick's room bearing a tray. She'd raided Aunt Irene's pantry and found crackers and tuna fish and peaches and English peas. It wasn't fancy, but the major food groups were here. She figured Nick would need plenty of protein and vegetables to heal well. And quickly. Like it or not, they didn't have much time.

He'd slept most of the day, awakening when she cleaned his wound or gave him his medicine. If he was in a lot of pain, he hid it well. He never complained. Lenny had said the wound was only a scratch, but it looked like much more than a scratch to Shea. The damage was deep, the furrow ugly. It pained her to look at it, but she did what she had to do without complaint. What choice did she have?

"Taggert?" she whispered, wanting to wake him gently.

"Nick," he said in a low, clear voice as he came awake

and rose carefully to a sitting position. "After all, we have slept together."

The memories of last night's closeness made her heart jolt and her face grow heated. She hoped there wasn't enough light for him to see her blush. "Behave yourself."

"Never," he said promptly, and with an unexpected touch of humor.

"I brought you dinner. I hate to wake you, but I want you to eat before it gets dark."

Nick pushed himself into a sitting position, using his arms. He'd removed his shirt hours ago, thanks to the heat, and beneath the thin quilt all he wore was a pair of boxer shorts. Shea tried to think like a nurse, or a doctor. Professional, distanced, unaffected.

But he had such a *nice* chest, lightly dusted with dark hair and firm and…just a little too thin. She wondered if he'd lost weight during his ten months in jail. The very idea of him locked away in that awful place made her want to cry. Fortunately, Shea Sinclair never cried. It was unprofessional and childish.

She placed the tray on his lap and scooted the hard-back desk chair to the side of the bed, where she sat. Nick ate in silence, and she waited.

"Aren't you going to eat?"

"I ate in the kitchen an hour ago," she said.

"I could've come downstairs—" he began.

"No," she interrupted. "I don't want you pulling that again until you're better. What if you'd fallen?"

"And broken my neck? Story over. An unhappy ending, but then, what do you expect?" He sounded angry.

She ignored the anger. He was hurt; he was a fugitive. He was angry at the world. She felt compelled to fix all that. To repair his leg and his life and find the truth.

"I watched the evening news," she said softly, wondering if she should tell him everything.

He nodded simply, unaffected. Unsurprised.

"They're searching all over for us, but it looks like they're concentrating on your old friends, for now. Someone gave them a tip that you might've gone to Mississippi to an old army buddy's farm."

Nick listened, but he said nothing.

"They found my car at Lenny's, along with the gun you took and what was left of our clothes."

This news made Nick's head snap up. His eyes narrowed. "We knew they'd find it eventually. Is Lenny okay?"

"He's fine." She smiled, remembering watching the gruff old man play to the camera. "He said he had no idea you'd left the Saturn and taken his truck, and then he said you could have the truck because he knew you weren't guilty."

"And they actually aired that opinion?" Nick asked dryly.

"The station I watched did. Lenny has a good face for the camera. And he defended you well."

Nick shook his head and sighed. "What a mess. I never wanted Lenny to get in trouble over this, and your family must be worried sick."

"No," Shea said sensibly. "I called Mark last night and asked him to tell them I'm okay. They won't worry."

Nick put his fork down. His eyes flashed dangerously. "You did what?"

"Relax," she said in a soothing voice. "I called from my cell phone when we were out in the middle of nowhere. I didn't call from this area, and I didn't use Aunt Irene's phone."

He nodded and returned to eating. He ate slowly, as if he didn't have any appetite but knew he needed the food.

"Tomorrow, if you feel up to it, I want to start taking notes."

"What kind of notes?" he asked, setting the half-finished dinner aside.

"I want you to tell me everything about what happened the night Gary Winkler was murdered."

He nodded solemnly.

"Do you have any ideas about who might've killed him?"

Nick shook his head. "Could've been anyone. To be honest, no one liked Winkler. He was a coarse-mouthed, unbearably rude excuse for a human being."

"We'll start a specific list tomorrow, if you're up to it." Shea reached for the tray, wanting to get all the dishes cleaned up before it turned dark. Once night had fallen she'd go on to bed. What else was there to do?

Nick grabbed her wrist and held her there, leaning toward her. Her hands gripped the tray. If she tried to jerk away the dishes and leftovers would fly everywhere, and besides, his grip was so tight she wasn't sure she could manage to free herself. A wounded man who had lost as much blood as he had shouldn't be so strong.

"Are you going to sleep with me again tonight?" he whispered.

"No," she said softly, unable to look him in the eye.

"Why not? It's not like I'm in any shape to do anything but sleep."

She shook her head. Heavens, she was tempted. It had been nice, to snuggle against him when she got cool in the night, to bury her nose against his chest. It had been nice not to be alone. Still, it was a *very* bad idea to even consider allowing last night's sleeping arrangements to continue.

"I liked it," he said softly. "I liked waking up in the middle of the night and feeling your body against mine. You were warm and soft and smelled so sweet. You smell sweet now."

"I'll be right next door if you need anything."

"I need you here," he whispered.

"No."

He sighed his acceptance. "Then kiss me good-night?"

She shook her head, but lifted her face to look at him. His eyes smoldered and his lips looked soft and inviting. Good heavens, what was she going to do when he was well? How was she going to handle this appealing man?

She leaned forward, her lips heading for his rough, stubbled cheek, but he shifted at the last minute and her lips touched his.

His lips were soft, easy, and he didn't try to make the caress more than it was. A sweet, tender good-night kiss. When she pulled away, bringing the tray with her, he didn't try to stop her.

"Good-night, weathergirl," he whispered.

For once she didn't correct him, but hurried from the room with the tray of his unfinished dinner in her hands. What on earth had she gotten herself into?

Chapter 6

"There has to be another reason," Shea said, pacing through the dining room and twirling a pencil in her slender fingers. "I just can't believe that the police would consider Winkler painting his house green a motive for murder."

Nick sat in a solid dining room chair, his bandaged leg resting atop another chair. His mind should be on the questions, but he found his attention wandering to the red shorts and navy blue tank top Shea wore. They hugged her body and showed off her fine legs. Watching her pace was sheer torture.

He dragged his mind to the matter at hand. "They made a big deal out of the fact that I'd built the house, suggesting that I suffered some kind of artistic outrage."

"Did you?" she asked, glancing at him warily.

"A little, but…you're right. That wasn't enough, not even for the morons investigating my case."

"So?" she asked impatiently.

"Sit down," he ordered softly.

"I can't."

"You're making me dizzy."

She sighed and grabbed another chair, placing it where she could see him but wasn't sitting too close. He couldn't help but notice the hint of wariness that touched her eyes. Ah, she tried to pretend all was well, but Shea wasn't completely oblivious to what was happening between them.

"All right. What other motive did they have?"

Nick didn't like to think about Lauren. He'd had such foolish hopes where she was concerned.

"The night of the murder, I had a barbecue at my place," he said, glancing out of the dining room window to the ancient trees that shaded the old house. Shea surely knew about the barbecue already. It had been part of the sordid story. "I'd invited all the neighbors. Have you see the neighborhood?"

He turned his eyes to her and she gently shook her head.

"It's a double cul-de-sac, and I built ten of the houses on that street, including mine and Winkler's. I knew everybody, the weather was just starting to turn cool and nice, and hell, it seemed like a good idea at the time." He had never told anyone everything, but... "I was going to ask my girlfriend, Lauren, to marry me, and I wanted her to meet all the neighbors. I wanted her to feel at home there."

Shea's eyes went wide. "I knew your girlfriend was at the barbecue that night, but I didn't have any idea your relationship was that serious."

Nick shrugged his shoulders as if he didn't care, and turned his gaze to the window again. His contractor's mind noted that the frame needed a fresh coat of paint, that the glass was old enough to give the view beyond a distorted cant.

''Apparently it wasn't all that serious. For Lauren, anyway. Winkler was...have you seen his picture?''

Again, Shea nodded silently.

''He didn't seem like anything special to me, but apparently he was a bit of a ladies' man. I don't know how such an ass gets anywhere with women, but apparently Gary had a gift.''

Shea looked like she knew what was coming.

''Winkler took one look at Lauren and spent the rest of the evening dogging her. Bringing her drinks when her glass was empty, patting her on the butt when she passed, smiling and winking and saying God knows what when he got a chance to corner her.''

''What a jerk,'' Shea muttered sympathetically.

''Unfortunately, Lauren didn't seem to mind. I think she was flattered that he gave her so much attention.''

Shea frowned. ''Wasn't his wife there?''

''Yep. Poor Polly, she's one of those mousy women who lets her husband walk all over her. I caught her watching what was going on, every now and then, but for the most part she ignored Gary. She talked with the other wives, about recipes and Halloween decorations, since the holiday was less than two weeks away, and pretended everything was just fine.''

''But not you,'' Shea said softly.

''I was never very good at letting things go,'' Nick said solemnly. ''I warned Gary once to keep his hands off my woman—taking him aside so I wouldn't embarrass anyone.''

''I'm guessing that didn't work,'' Shea sighed.

Nick shook his head, getting angry all over again. ''He took it as a challenge and moved things up a notch. He drank too much beer and poured Lauren too much wine. They danced to the radio and laughed and whispered.

While I was flipping burgers they had themselves a good old time.''

He had never told anyone everything, but if Shea Sinclair was going to stay in this with him, she deserved to know all the ugly details. "Then they disappeared. No one else seemed to notice. The kids were playing ball, the men were talking golf, the women were talking recipes. I went looking for Lauren and Winkler and found them in the laundry room. If I'd been two minutes later, they would've been doing it right there on the dryer.''

He'd never forget the sight. Lauren sitting on the dryer, her legs wrapped around Winkler. One hand on his neck, the other reaching down between his legs as they locked their mouths together. That low moan coming from her throat had shattered all his stupid, idyllic plans.

"Oh my God," Shea whispered. "Why didn't I hear about this?''

"Only the three of us knew. Winkler was dead, and Lauren wasn't about to tell everyone that she was drunk and wrapped around my neighbor in the laundry room while I was asking the neighborhood ladies if they wanted onions on their damned burgers,'' he snapped.

"But everyone knew that he'd been hitting on her and that I didn't like it,'' he added soberly. "They all saw me drag his sorry ass out of the house and tell him to go home and not come back unless he wanted the beating of his life. When we were where no one else could hear, I told him to keep his grubby hands off Lauren and to keep his dirty mouth shut. He left with a big grin on his face, and poor Polly followed dutifully behind." Nick locked his eyes to Shea's. "Honey, that's motive.''

"Yes it is,'' she whispered.

"But I didn't kill him.''

"I know.''

He shook his head in disbelief. She seemed so sincere,

so naively confident. "How do you know? How do you know I'm not just the best liar you've ever met?"

She grinned and his gut turned over. "I have great instincts. Growing up with three older brothers will do that to a girl." Her smile faded. "I don't think you're a great liar, Nick. I'll bet you're a lousy liar. You're too straight-forward to be good at it."

"Too bad the jury didn't have your instincts," he said bitterly.

Shea shrugged her shoulders and scribbled in her spiral notebook. "We can't worry about that now. All we can do is move forward. So, who else wanted Gary Winkler dead?"

"Everybody," Nick whispered. "Damn near everybody."

She'd wanted a list of possible suspects. She just hadn't expected that the list would be this long.

Nick looked good today, much better than he had yesterday. His eyes were lively, bright and alert, and he wasn't quite so pale, though he could definitely use a few days in the sun. He simply looked stronger. Healthier. She wasn't certain she was prepared to face a healthy Nick Taggert just yet.

"Okay," she said calmly, "so no one liked him. Other neighbors were upset by him painting his house chartreuse and not mowing his lawn regularly."

"And when he did mow," Nick added, "it was at the first appearance of sunlight on a Saturday or a Sunday morning, while everyone else was trying to sleep."

"Annoying, but hardly motive for murder."

"The media made 'annoying' work for me," he said darkly.

Shea gave him an apologetic glance. "If he'd hit on

Lauren, he'd hit on other women. You said he had a reputation as a ladies' man. Any names?''

"Just gossip. A woman where he worked quit after their
affair got ugly, I hear.''

"A name?''

Nick shook his head. "Pearl, Ruby…something like
that. I can't remember.''

"Did anyone check this woman out?''

"I don't know. I told Norman about it, but he said the
cops weren't exactly interested.''

"They already had you,'' she said angrily.

"Exactly.''

She leaned back in her chair and propped her bare feet
on Aunt Irene's old oak table. This task she'd set for herself was much easier when she was not looking directly at
Nick. With his blue eyes and his nice mouth and that snug
black T-shirt he wore, she kept getting distracted. "Anyone else?''

Out of the corner of her eye she saw Nick shake his
head. "He was a shark at work. He bragged once about
taking some poor schmuck's software idea and tweaking
it a little and calling it his own.''

A woman named after a jewel, a computer nerd, an annoyed neighbor, any number of jealous husbands… "What
about Lauren?''

"What?'' Nick asked, snapping his head up.

Shea made herself look him in the eye, trying to gauge
his reaction. "Would she kill Gary and plant the evidence
to convict you?''

"No,'' Nick said quickly, confirming Shea's suspicion
that he was still in love with the woman who had fallen
for Gary Winkler's charms in the laundry room.

Shea lowered her eyes and leaned back to leaf through
her pages of notes, trying to calm the furious pounding of
her heart. Lauren had been faithless and Nick still loved

her. He defended her, when he should be latching on to any and all possible suspects.

"Okay," she said calmly. "The key to the conviction has to be the blood and green paint that was found in your kitchen." Not much, just a drop of each. No fingerprints had been found directly on the damning evidence of Gary Winkler's blood and a touch of bright green paint, though. That in itself should have raised a red flag for the investigators. "Someone must've deliberately placed it there. Since Winkler was killed in the middle of the night, let's assume it was planted there the next day. Who was in your house?"

Nick shook his head. "I've been through this a thousand times. Polly Winkler came by early to collect a dish she'd left the night before. That was just a half hour or so before she discovered the body in her backyard. Norman came by, to see if I wanted to go golfing. A fourth had backed out at the last minute. I declined."

"Norman Burgess, your lawyer?"

"My lawyer, my neighbor and my friend," Nick snapped defensively.

"Anyone else?" Shea asked calmly.

"Lillian Casson, the Winklers' next-door neighbor, came by to collect a dish as well, and after the murder was discovered, two other neighbors stopped by. Tom Blackstone and Carter Able."

"Any one of them could've taken a Taggert Construction T-shirt from the laundry room the night before and dropped it in the storm drain with the baseball bat, then planted the blood and paint that next morning."

Nick shook his head. "I can't believe any one of them could be so cold-blooded."

Shea leaned forward, watching him for reaction. "Where was Lauren?"

He fixed his intense blue eyes on hers and her heart

hitched. "She was there. I let her spend the night on the couch, since she was too damn drunk to drive home."

"Nick," Shea said, using her most sensible voice. "One of these people killed Winkler and pinned it on you."

"I just can't believe—"

"Believe it," she interrupted. Personally, her money was on Lauren. That rush of indignant anger wasn't fueled by jealousy, was it? Of course not!

"Do you still love her?" she asked softly.

Nick's eyes hardened. "No."

"But you did, once?"

He hesitated. "I suppose."

"You were going to ask her to marry you," she said defensively. "You must've loved her."

He took his eyes from her face and stared out the window. She'd caught him doing that several times this afternoon, when he didn't want to answer her probing questions.

"I thought she wanted the same things I did," he said softly. He shrugged his shoulders as if he didn't care. "I was wrong."

"What do you want?" He didn't answer right away so she added, "I'd really like to know."

He continued to stare out the window, and for a long moment Shea though he wasn't going to answer. "A house," he said in a low voice. "Nothing fancy, but something comfortable and safe, with a swing on the front porch and a swing set and a fort out back for the kids."

Her heart hitched. "Kids?"

"At least four." He pinned his eyes on her again. "You had that, didn't you? Two parents, three brothers, a house that was warm in the winter and cool in the summer. The white house with the picket fence and a nice green lawn and laughter coming from behind solid doors that kept out everything ugly and mean."

"Yes," she whispered.

"I didn't," he said. "So I thought I could manufacture that life for myself and a wife and a few kids. I came close." He shut himself off with that statement. Turned off his emotions like he'd flipped a switch that shut everything down. "But I guess it wasn't meant to be."

"When this is over you can—"

"Start all over?" he snapped. "I don't think so."

"It's not too late," she said, closing the cover of her notebook. "You're still young."

He laughed darkly. "Thirty-two never felt so old. It's not the time, weathergirl, it's the will. I don't have it anymore."

"You'll have it again," she said optimistically, wanting that warm, normal life for Nick. After all he'd been through, he deserved it. "You'll see. Once all this is behind you, the will and the drive and the desire will come back."

Nick pinned cold eyes on her. "You'd best not be talking about desire around me, weathergirl. I'm not completely disabled."

He tried to annoy her by calling her "weathergirl," tried to scare her by acting sinister, by glaring at her with a threatening and seductive gleam in his blue eyes.

But she'd been right. Nick Taggert was a terrible liar. He did like her, he did want her—but he would never hurt her.

"I think it's time for you to get to bed," she said, rising to her feet.

He lifted his finely shaped dark eyebrows.

"Don't give me that, Taggert," she said roughly. "You're not so tough."

"I'm not," he said as she helped him to his feet.

"You made it down the stairs on your own, once," she said, wrapping her arm around his waist and heading for the stairs. He leaned against her, warm and snug and familiar, using her for support but not weighing her down. It had become a rather comfortable ritual, the way their arms snaked around the other's waist, the way they stepped in tandem. "When you can make it up on your own, then I might start to worry."

He grumbled.

"Until then," she said, "save your growls and glares. You don't scare me."

"You have no common sense at all," he grumbled.

"Please, if I need to hear *that* I'll call Dean."

Nick smiled as they began to make their way slowly up the stairs. "You're tough, weathergirl."

"Call me 'weathergirl' again and I'll bloody your nose. Again."

His grin, a reluctant smile on a beard-roughened face, seemed real enough. "Fair enough."

"And Nick," she said, softly and with a new seriousness. "Don't give up on your dreams. What you want is very nice. Very warm and real. You'll have it, one day."

He didn't argue with her, but he didn't agree, either.

"What about you?" he asked as they slowly climbed the stairs. "What do you want?"

"Right now career comes first," she said, nodding her head for emphasis.

"What about kids? A husband?"

"I plan to have both, one day, but not in that order," she teased.

"One day," he said softly.

"I can't think about that now," she answered seriously. It was too much. She knew women who tried to have it all, but it never worked. Something suffered. The career. The family. The marriage. "I mean, I see other people with kids and they seem very happy, but I can't imagine myself taking that route." Not now, maybe not ever.

"You'd make a great mother." Nick leaned into her as they reached the top of the stairs.

Her heart hitched. "And why would you say that?"

"You're taking very good care of me, and you don't take any crap from anybody." There was a touch of teasing in his voice again. "Every boy should have a mother who can tend a bloody wound without throwing up, and then send him to bed with no supper when he misbehaves."

No one had ever told her she'd make a great mother before. Surprisingly, she took it as a grand compliment. And then Nick grinned down at her, and her heart nearly pounded through her chest.

Luther leaned back in his chair and glanced up at the three men who hovered over his desk. He didn't need this, not today. The one with the ponytail was an ex-cop, a P.I. now. The one in the crisp gray suit was a Fed. The other one was a damned cowboy. They were Shea Sinclair's brothers, and they were all very angry.

"Anything I can do to help find Shea, I will," he said. "I've offered my assistance to the FBI, but they don't seem to want any help." Since Shea's brother was a federal agent and the kidnapping had actually taken place on camera, the FBI had eagerly jumped all over it. The case was too high-profile to allow a local to participate. He'd been rudely brushed off. "But if I can help you guys, just say the word."

"You called her Shea," the cowboy said, narrowing one eye. "Do you know her?"

Luther recalled their one disastrous date, set up by the ever hopeful Grace Madigan. "She's a friend of a friend."

"I want to see everything you've got on Taggert and the Winkler murder," the P.I. demanded.

"It wasn't my case," Luther explained, reaching for a

peppermint in the candy dish by the phone. "I'm afraid I don't know much."

"Whose case was it?" the Fed asked in a deceptively low voice.

"Daniels's," Luther said as he unwrapped the peppermint. "He's out sick today." The coward. His case had blown up in his face, a killer had kidnapped Shea on camera and Daniels decides to stay home pretending to have a tummy ache.

"He's gonna be sick if he doesn't get his ass down here," the cowboy grumbled.

"Let me give him a call," Luther said calmly, popping the candy into his mouth and reaching for the phone.

Daniels answered on the third ring, sounding tired and sleepy, but not exactly deathly ill.

"Shea Sinclair's brothers are here looking for the Taggert file," Luther said, his eyes on the Fed.

Daniels's response was obscene.

"One of them is a Deputy U.S. Marshal," Luther added. "I think he'd like to discuss the case with you."

Daniels was quiet for a moment, then he hemmed and hawed. All the while, Luther watched while Shea's brothers got stonier and more eagle-eyed. A vein in the Fed's temple bulged. The P.I. flexed his fists. The cowboy cracked his knuckles.

"Just give him the folder," Daniels finally said. "It's in my bottom righthand drawer."

Luther was a little surprised Daniels folded so quickly, but he agreed and hung up the phone.

"You're in luck," he said as he led the Sinclair brothers across the room to a messy, folder-laden desk. "Daniels is actually willing to share."

"He can't get his sorry ass down here?" one of the brothers muttered behind him. Luther's money was on the cowboy.

Luther retrieved a slim folder from the bottom drawer and handed it over to the Fed. "It's all yours."

The man in the gray suit practically sneered. "This is it?" He opened the manila folder and flipped through. "This is all he's got?"

Daniels was a lazy cop, always taking the easy way out. Sinclair was right: that folder should've been three times as thick. Would've been, if Daniels had done a decent job of investigating the crime.

"This Daniels might've been the primary, but he must've worked with a partner, right?" the P.I. asked angrily.

"He had a partner at the time," Luther said, searching his memory. "But Fred was about to retire, and I don't think he spent much time on this case."

"Where is this Fred?" the cowboy asked through clenched teeth.

"Arizona, I think."

Together the brothers glanced through the thin file. The scant information there did not improve their moods.

"You know," Luther said, sucking on his peppermint, "Daniels probably kept a lot of the information on the case in his head." He tapped his own temple as he returned to his desk. "You should talk to him directly." He sat down, grabbed a notepad and scribbled down Daniels's address.

He ripped the piece of paper out of the notebook and handed it to the closest Sinclair—the P.I. with the ponytail. "I'm sure he wouldn't mind if you fellas dropped by to discuss the case."

As the Sinclair brothers left, Luther experienced a rush of satisfaction the likes of which he hadn't felt in a very long time. He even smiled as the door closed behind the cowboy.

Chapter 7

It was time to call Mark again, but she was getting nervous about the prospect. Shea didn't think anyone would be monitoring her cameraman's phone calls, but anything was possible.

She didn't dare call anyone else, not yet. Her parents had caller ID, and would be no help at all in any case. Grace had caller ID, too, darn it, and her husband, an ex-cop, would surely take whatever useful information he gathered about her whereabouts to the police. Shea and Mark worked together well, but they didn't socialize and no one would suspect that he'd be the one she'd call, given the opportunity. Except Boone, she thought with a grimace, and Grace, since she'd already passed along a message through Mark.

Life had been much simpler before caller ID, Shea thought as she reached for the yellow phone on the kitchen wall.

It was early morning, not yet six, and she woke Mark up. He grumbled a groggy hello into the telephone.

"Mark?" she said softly.

"Shea!" He was instantly awake, and through the phone lines she heard his bed creak as he shot up. "Are you all right?"

"I'm fine," she said calmly. "Do you have a paper and pencil?"

She waited while he fetched what he needed, tapping her bare toes nervously on the kitchen floor.

When Mark was back on the line, she gave him the names of her suspects, placing Lauren at the top of the list and including the co-worker who'd had an affair with Winkler, Pearl or Ruby or whatever, and everyone who had stopped by Nick's house the day after the murder. One of them had planted the evidence.

"Give this information to Boone and to Grace." Shea bit her bottom lip. "And I can't call you anymore," she added softly.

"Why not?"

"Boone's going to get suspicious after this second phone call. Grace, too. They'll probably try to tap your phone. It wouldn't be legal, but that won't stop either one of them."

"You need to be able to call someone, Shea," Mark barked. "Dammit, we want to know you're all right! I'll go nuts if you just…disappear."

Shea smiled. "He's not going to hurt me, I swear."

"Not good enough," Mark grumbled.

"I don't know what else to do."

"I do," Mark said, his voice brighter than before. "I have a friend who lives next door. No caller ID, and no possible reason for anyone to tap his phone. Call me there in two days. I should have something by then. Seven o'clock in the evening, after I get home from work." He rattled off the number, and Shea scribbled it down, relieved to have a point of contact.

"Take care of yourself," Mark said warmly as Shea said goodbye.

She hung up the receiver and stared down at her notes and the phone number, feeling that she'd accomplished something by touching base with Mark and setting up the next phone call. When she lifted her head and saw Nick standing in the doorway, staring at her with those cold blue eyes, she couldn't help herself. She jumped. And surely that was *not* a squeal coming out of her mouth!

"You should be in bed," she chastised him, when her heart beat normally again. She tried her hardest not to stare at his bare chest. A man shouldn't look so good in nothing but a pair of jeans. She shouldn't be fascinated by a naked chest and big bare feet, by the height and leanness of a body. Every man on earth had legs, and arms, and a chest. She sighed, giving in and admitting that not many of them were put together quite this nicely.

"So should you," he said.

"I haven't been shot," she countered.

But she might've been, she remembered. She'd been running from Nick and he'd fired a warning shot and threatened to shoot her in the leg. She remembered, too well, the blast of the gunfire, the sight of him kneeling on the ground with that pistol pointed at her.

"Back there on the mountain, right after you escaped," she began in a soft voice. "Would you really have shot me if I hadn't stopped?"

He hesitated. Ah, he hadn't hesitated at all when she'd asked him the first time.

"Probably," he said. He looked her up and down, and a fire grew in his eyes. Something smoldered there, and she realized belatedly that she was wearing one of Susan's old nightgowns. It was plain, ordinary, long and white and worn. And with the morning light streaming through the kitchen window, Nick could no doubt see right through it.

She nonchalantly brought the notebook to her chest, trying to cover her breasts. His eyes remained riveted below her waist.

"But I'm glad I didn't have to," he added huskily. "It would be a shame to scar those legs of yours." He very slowly lifted his eyes to her face, taking his time, and gave her a crooked smile that set her heart to pounding. "A real shame."

He hadn't felt this kind of raw heat for a woman in a very long time. Maybe never. Nick wrote off his raging lust to the fact that he'd been in jail for the past ten months, and tried to cool his heated response.

Shea Sinclair was a reporter, and she was doing her job. Nothing more. She had no interest in him beyond what kind of ratings she'd get on her news broadcast when this was all over.

So why did she look at him this way? Like she felt the same attraction he did. Like she wanted him, here and now.

"Come on," she said sensibly, coming toward him with that damned notebook held over her breasts, the thin white cotton of her nightgown dancing around her slender legs, her bare feet stepping gingerly across the kitchen floor. "You need to get back to bed. You are a terrible patient." She didn't look at his face as she chastised him for leaving his bed, but kept her gaze firmly on his chest.

When she reached him, she fluttered her fingers in a silent order for him to turn around, to clear the doorway so she could pass. He didn't move.

"Why are you doing this?" he asked. "Why are you still here?"

Shea shuddered. She tried to hide her reaction, but he saw her slight response. "I told you, I can't allow an innocent man to go to the electric chair or to prison for the rest of his life."

"So, you're like a modern-day female Lone Ranger," he said dryly.

She lifted her head and pinned warm, hazel eyes on his face. Ah, he'd made her angry. Her cheeks were flushed pink; her eyes danced. "I don't suppose it ever occurred to you to simply say thank-you, to be grateful that someone believes in your innocence, to be content with—"

He grabbed her chin and whispered, "Thank you," as he lowered his head to kiss her. Her lips were soft and sweet, surprised and...yielding. She didn't fight; she didn't pull away from him and protest his audacity. After a moment, she kissed him back.

This would work. Maybe she was in this for her damned story and justice, but that didn't mean they couldn't enjoy one another, that they couldn't behave as any two healthy adults who were attracted to one another might behave. Sex for the sake of sex, something hot and memorable to break the tension and cure this heat and pain in his body. He wanted her beneath him again, in that soft bed upstairs, but this time he wouldn't fall asleep. This time would be different.

He took the notebook from Shea and dropped it on the floor, never breaking the gentle kiss. She didn't protest as the notebook slipped from her fingers. But then, she probably didn't realize that her nipples were so hard they were prominent beneath the thin cotton nightgown. She probably didn't realize what an arousing sight she was.

Then again, maybe she did.

Shea slipped her arms around his neck and parted her lips slightly, and Nick went hard, blood rushing to his loins and leaving him light-headed. Thank goodness he leaned against the doorjamb...though falling to the floor with Shea in his arms didn't seem like such a bad idea, at the moment.

There was nothing awkward about the way they came

together, as if they knew one another well. Her lips moved, softened, sucked lightly against his. All they'd shared was one simple, sweet good-night kiss, but this heated and arousing caress seemed familiar, like a good memory any man would savor.

It was Shea who pulled away, a slight frown on her pretty face. "Why did you do that?"

"Why not? Seemed like a good idea, that's all."

"Well," she said, trying to sound firm but falling far short, with her well-kissed lips and thin nightgown and breathy voice. "It was not a good idea."

"It was just a kiss, weathergirl. A simple thank-you."

She lifted skeptical, narrowed eyes to him. "That's your way of saying thank you?"

"Yes," he whispered.

"Well…" She slipped past him and into the dining room. "You're welcome, and don't thank me again."

"Why not?"

She grabbed her notebook from the floor and headed for the stairway. "I don't want to feel this appreciated," she mumbled.

Nick smiled as he watched her climb the stairs. He didn't quite have the strength to leave the support of the doorway, not just yet. At the landing she turned and looked down at him. Surely she didn't know that the window behind her made her nightgown damn near transparent.

"And if you have the strength to…to thank me like that, you can surely make your way up the stairs on your own." Chin high, eyes clear, she looked downright defiant.

"Yes, ma'am," he said softly, knowing it would be awhile before he could possibly climb those stairs.

Once Nick started to recover, he healed quickly. In the two days since he'd *thanked* her, he'd eaten more, and he

got around on his own with no problem but for a slight
limp.

She needed to make a trip to the grocery store for more
food, but what if someone recognized her? Not everyone
in Marion knew her, but she had a number of old friends
here, people who knew Aunt Irene and had met Shea during her summer visits. Besides, strangers really stood out
in this small town.

But Nick needed protein to heal, and she'd used up all
the tuna in the cupboard and they were out of eggs. He
had to eat well to improve, to get his strength back.

She still felt his kiss. His 'thank-you' had been different
from the first kiss, when he'd been delirious and she'd only
kissed him to hide his face from the state trooper. And it
had been very different from the sweet good-night kiss that
had kept her up half the night. The thank-you had been
very…involved. Very nice. It would be too easy to fall for
Nick Taggert, and she didn't have the time or the incli-
nation for a romantic involvement.

With the man who had kidnapped her! Wasn't that a
syndrome, or something? She did not want to be a cliché?

Still, she had to admit that Nick could be very sweet.
Tough as he was, cynical as he could be, he wanted such
ordinary things from life. Justice. A home and family.
Swings. She hated to see him give up those simple dreams.

She heard a grunt from the parlor, and afraid that Nick
had hurt himself again, she hurried through the kitchen and
parlor and found him on the floor…doing push-ups.

"Stop that!" she demanded sharply.

Nick ignored her and continued with his exercise. Wearing nothing but his jeans, he concentrated on the matter at
hand. Keeping his body rock hard and perfectly aligned as
he pushed himself up and slowly lowered himself down
so that his nose touched the floor. His muscles bunched,

and he'd already worked up a sweat. Oh, she did not need this!

"For goodness sake, stop it!" she commanded.

He did as she asked, ending his exercise and sitting on the floor to look up at her. She could see the strain on his face, the pain in his eyes.

"Are you insane?" she asked.

"I think…maybe," he said with a half smile.

"What are you doing?"

He rose slowly and gingerly to his feet. Oh, she wished he'd remained on the floor. Standing, he was too tall, too menacingly tempting. And his bare chest was practically in her face.

"I need to start training."

He needed to heal, to grow stronger. But was she ready for him to be completely well? Strong and healthy and…oh dear, how would she resist him then? "I'm going to the grocery store. Do you want anything?"

His eyes lit up. "A pack of condoms?"

Shea swallowed hard and tried to maintain her composure. "Be serious."

"I am."

"Fine, I'll pick out food on my own. If I come home with something you don't like, that's just too bad."

"Anything but spinach," he said, making his way to the couch and sitting slowly, favoring his injured leg.

Shea fetched the ottoman from in front of the wing chair and placed it where Nick could rest his leg on it. "I don't see how pushing yourself is going to help matters," she said testily, watching as he lifted his leg to the ottoman.

"I have to get my strength back," he said.

"What's the hurry?"

He laughed darkly. "What's the hurry? Every lawman in Alabama, and quite a few from out of the state, is looking for us. Then there are your brothers to contend with, and your uncle the judge.''

''But some things can't be rushed,'' she said sensibly. ''You can't...''

She squealed when Nick reached up, grabbed her wrist and pulled her down to sit beside him. She landed too close. Hip to hip. Thigh to thigh.

''I don't have the luxury of time, Shea,'' he said in a low voice. ''Some things need to be rushed, like it or not.'' The way he looked at her, she had to wonder if he was talking about his leg or something else. She figured... something else. This thing between them was like a monster that grew every day. It was strong; it was powerful. It most definitely had fangs.

Nick lifted his hand to her face, trailed his fingers down her cheek. Her heart fluttered and her nipples hardened. ''We could be good together, Shea.''

She swallowed hard.

''And I want you so bad. If the situation was different, I'd wine and dine you. I'd bring you flowers and candy and charm you until you just couldn't stand it anymore.''

She had no doubt but that he could do just that, if he put his mind to it.

He didn't take his hand from her face, but continued to touch her with gentle, exploring fingers. ''We're two adults, neither of us is involved in a serious relationship, and you can't say the temptation isn't there.''

''No, I can't,'' she admitted. ''But I've only known you for a few days.''

''What difference does that make?''

''You kidnapped me!''

''I tried to let you go.''

Shea licked her lips. She couldn't say she wasn't tempted. ''You shot at me.''

''But I didn't actually shoot you.''

She wondered, still, if he would have shot her if she'd kept running. Somehow she doubted it, no matter what he said. "It doesn't make sense to even think about starting a relationship during a crisis of these proportions. We're caught up in the heat of the moment, but it's not...this is just..."

He kissed her neck, buried his face there and whispered against her shoulder, "I'm not talking about a relationship, Shea. I'm talking about sex. We're two relatively healthy adults, the attraction is there, we're going to be together for God knows how long." His hand settled high on her side, his thumb brushing the swell of her breast. "You said you didn't have time for romance. When was the last time you let a man into your bed, Shea?"

That would be a tough question to answer. "You're talking about casual sex," she whispered. "A quick tumble."

"I didn't say anything about *quick*," he whispered back, kissing her neck again. Oh, she loved the feel of his mouth there, beneath her ear. She loved the heat and smell and weight of him, leaning into her. It would be so easy to say yes, to give him what he wanted. What she wanted.

She more than wanted Nick, she liked him. She liked him a lot. When was the last time she'd met a man she liked so much? The men she worked with were all caught up in their careers, just as she was. They were selfish, controlling, pretty-boy jerks, for the most part.

Nick was smart, but he didn't play games. He'd been treated badly, by Lauren, by the press, by the police, but he hadn't whined, "Why me?" Not once. He wanted to do something about his problem. He wanted to fix this mess himself. And he wanted her.

He didn't pretend he wanted anything more from her than sex. He laid it all on the line, and as he kissed her neck and settled his hand more securely on her breast, she was tempted. She was sorely tempted. And maybe it was time. Maybe she'd waited long enough.

It took all her willpower, but Shea placed her hands on Nick's chest and pushed. He didn't persist, but moved obediently away from her. "I don't have casual sex," she said, hoping she didn't sound like a complete prude.

"Too bad," he whispered, moving away to lay his head back against the sofa and close his eyes. She was so tempted to reach over and push back that lock of black hair that fell over his sweaty forehead, to lean over him and into him and wrap her legs around him....

Too bad, indeed. If she was a different woman, she'd jump at the chance to sleep with a man like Nick. She would follow her instincts and surprise him right now, with a caress and a kiss and an offer he wouldn't refuse. He was charming, good-looking, strong, and he had a great body. She should know. She'd seen almost all of it! Yes, Nick Taggert was everything a woman might look for in a lover.

But she wasn't what any man was looking for, not where sex was concerned. Men like Nick wanted women who were experienced, who could give and take and enjoy, who could make a man feel good and then walk away with a smile and no regrets. Good heavens, she didn't even know where to start.

Well, she had a pretty good idea where to *start,* but when it came to practical experience, she had none. And she wasn't about to tell Nick that she was a virgin!

Chapter 8

A wide-brimmed hat and a polka-dot scarf disguised her hair, and a pair of Aunt Irene's largest sunglasses covered her eyes. She had no choice but to walk to the Jitney Jungle, since the truck was too recognizable and was sure to be spotted by the Marion police as it rumbled through town, and Uncle Henry's Cadillac was well known. Shea didn't need that kind of attention turning her way.

Nick had asked if she wanted him to come along, but his leg was not strong enough. They both knew it. Besides, he was more recognizable than she was! She could alter her appearance to something more casual than was ever shown on television, with no makeup and the borrowed accessories, but Nick...there was no disguising that face of his. He hadn't argued for long, but finally agreed that it was best if she went alone.

Thankful that she hadn't run into anyone she knew, Shea entered the kitchen and gratefully set the three plastic bags of groceries on the counter. The house was quiet. Too quiet. She locked the door behind her and took the meat and eggs from one bag, putting them in the refrigerator. The walk wasn't a long one, but on a hot day like this she wasn't anxious to leave the groceries out any longer than was necessary. She took the other items into the pantry and arranged them neatly on the shelf. What was here would have to last them awhile. She didn't have a lot of cash left, and writing a check or using her charge card was out of the question.

She removed her disguise and dropped the items on the kitchen table, ruffling her hair and glad to be free of the hat. It had shaded her face from the sun and added to her disguise, but it was too hot to wear a hat!

As she had while she'd put the groceries away, she listened for Nick. Grunting, mumbling, moving about the house. She heard nothing. Maybe he was taking a nap. He needed to do that, after this morning's foolish exercise, but somehow she doubted he was upstairs in Carol's lavender bedroom, napping the afternoon away.

And then it hit her. He was gone. She actually felt dizzy for a moment. He'd just been waiting for her to leave the house so he could make his getaway. He'd tried to dump her once. His chance had come again and he'd jumped at it.

She left the kitchen, somehow sure she wouldn't find him in the dining room or the parlor. And she didn't. She climbed the stairs quickly, listening for sounds of movement on the second floor. All was silent. Just to be sure, she checked each and every room. The silence grew, and she felt something grow inside her. Panic. A sense of loss.

Nick was gone.

But he couldn't have gotten far, she thought, hope springing up inside her. She had the keys to the truck in her purse, the purse she'd carried with her to the grocery store, and no matter how desperate he was to get away,

Nick was not foolish enough to steal a judge's long white Cadillac. With vanity plates, no less.

She left through the kitchen door, peeking through the separate garage as she passed on her way to the barn. The Caddy was there, safe and sound. She'd told Nick where the barn was, hadn't she? Out back, beyond the line of trees, hidden from view by thick summer foliage. In the wintertime, when the trees were bare and the kudzu was dormant, you could see the old barn from the kitchen window. Weathered and dilapidated, it looked to be a hundred years old. And might be, for all she knew. The house was almost that old.

Before she entered the barn, she caught sight of the truck through the open door. The relief she felt was tangible, and was followed by a rush of anger. Where the hell was Nick? As she stepped into the doorway she saw him, sitting in the driver's seat, his hands on the wheel, his eyes locked to hers.

"Going somewhere?" she asked calmly as she approached the truck.

"I thought about it, but someone took the keys."

"They're in my purse," she said, leaning against the driver's door and peering in through the open window. She felt oddly betrayed. How dare he try to desert her like this? "You're not ready to leave, not just yet."

He locked those ice-blue eyes on her and her heart skipped a beat. She couldn't help but remember the kiss, the offer she already regretted turning down. What if she never again felt like this? What if no other man but this one could send her heart racing and her knees trembling?

"You're a good person," he said softly. "I don't want you any more involved than you already are."

It sounded like an excuse, but she believed him.

"If we part company now, you can still claim you were

kidnapped and held against your will all this time. No one has to know you helped me.''

She opened the truck door and offered her hand, in case Nick needed assistance leaving the driver's seat. He moved easily, didn't need any help, but he took her hand anyway. Sparks flew the minute their fingers touched. She felt it and so did he. What would she have done if she'd come home and found him truly gone?

''I'm already in too deep,'' she confessed. ''If the state trooper ever makes the connection—''

''What state trooper?'' Nick interrupted, pulling her close.

She bumped into his chest, and decided to stare at the buttons of the checked shirt Lenny had given him instead of looking into his face. ''I had to stop for gas on the way here,'' she said simply. ''A trooper came in, and I…I pretended you were my husband and we were on our way to Florida to see my mother.''

''You lied.''

Shea nodded. ''And then the trooper came outside, and you took off your hat, so I…I kissed you so he wouldn't see your face.'' Her face flushed warm, and she could only imagine how brightly she blushed. How embarrassing! ''It was necessary,'' she said in a matter-of-fact voice.

He cupped her chin in his hand and forced her to look up, into his eyes. ''You shouldn't have done that,'' he whispered.

''He didn't recognize me. He might never make the connection.''

Nick towered above her. ''And then again, he might. Dammit, Shea, I don't want you involved in my mess! I want you out of here!''

''I think it's too late for that,'' she said softly. ''I'm already involved.''

Nick ignored the urge to kiss Shea again, taking her arm and leading her out of the barn and toward the big white house. At least now he knew why her taste and smell, her gentle kiss, had seemed so familiar. She'd lied and then kissed him in order to hide him from a state trooper! Foolish woman.

He had never intended to involve her this way, to pull her into his own hell and make her a part of it. She was a good person, and while he might make fun of her sense of justice and old-fashioned views on sex, he also admired her. She knew who she was and what she wanted. Few people were so lucky.

"If he remembers you, we'll say I had a gun and I forced you to kiss me."

"I will say no such thing!" she said. "Besides, the gun was back at Lenny's and there isn't another one."

"I will not have you thrown in jail for helping me," he insisted. "As a matter of fact, I don't want your help anymore. My leg is better. I can handle things from here on my own."

"No way."

"Not enough story for you?" he snapped. "What else do you want?"

"I want to find out who really killed Gary Winkler."

"You can't do that from your Aunt Irene's house."

"We can start, but you're right. To finish this we'll have to go back to Huntsville."

He shook his head as he reached for the kitchen door. "There is no *we,* weathergirl. Get that through your head."

The door slammed behind them, and Shea took the time to lock it. She was a careful girl. "There is most definitely a we, Nick Taggert," she said as she turned to face him. "You might not like it. I might not like it. But there is most definitely a *we.*"

She took his arm and pulled him gently toward the din-

ing room. He followed willingly, watching the back of her
head, the curve of her neck and the seductive swell of her
butt in those tight denim shorts. She didn't stop in the
dining room or head up the stairs, but led him into the
parlor and to the sofa where he'd kissed her, where he'd
propositioned her and been turned down flat.

"Sit down," she ordered, releasing him to sit where he
had before, with the ottoman at his feet. He propped up
his throbbing leg and tugged gently until Shea sat down
beside him.

He placed his arm around her shoulder, and she didn't
protest, but laid her head there and relaxed. She seemed
to melt into him, soft and compliant, restive and anxious.
All that and more. When had he decided that it was his
duty to protect her? He had kidnapped her, threatened her
and frightened her. If anyone else did those things to Shea
he would be sorely tempted to kill the guilty party.

"I just don't want you hurt," he said softly. "Dammit,
you shouldn't be here."

"What would you have done without me?"

Bled to death in the middle of nowhere, most likely,
though he wasn't prepared to admit that fact out loud. "I
would've done fine without you."

She snorted. "Unlikely."

"Want me to thank you again?" he teased.

She hesitated, and his insides twisted. "You'd better
not," she whispered.

Ah, she was close to giving in, to collapsing. But Shea
didn't have casual sex, and he didn't have time for anything else.

She snuggled against him and rested one arm across his
midsection. Did she have any idea what she was doing to
him?

"I thought you were gone," she said softly. "And I
guess if I'd left the keys to Lenny's truck you would be."

"Yep," he admitted.

"You're not ready to be on your own, and I'm not ready to let you go."

"We don't have a lot of time—"

"I know," she interrupted. She lifted her head and glanced up at him, looking so clean and pretty and naive he wanted to soak her up. He wanted to inhale her, absorb her. Just when he had begun to believe that there was no such thing as honesty and goodness in the world, just when he'd begun to believe that everyone was against him...in walks Shea Sinclair to turn all his beliefs upside down.

She raised up and kissed him briefly, surprising him. "I wish we'd met differently, like you said before. I wish a friend had introduced us and we went on a date, dinner and a movie, and at the end of the evening we could be surprised that we actually liked each other." She kissed him again, the touch as brief and light as the last time. "You could ask me out again, and we'd do something silly the next time. Miniature golf, maybe. Or bowling. I'd expect to find out you're competitive and overbearing and you'd expect me to be bossy and too chatty for your tastes, but we'd surprise one another again and have a good time." She placed her hand on his neck, threading her fingers through the hair at the back of his head. "And then on the third date, I'd cook for you. You'd come to my apartment expecting something dreadful, but I'd surprise you again." She smiled. "I'm a pretty good cook."

"I know," he said huskily.

"And then..." she began, her hazel eyes locked to his.

"And then what?" he prodded when she became silent.

But his imagination took over with no help from Shea. And then he'd seduce her. Or she'd seduce him. Is that what she was trying to do now? Is that why she was leaning into him, her hand on his neck, her eyes glowing...

Oh, no. Girls who didn't have casual sex were looking

for love. And that's what he saw in Shea's eyes as she gazed at him. Love. She was so naive her heart was in her eyes, hopeful and romantic.

He liked Shea, and he wanted her so much he hurt with it. But there was no room in his life for love. He wouldn't lie to her about that. He wouldn't tell her what she wanted to hear just to get what he wanted. She deserved better.

Before he could come up with a proper response, a shadow fell over them. Without letting go of one another they looked up.

Nick saw the revolver first. It was a big one, and it was pointed directly at him. The revolver was gripped in two pale, wrinkled hands. Next he saw the dress, a monstrosity of pink and purple flowers. Pearls hung at the neck, below a face as wrinkled as the hands. He met suspicious, narrowed eyes beneath blue-gray hair sprayed to within an inch of its life.

"You don't *look* kidnapped," a shaky voice said.

Shea would've disengaged herself from Nick's arms, but she was afraid if she backed away Mrs. Wilton would shoot. Since the gun she held was pointed at Nick's chest…

"Mrs. Wilton," she said, trying a smile. "We didn't hear you come in."

"I can't imagine why not," the old lady answered sarcastically. "You have some explaining to do, Missy."

Maude Wilton, and her sister, Abigail Bates, lived in the house next door. The widowed sisters were both in their eighties, and had lived together in that old house for more than twenty years.

"Why don't you put the gun down first," Shea said calmly. "Then we can talk."

Mrs. Wilton eyed Nick suspiciously. "I think I'll keep the gun right where it is, for the time being."

Shea explained, as succinctly and quickly as possible, that she was fine, that Nick was innocent and that they were in hiding until they could prove his innocence. As Shea told her story, the gun dropped and Mrs. Wilton's wrinkled face took on an excited glow.

"This is so exciting!" the old woman said as she dropped the revolver into the oversize white purse that hung from her shoulder. "Just like *Murder She Wrote* or *Matlock*." She winked at Shea. "I love that *Matlock*."

Nick got right down to business. "Did you tell anyone that you saw us in the house?"

Mrs. Wilton looked properly confused. "Of course not. I didn't even know you were here until I came into the parlor to water the African violets." Shea glanced toward the doorway and saw a watering can on the marble table. "You two were too busy to hear me, I imagine," she said with a disapproving narrowing of her lips.

"Why the firearm?" Nick asked.

"Oh, I always carry a gun with me these days." She leaned slightly forward. "A girl can't be too careful, you know."

Mrs. Wilton sat in the wing chair and fanned herself with her hand. "I can't remember the last time I had so much excitement. I need to sit a spell."

Nick glanced at Shea, his eyes full of questions. Could they trust the old lady? Did they have to leave this place right this minute? Where would they go?

"Mrs. Wilton," Shea began carefully, leaning slightly forward on her sofa. "Can we trust you?"

"Of course you can, and call me Maude." She gave Shea a bright smile. "You're all grown up now."

Shea responded with a smile of her own. "No one can know we're here. Please…"

"Oh, I won't tell anyone, not even Abigail." She leaned forward and lowered her voice. "She can't keep a secret.

Never could. If I tell her you two are here it'll be in the next edition of the Selma newspaper.''

Maude pinned her eyes on Nick, and her smile dimmed. ''So, you're innocent.''

''Yes, ma'am.''

Her smile drifted back. ''Ma'am. I like that. So few young men have manners these days. Still, it isn't exactly the best of manners to kidnap young ladies.''

''He tried to let me go—'' Shea began, but Nick grabbed her wrist and squeezed, silencing her.

''Yes, I kidnapped Shea,'' Nick said, his eyes and his full attention on Maude. ''When this comes to a head, I want everyone to understand that she was held against her will the entire time. Is that clear?''

Maude wrinkled her nose. ''You're trying to protect her. That's very gentlemanly of you. Naturally I will do and say what's best for Shea.''

Nick nodded, satisfied.

''I don't need you two covering my involvement in this,'' Shea said indignantly, ''and I won't have Nick accused of something he's not guilty of, like holding me hostage all this time.''

''You're not going to jail,'' Nick said, glancing down at her. ''I won't have it.''

''And you're not going back,'' Shea whispered. ''I won't have it.''

Maude was beaming when Shea looked at the old woman again. ''What can I do to help?'' she asked.

''Nothing, really,'' Shea said. ''Just don't tell anyone we're here.''

''Food,'' Maude said with a lift of her eyebrows. ''You must need food.''

''I went to the grocery store this afternoon,'' Shea said. ''We're fine for a few more days.''

Maude tsked and shook her head. ''You shouldn't have

done that. What if someone had seen and recognized you?''

Shea shrugged her shoulders. ''I didn't see any other way.''

Anxious to help, Maude straightened her spine and nodded her head crisply. ''From now on, if you need anything you send me out for it. Your face is too well known. Heavens to Betsy, Shea, you've been all over the news.''

''I know,'' she muttered.

''We'll just be here a few more days,'' Nick said. ''As soon as we have a few answers and my leg is sufficiently healed, we'll be out of here. I don't want to involve you any more than I want to involve Shea. This is my fight, not yours.''

Maude raised her eyebrows indignantly. ''Young man, sometimes even the best of us needs help.'' She jumped as if surprised, reached into her large handbag and withdrew what Shea at first thought was another gun. She soon realized it was a cell phone. ''Whatever you do, don't use the telephone here to call anyone.'' She leaned forward and lowered her voice. ''The coppers might trace the call. I got this cell phone from a company in Birmingham, so that's what comes up on caller ID. Birmingham and the number. You can block the number, though, unless the person you're calling has that thing where they don't take private calls.'' She fluttered her fingers. ''Annoying cusses, each and every one of them. In any case, it would probably be a good idea if you called your folks. They must be worried sick.''

''I already called a friend and had him relay a message to my parents and my brothers, so they won't worry.''

Maude laughed. ''Your brothers? Not worry? Good heavens, they've probably torn Huntsville apart by now.''

Shea didn't feel like laughing. ''Probably so.''

Chapter 9

Maude was not quite five feet tall, Shea realized as she followed the woman to the kitchen. She was softly round, with wide hips and a massive bosom and a penchant for pastels and pearls. Shea remembered the woman bringing her and her cousins cookies and lemonade, pies and cakes, and offering comforting, mothering bear hugs when it was time for her to go home.

The old woman glanced over her shoulder as they reached the kitchen. Her gray eyebrows twitched and she flashed a smile. "He's a hottie."

"Maude!" Shea said, shocked.

"Well, he is. Don't tell me you didn't notice." Maude pursed her lips and raised her eyebrows. "You were so busy noticing you didn't even hear me come in, put down the watering can, open my purse and take out the revolver!" She didn't seem angry at all, but was clearly amused.

"It's been rather intense," Shea said by way of explanation.

"Love usually is," Maude said with a sigh.

Love? "I don't, uh, love Nick. I just met him a few days ago."

"A few days is plenty of time to fall in love," the old woman said wisely. "Why, I fell in love with my Walter the first time I saw him. I knew then and there that he was the only one for me." Her eyes went dreamy as she remembered her late husband. "We were married five days later."

"Five *days?*" Shea had known Nick five days....

That wasn't the way she had imagined love. First there was the initial physical attraction, and that could come quickly, immediately even, but then...two people had to get to know one another. They had to learn the good and the bad, the foibles and the quirks. You had to know what kind of movies and books a person liked before you could love him. Didn't you?

"Five days," Maude repeated. "And the honeymoon lasted forty-three years." Her eyes misted, but she continued to smile. "I used to look at him the same way you look at your Nick." She sniffled, cleared her eyes and straightened her spine. "So we'd best get crackin' to prove him innocent so you two can get on with what's important."

That "we" terrified Shea. Maude apparently assumed she was now a part of this drama. "It's very nice of you to offer your help, but really, Nick and I can handle it."

Maude ignored her protest. "I'll bake some cookies and bring them by tonight. That boy needs fattening up, and it wouldn't hurt you to put on a few pounds."

"That's very sweet, but—"

"I can make the police chief a cake—he loves my lemon pound cake—and take it to him and see what kind of information I can cajole out of him. If the coppers suspect you two are in the area, we should know about it."

"Yes, but—"

"Do you think Nick likes chocolate chip?"

Shea sighed and surrendered. "I imagine he does."

"Good." Maude beamed as she headed for the door. "And don't you worry. I won't tell Abigail a thing. She lives in her own little world, anyway, painting those pictures of hers."

"She's still painting?"

Maude nodded and snorted in disgust. "Fruit. After all these years, all she can paint is fruit. Bananas, apples, oranges, the occasional grape." She shook her head. "You'd think she'd want to paint a flower now and again, but no. She says fruit is her *specialty*."

Maude left the house with a roll of her eyes, and Shea smiled as she watched the old woman march across the lawn toward her own house.

But her smile faded as she made her way through the dining room and back to the parlor and a waiting Nick. Love? Shea's stomach knotted; her mouth went dry. Maude hadn't really seen anything so extreme happening here. Her musings were no more than a sentimental old woman's fantasy. Maude was just confusing love with physical attraction.

Shea stopped in the doorway and stared at Nick. His eyes were closed. His face was too pale.

And like it or not, he was the one. Maybe she wasn't ready to call what she felt *love,* the word Maude bandied about so easily. But heaven help her, Shea had never felt this way about a man before. She'd never looked at a man and felt her body respond. She'd never been compelled to touch a man. A hand here, a kiss there. He made her feel like a woman. No one had ever made her feel this way.

No matter what was to come, she wanted Nick to be her first. She'd waited all this time. She'd saved herself for the right man, the right time.

The situation was far from ideal, but she wasn't going to be a coward. Not this time.

Nick munched on a chocolate chip cookie and watched while Shea talked on Maude's cell phone and took notes. She sat at the dining room table, the early evening summer sun streaming through the window and illuminating her to perfection. From his seat across the table he watched the rise and fall of her breasts beneath the white tank top she wore, the working of her slender throat, the occasional spark of wonder and excitement in her warm eyes.

He had never known anyone like Shea. He hadn't even believed that women like her existed. His own mother had never been so caring, and the women who came in and out of his life…none of them had been this warm and real. He had never felt the urge to wrap them up in his arms and shield them from the world.

He never should've kidnapped Shea, but he wasn't sorry. If that was what it took to know her, he couldn't be sorry.

She hit the disconnect button on Maude's cell phone and flashed him a brilliant smile. "Okay, things are rolling."

"What kind of things?" he asked calmly, making damn sure he didn't give away his train of thought.

"First of all, Grace found the woman Winkler had been having an affair with, the one who got fired? Her name is Coral, and after she left the company Winkler was with, she ended up with a better job than the one she had before."

"We never did figure out how she could've planted the evidence. Since she's better off than she was before …"

"We can cross her off the suspect list."

"Why is that good news?" Nick asked.

"We can't do anything until we narrow the list of suspects."

Nick nodded in agreement. "What else did your friend find out?"

Shea's smile faded. "You won't like this next part."

"There hasn't been much in the last year I have liked. Go ahead, hit me."

"Lauren is engaged to be married."

He expected to be outraged, but he wasn't. He'd found out in time what she was like. "Poor bastard," he muttered.

His response generated a soft smile from Shea. The smile didn't last. "To Norman Burgess."

Now Nick felt like someone had kicked him in the gut. "Norman?" His lawyer, his friend. How long had this been going on? Is this why Norman's wife had left him? Months ago. Long before the trial ever started. Nick expected anything of Lauren, but dammit, he expected better of Norman.

"Grace hasn't found anything incriminating on the other neighbors, but she's still looking." Shea's eyes softened. "I'm sorry, Nick."

"No need to be sorry." He quickly left the table, turning his back on her and heading for the kitchen.

He made a beehive for the counter and the plate of Maude's cookies, but instead of taking one he placed his hands on the counter and closed his eyes. Could things get any worse?

Shea's bare feet shuffled across the floor. He heard her approaching, steeled himself against the inevitable contact.

"What a jerk," she said softly, wrapping her arms around him and laying her head against his back. "But Nick, this is surely grounds for a new trial. If you had a decent lawyer, and a thorough investigation..."

"You're right," he said dryly. "I could be cleared of murder and get a life sentence for escape and kidnapping instead."

"Don't say that," she whispered.

He turned in Shea's embrace, wrapping his arms around her, losing himself in her soft warmth. "It's the truth," he whispered.

"Do you really think I'd let them convict you of kidnapping? No way. I'll tell them you tried to let me go and I refused, and if that's not enough, I'll tell them we planned it all along, that it was a publicity stunt."

He grabbed her chin and jerked her head up so she had to look him in the eye. "You will not," he insisted. "I won't have you going to jail. I won't stand for you going to that awful place, not for a minute."

Her smile faded. "For as long as I can remember, my brothers protected me. I don't need or want another man shielding me from life. I'm not a child."

"I know that very well," he said huskily.

"I'll do what's right and what's best, and I don't want you trying to stop me, Nick." Her eyes were wide and warm, soft and pleading. "We're partners in this, no matter what."

Partners. He'd never had a partner, in anything. He'd had employees, he'd had comrades in arms, he'd had women who came in and out of his life as it suited him. Even Lauren had never been a partner. She'd been a means to an end, the wrong woman who was in the right place at the right time.

Nick lowered his mouth to Shea's. Dammit, she looked like she needed to be kissed, like she wanted to be kissed. She melted in his arms, falling against him, parting her lips very slightly and breathing deep and slow.

He cupped her breast and flicked his thumb over her hardened nipple. She never bothered with a bra when she wore these old tank tops, and he had noticed the way she filled out the fabric, so soft and tempting. Yes, he had definitely noticed. She took in a deep breath, perhaps surprised by his boldness or the intensity of the sensation, but she didn't back away. She flicked the tip of her tongue in his mouth and leaned into his hand.

Already he was hard, ready to take her here, or on the stairs, or on the kitchen table. He didn't care where, but dammit, it needed to be soon.

Did she know what she was getting herself into? She'd said she didn't do casual sex. Of course, there was nothing *casual* about this. It was intense, overpowering. Unstoppable.

He slipped his hand beneath her tank top to trail his fingers along her bare flesh, to touch her breasts again, without the thin cotton fabric between his hand and her silky skin this time. Her breathing changed, and she held him tight, as if she needed to hold on to keep from falling to the floor.

He moved his mouth to her neck, marveling at the way he treasured the taste of it, the feel of her skin against his mouth. She threaded her fingers through his hair and held on, taking deep, heated breaths.

"I feel…" she whispered. "I feel misty."

"Misty?" he asked with a smile, dragging his mouth from her neck to her shoulder.

"Misty," she repeated. "And hot. And…and I throb. Nick, I throb everywhere. Oh, my."

She sounded pleasantly surprised, taken aback, as if she'd never…

Nick raised his head to look her in the eye. He needed to see her reaction to his question. "Shea, you said you didn't have casual sex."

"This isn't casual," she insisted breathlessly. "This is—this is…"

Love. She didn't say it, but he saw it in her eyes, heard it in her voice.

"Shea, are you a... You have done this before, haven't you?"

She held on tightly. "What difference does it make?"

That was a yes. A damned yes! "You're a virgin, aren't you?"

"I suppose," she said, unsmiling. "But it doesn't make any difference," she whispered. "I want you to be my first. I've never wanted anything the way I want this."

She'd waited all this time for the right man. Someone who was headed for prison or a life on the run was *not* the right man. No matter how much he wanted to be.

Shea fought dirty. She reached out and began to unbutton his shirt. Every move was seductive, every flick of her fingers pushed him a little further beyond his limits. When the shirt was unbuttoned, she spread it open and laid her hands on his chest.

"I've wanted to do this for days," she said softly, watching the play of her hands over his chest, the flick of her slender fingers over his flat nipples. "And this." She leaned forward and kissed him, first in the center of his chest, then on each nipple, her soft lips lingering, teasing.

He thought of walking away, of dredging up every ounce of dignity and honor he had left and pushing this woman away. But he couldn't.

Moving as slowly and deliberately as she did, he dragged the tank top over her head and dropped it to the floor. In the last light of day, soft rays breaking through the yellow curtains in the kitchen window, she was warm and incredibly soft, her breasts full and firm, her waist tapered and her belly flat. He'd never seen skin so smooth, so flawless.

She wasn't shy, not even when he lowered his head to take a nipple into his mouth. He savored the feel of her against his tongue, but more than that he savored her reaction. Her heart raced; her knees trembled. He knew that if he touched her, she would be wet. Wet and ready for him.

But he took his time, caressing one breast and then the other, trailing his fingers over her bare skin and delighting in her unrestrained response. Slipping his fingers just inside the waistband of her shorts, he caressed her gently, touched and stroked and explored unseen skin.

When he put his mouth to hers again she pressed herself against him, her soft breasts against his bare chest, her belly against his, her arms tight around him. She parted her lips and teased him with her tongue, moving it in and out, in and out, until he couldn't take any more.

He reached down and popped the snap on her cutoff jeans, lowering the zipper slowly. She parted her legs, offering herself to him openly and hungrily.

His mouth was clamped to hers when he slipped his hand inside her panties, over her mound, and touched her intimately. He was right: she was wet. Hot and slick and eager. He cupped her mound, pressed his palm against her most sensitive spot and teased her with the tips of his fingers.

Again her reaction was genuine and intense, as powerful as anything he'd ever known. She parted her thighs farther and rocked against his hand.

The kiss continued while he stroked her, the caress becoming stronger, longer, more rhythmic. Her breath came hard and fast, her body shook, and when he slipped his finger inside her she cried out, coming apart with a deep tremble and a glorious spasm.

The climax died, but the kiss continued. Softer. Easier. And then she reached for the zipper of his jeans.

He grabbed her wrist and moved her hand away. "No," he protested huskily.

"But we're not finished," Shea whispered, still breathless.

"We are most certainly finished," he said, placing his hands on her shoulders and gently pushing her away from him. She was flushed, breathing deeply and shaking slightly. And God, she was beautiful! He wanted her. He wanted to carry her upstairs and make love to her all night.

But he wouldn't. "You waited all this time for the perfect moment," he said. "I kidnapped you. We have no future. I won't...I don't want you to do anything you might regret in the morning."

"I won't," she insisted. "I wouldn't—"

"You don't know that," he said, walking past her and heading for the stairs. Dammit, he couldn't look at her any longer! Topless, shorts unzipped and pushed low on her hips, face flushed and lips well kissed, she was too tempting. He already felt like a damned saint, walking away.

"But Nick..."

He heard her behind him, knew that at any moment she would come up behind him and put her arms around him and he would be lost.

If noble wouldn't work, maybe crude would. "Besides, I don't sleep with virgins. It's messy and painful, and I just don't have the desire to break in an untried woman."

She stopped following him; he knew it. The house went completely silent.

"You needed to get off and I did what I could to help you out," he said as he began to climb the stairs. "Seems like the least I can do since you've been working so hard to help me."

He expected something heavy to come flying toward his head at any moment, but no projectiles came his way. No harsh words, either. All remained silent, and he didn't look back. By the time he reached the first landing, Shea had left the dining room.

Maybe that hadn't been too smart. He'd probably wake tomorrow morning and find his bed surrounded by cops.

At the moment, he didn't particularly care.

* * *

Luther Malone had a suspicious nature. He wasn't surprised when Grace and Ray invited him over for dinner. He saw them often. But when he found that Grace had prepared all his favorite foods, and no single, eligible, suitable woman had been invited to join them, he was immediately on alert.

"So," Grace said as she placed the roast, the final dish, on the table. "How are things at work?"

How were things at work? If she read the paper, she knew darn well how things were. "If we had a popcorn machine and an organ grinder we could call it a circus."

Ray, sitting at the head of the table, laughed. Grace just smiled and took her place next to her husband and across from Luther.

She'd begun to pass the vegetables his way when Ray nudged her. "Go ahead," he said. "Get it over with."

"Over dessert," Grace said softly.

"Now." Ray Madigan gave his wife a loving but stern look, then kissed her briefly on the mouth. "Now," he said again, in a softer voice.

Grace sighed and turned her eyes to him. "Luther? Do you trust me?"

"About as far as I can throw you," he said honestly.

She arched her dark eyebrows. "You shouldn't speak that way to a pregnant woman."

"You're not even far enough along to be showing yet," he grumbled.

"Yes, she is," Ray said, a sparkle in his eyes as he looked down and placed his hand over Grace's belly. "Just a little."

This was disgusting.

"You're going to milk this pregnant thing for all it's worth, aren't you?" Luther mumbled.

Grace grinned. "Why not?"

"Go ahead," Ray urged. "Tell him."

"You know Shea Sinclair is a friend of mine," Grace said with wide-eyed innocence.

"Yep." It hit him then. Shea was Grace's friend, and Grace hadn't said a word about the kidnapping. She hadn't asked a single question about the case. "Why aren't you hysterical?"

"See, I got this phone call..."

"From Shea?" Luther barked. "God, Grace!"

"No," Grace interrupted with a quick shake of her head. "From her cameraman, Mark. Anyway, he said she was okay, and said she wanted me to look into the Winkler murder. Apparently she thinks Taggert is innocent."

"You're not surprised," Ray said immediately. "You already knew, didn't you?"

The Sinclair brothers had finally realized why Mark was so sure Shea was fine when he'd passed along the message. But they had asked him to keep the news that Shea was a willing hostage to himself. They didn't want to see their sister go to jail for aiding and abetting, and to be honest, neither did Luther. They were tearing the state up searching for her. They'd decided to start with her friends in Huntsville and then work out from here. Luther almost felt sorry for Taggert.

"I had a suspicion," he said cryptically.

"The thing is," Grace said, "I think she might be right about Taggert. Daniels did a lousy job of investigating the Winkler case."

Ray and Luther both mumbled their unflattering opinions of Daniels.

"I've been investigating the case—"

"You've been *what?*" Luther interrupted.

Grace bit her bottom lip. "Mostly I've been looking into the backgrounds of Winkler's other neighbors and a few of the people he worked with. I don't have anything solid, but there are a number of details that just don't look quite right. I have a couple of friends following a few muddy money trails.''

"Hackers?" Luther deadpanned.

"Friends," Grace reiterated. "If I give you what I have, will you look into it? I'll keep looking, and I promise I'll give you everything I find."

Luther pinned accusing eyes on Ray. "Did you know about this?"

"For a couple of days. But it's Grace's case," Ray said defensively. "Not mine. She's making the calls on this one."

Luther shook his head. Ray had once been a damn good cop, and he was a brilliant P.I., but he had let a woman wrap him around her little finger. "You should have come to me right away."

"I'm coming to you now," Grace said softly.

Luther glanced around the laden table. Roast beef, mashed potatoes and gravy, homemade biscuits, corn on the cob, green beans and carrots in a honey glaze. He should order her to stay away from the case, to keep her nose clean, to spend her time eating pickles and ice cream and knitting booties. But in truth he was as bothered by this case as she was. Things didn't quite add up.

"Can we wait until after dinner?" he asked, surrender in his voice.

Grace's smile was brilliant. "Sure. And I have jelly doughnuts for dessert."

"You're a wicked woman, Grace Madigan," he said as he dug into the mashed potatoes.

Chapter 10

Shea danced around the kitchen in her bare feet as she prepared a late breakfast, feeling oddly content.

It had taken her half the night, a few tears and more than a few hotly whispered threats directed toward Nick's favorite body parts, but the truth had finally dawned on her about three in the morning. She chastised herself for not seeing it right away.

Some tough guy Taggert was, she thought with a fond smile. He'd probably swear there wasn't an ounce of gentleman in him, but he was wrong.

A soft knock interrupted her song, and she peeked through the kitchen window to see Maude, resplendent in pale blue and yellow and the requisite pearls, nervously bouncing on the balls of her feet outside the door. Shea admitted her with a bright "Good morning."

"Almost good afternoon," Maude said as she closed the kitchen door behind her. But not before surreptitiously glancing down the driveway and to the woods at the rear of the property. Searching for coppers, no doubt. And then she glanced at the sizzling ham on the stove, and her eyebrows shot up.

"We had a late night," Shea explained, turning down the music and taking her biscuits from the oven.

"I can imagine," Maude said with a smug smile. "Anyway, I came to tell you that the police chief doesn't know a thing. He's aware of the kidnapping, of course, and on the lookout for you two, but I don't think he even realizes that you're Irene's niece."

"That's good."

"I didn't actually talk to the police chief, but I did have a nice long conversation with a civilian volunteer. T.J. Thayer. He adores my lemon pound cake, too, and he dearly loves to talk business. He'd very much like to be a cop, but I don't think he'll ever make it. He's a nice boy," Maude said, leaning in to share this tidbit in a lowered voice. "But not the brightest crayon in the box, if you get my drift."

"Especially not when you're plying him with lemon pound cake," Shea added with a grin.

"Every man has his weakness," Maude revealed with a wise nod of her head.

Shea wondered, just for a moment, what Nick's weakness was.

"I brought you a couple of things," Maude said, all-business again. She opened her huge handbag and handed Shea yet another cell phone. "If you need to make another call, use this one. I borrowed it from the chief's aunt, Miss Caroline. I told her mine was on the fritz and I was afraid to get on the road without a cell phone. In case of emergencies, you know."

"The police chief's Aunt Caroline," Shea repeated as she took the phone.

"Tomorrow I'll bring you another one. That ought to

keep the coppers on their toes.'' She flashed a girlish grin and shrugged her shoulders.

''You're having way too much fun with this,'' Shea observed.

''I haven't had this much fun in ages.''

''I don't want to get you in trouble.''

Maude winked at her. ''You won't.'' She removed another item from her bag, a sloppily folded paper. ''And there are a few items of interest in the Selma morning paper,'' she said with a sigh. ''You'd better check it out.''

With a flourish, Maude produced more cookies. Devil's food with chocolate icing and colored sprinkles, and sugar cookies in the shape of an assortment of guns and badges. She'd found the old cookie cutters in her pantry and thought them appropriate for the occasion.

Maude left after delivering the supplies, taking her own cell phone with her and leaving Miss Caroline's in its place. Shea decided Maude had been watching way too much *Matlock*.

She unfolded the paper, read the pertinent article on the front page and slapped it on the counter with a muttered curse. She shouldn't be surprised.

Alone again, Shea turned the music back up and danced while she placed the biscuits on one side of a large plate and took the ham out of the skillet and piled it on the other side. Okay, this was a complication, but it wasn't an unexpected one. She turned around, ready to run upstairs and wake Nick, but she found him standing in the doorway. Watching intently.

''Playing at being a Supreme?'' he asked lowly and coldly.

''No,'' she answered, not quite ready to smile at him. ''A Vandella.''

He raised his eyebrows in a silent question.

"You know, Martha Reeves and the Vandellas. For years it was my greatest ambition to be a doo-wop girl."

"A doo-wop girl."

She carried the plate toward him. "You know, doo-wop, doo-wah, slinky sequined gowns, very high heels, the occasional hip thrust." She suppressed the urge to demonstrate. Not yet. "Unfortunately, I can't sing. I can't even doo-wop properly."

"Seems to me like you were doing fine," he said as he looked her up and down.

She pushed past him and placed the plate of ham and biscuits on the dining room table. "I've been thinking," she said as she returned to the kitchen for two cups of coffee and two small plates. "What about Winkler's wife?"

"Polly?" Nick shook his head as he made his way to the table. "No way. I never heard her raise her voice or complain in any way. She was always quiet, always taking whatever Winkler dished out."

"In public," Shea said, taking a seat across from Nick. "You have no idea what their private life was like."

"That's true, but she always struck me as being very meek."

They piled their plates high, and Shea added sugar to her coffee. They both did a great job of ignoring what had happened yesterday as they began to eat, but the tension built gradually and steadily. Finally, Nick lifted his head to stare at her.

"Why are you still here? I half expected to wake up this morning and find you gone."

Shea cast him a weak smile. "I thought about it," she admitted. "For about ten minutes. But I've got your number, Nick Taggert, and I never quit. We're in this together, like it or not."

"What if I don't like?" he asked tersely.

"Too bad," she snapped.

He shook his head. "My leg is stronger. I'm doing well. I'm ready to go back to Huntsville and finish this. Alone."

"No," Shea said, popping a small piece of biscuit into her mouth.

Nick raised his eyebrows. "No?"

"I've come this far and I'm not turning back."

She could look into his eyes and tell he was thinking of ways to dump her, to continue without her help. "We're in this together, Taggert," she repeated. Leaving the chair, she made her way calmly to the kitchen, retrieved the newspaper and tossed it on the table, where it landed beside Nick's coffee.

"You can read the details for yourself," she said calmly, "but the gist of it is the state trooper finally made the connection. He identified me and the truck, and even though he didn't see your face, he naturally assumes you were the man in the front seat."

Nick glanced at the article and cursed.

"Sorry, but it looks like you're stuck with me until this is over, Taggert. Like it or not."

It didn't matter how strong he got, how quickly he recovered. There was no way he could walk away and leave Shea to handle the firestorm on her own.

Nick did another push-up on the parlor floor. He tried not to think about the trial any more than he had to, but in his mind he could still hear the jury foreman reading the verdict. *Guilty.* Panic had swept through his body, and he'd known the only way to prove himself innocent was to find the real killer himself. Running had seemed like the right thing to do at the time.

He regretted that impulsive move now. Not because he wished to be back in the Madison County Jail, not because he trusted anyone else to clear his name. But because he'd dragged Shea into this mess and he didn't see any easy way out for her.

She was feeling domestic today. She'd taken his jeans and checkered shirt and underwear to wash, and given him a pair of her uncle's shorts and one of Lenny's T-shirts to wear while she did the laundry. The khaki shorts were too big, and were held up with a narrow leather belt, but the white cotton T-shirt had shrunk so it fit well.

He'd draped the T-shirt over the sofa while he exercised, knowing that in his condition he'd work up a sweat quickly. As he pushed his body to the limit, he thought about Shea. Listened to her puttering through the old house.

Their clothes were in the washer, she'd been cleaning the kitchen and she'd used the last can of tuna to make a casserole that was bubbling in the oven. She'd gathered together all her notes, the map he'd drawn of the cul-de-sac, and the borrowed cell phone, placing it in a neat pile on the dining room table.

He hadn't said a word, but she knew it was almost time to go, and she was getting ready. Cleaning up, using the last of their supplies, gathering what they'd need for the trip.

Back to Huntsville, he imagined. He wouldn't make Shea live on the run, and those were his only two choices. Run, or return and get about the business he'd set himself to when he'd escaped. Finding Gary Winkler's killer.

Shea suspected Lauren, but Nick had thought that impossible. Until he'd learned that she and Norman were involved. How long had that been going on? She also suspected Polly, but Nick couldn't see the timid woman cracking her husband's head with a baseball bat and then coldly pinning the murder on someone else.

What about the men Winkler worked with? He had not been a popular guy, and had been downright unscrupulous.

His other neighbors? Shea's friend, the P.I.'s wife, hadn't found anything incriminating there, but more than ten months had passed since the murder. Any evidence was now going to be tough to find.

Maybe impossible.

"Enough," Shea's soft voice called from the doorway between the parlor and the dining room. "You're going to hurt yourself."

"No, I'm not." Looking at her would hurt, lying to her again would hurt. Physical pain he could handle.

"Dinner will be ready soon. I made a casserole, and Maude brought over a pan of lemon squares."

Nick stopped, pushed himself up one more time and then scooted into a sitting position on the hardwood floor. He made himself glance up at her with emotionless eyes.

"I've been thinking," he said. "About that state trooper."

Shea crossed her arms over her chest and shifted her feet. She looked defiant, as if she knew what was coming and had already decided that she didn't like it.

"Were there cameras in the store?"

"I don't think so. At least, I didn't see any."

"Did the trooper get the license plate off the truck?"

She shook her head. "Apparently not. If he did, they're keeping it out of the paper. Besides, he was parked in front of us, not behind. I never saw him circle around to check the plates."

His heart had damn near come through his chest when he'd seen that article this morning, the article that implicated Shea, that made her an accessory.

"Then it's your word against his."

Her expression didn't change, but for a slight hardening of the eyes. "So you want me to lie?"

"Yes." He rose slowly. His leg was better, if a little

weak, and thanks to Lenny's leftover antibiotic and Shea's careful cleaning, there had been no infection.

"No."

He ignored her. "I'm going to drop you off in Huntsville, in a day or two, and you're going to tell the police that you were held hostage the entire time."

"I'm not going to lie—" she began.

"Yes, you are," he said, taking the white T-shirt from the sofa and pulling it over his head.

"I won't let them believe that you kidnapped me and kept me hostage all this time."

"It doesn't matter what they think of me, Shea," he said, losing his patience. "I'm already in a world of trouble. A little more won't hurt."

"Besides," she said stubbornly, "I'm not leaving you until we find out who killed Winkler."

He walked toward her, past her when she stepped aside. "Then I guess I'll have to leave *you*," he said flatly.

She opened her mouth to protest, but said nothing.

The dishes were done, their clothes were clean and what was left of Maude's lemon squares were wrapped and sitting on the counter. Nick had gone to his room, to Carol's lavender room, right after dinner. He hadn't so much as glanced at Shea as he'd eaten, and he hadn't eaten much. When she'd asked him if he liked her tuna casserole, he'd said it was okay. His lack of enthusiasm had been underwhelming.

He had finished off the meal with a sugar cookie shaped like a western-style revolver, and Shea had munched on a sheriff's star.

Upstairs, all was silent. Maybe Nick was already gone, she thought as she climbed the steps with the notebook and her purse in her hand. Maybe he'd climbed out of the window and deserted her.

She tossed the notebook and her purse, with the newly borrowed cell phone in it, onto her own bed. There was a little bit of summer light left in the sky. Maybe she could look over her notes again, see if anything new came to her, something she'd missed before. She was too wound up to sleep, and she still didn't dare light a lamp that could be seen from the street.

The door to Carol's room was closed, and beyond, all was silent. In a day or two she and Nick would be gone, and if he was determined to dump her, she'd be hard-pressed to stop him. She had to sleep; she couldn't stay at his heels twenty-four hours a day.

She didn't doubt that he wanted what was best for her. The problem was, she was mightily tired of men deciding what she should and should not do.

Leaving her belongings on the neatly made bed, she crossed the hall and knocked softly on the door. No answer. She tried the knob, found it unlocked and took a deep breath for courage before entering the room where Nick slept.

Only he wasn't asleep. Wearing nothing but a newly washed pair of boxer shorts, he was lying on his back, hands behind his head, eyes on the door. On her.

"What do you want?" he snapped.

There was just enough light for her to see that his eyes were hard, his mouth thinned. A muscle in his jaw twitched.

"You never asked me," she said, her voice low. What if she was wrong?

"I never asked you what?" His voice was hard, less than kind. Why did he have to make this so difficult for her?

"You never asked me how I got to be twenty-five and still a virgin."

This time his entire body tensed. He tried to cover his

response by sitting up, leaning against the headboard and glaring at her. "That's none of my business."

"I think it is."

She gathered every bit of courage she possessed and crossed the room, noting as she neared Nick that his eyes were not completely cold, that his fingers twitched as if he were as nervous as she.

"I don't," he said, as she sat on the side of his bed.

She ignored him. "When I was in high school a lot of my friends experimented with sex. Some of them thought they were in love, others were just having fun."

"But not you," Nick said without emotion.

She ignored him. "It was a mistake for all of them, but it was a mistake I never got to make." She smiled crookedly. "Every time I even thought about getting serious about a boy, one of my brothers would pay him a visit. I don't know exactly what was said, but I was lucky to get a peck on the cheek after a date."

Nick almost smiled. The corners of his mouth twitched. "I can imagine."

"When I went to college I was ecstatic. Freedom! All my brothers were at least two hours away, and I would be my own woman." She shook her head. "But I wasn't going to have sex simply for the sake of getting rid of my virginity, and so many of the men there were..." she sighed "...not exactly mature."

"Why are you telling me all this?" Nick asked, sounding annoyed. "So no one at college measured up to your standards. Sounds like your tough luck to me."

Again, she ignored him. "Eventually I did meet a guy I liked a lot. We dated a couple of times and I still liked him. Things were headed in the right direction, and wouldn't you know it? Clint showed up for a surprise visit. Scared the bejesus out of this poor guy, who left and never called me again."

"Coward," Nick muttered.

She'd had the same thought, at the time. "For four years, every time I got serious about a guy, one of my brothers would show up to scare him off. It was like they had some kind of radar," she said, reliving the frustration she'd felt during her college years. "As soon as I even thought about having sex with a guy, one of them would show up." She'd hated her brothers then, and sometimes loved them again quickly when a potential lover showed his true colors.

"They protected you."

"They smothered me."

Shea shook her head. The light was almost gone. The room was gray; Nick's eyes were less distinct. "I graduated, got my job at the station and found my ambition. By this time I knew I didn't want to sleep with a man I didn't care about, and I was too busy to get to know anyone enough to care. The men I met were shallow, and as ambitious as I was, and...nothing ever clicked."

"And now here we are," Nick said dryly.

"And now here we are," she repeated. "I really, really care about you." The word *love* flitted through her mind, but she didn't say it aloud, knowing the mention of love would scare Nick away. "We don't have much time left. I can feel the minutes ticking past." She licked her lips. "If you were telling the truth last night, and the idea of sleeping with a virgin truly repulses you, tell me now and I'll leave you alone." She looked deep into his eyes. "But if you're just trying to protect me, I'd like to remind you that I don't need another brother."

She held her breath. Nick didn't respond right away, and with every heartbeat that passed, her worst fears grew. He really didn't want her.

He reached out and cupped the back of her head, drawing her close. "Trust me when I tell you that I have *never* felt like your brother," he whispered. "I just don't want to hurt you."

"You won't."

"You deserve so much better."

She laid her hand on his face, feeling the roughness of his five o'clock shadow, running her thumb over his lower lip. Somehow she knew it was tonight or never. And the thought of losing Nick terrified her. She had never been terrified like this before, not even when he'd kidnapped her.

"What if I never feel this way again?" she whispered. "What if I listen to you and walk away and...and give up? I don't want to give up on us. I don't think I can." She continued to touch him, her fingers on his neck and his chest and his face. "Make love to me, Nick."

He leaned forward and kissed her, and she felt the regret in his kiss. It broke her heart. "I don't know where I'll be in two days," he whispered against her lips. "Much less two months or two years from now. I'll touch you again, I'll let you touch me, but I can't take the chance of leaving you with a baby when—"

She smiled and kissed him quickly, then scooted off the bed. "You won't have to take that chance." She turned her back on him and hurried to her own room, dumped the contents of her purse onto the bed and grabbed the package she was looking for before rushing back to Nick's room. She stopped in the doorway and lifted the package of condoms between two fingers.

"A three pack," she said with a smile.

He wasn't as surprised as she'd thought he'd be. "Where did you get those?"

"At the grocery store." She walked to the side of the bed and dropped the condoms onto the bedside table. "I had a lot of time to think while I was walking," she said softly. "And most of all I thought about you."

He took her hand and pulled her down so she sat beside him. When he kissed her this time there was no regret, just a mirror of the passion she felt, a hunger that swept her away.

Nick moved slowly, as if he savored every brush of his mouth against hers, every soft caress of his fingers. Already her body throbbed, her knees were weak.

When he laid his mouth over her wrist she was surprised by the intensity of the sensations that washed through her. His touch was so loving, so tender and arousing. Most of the light of day was gone, but enough remained for her to watch the play of his mouth against her wrist, against the crook of her elbow, until he kissed the side of her neck and she closed her eyes in sheer delight.

"My turn," she whispered, lifting his wrist to her mouth, flicking her tongue over the pulse there. She trailed small kisses up his inner arm, then flicked her tongue over the tender skin at the inside of his elbow. He groaned, low and soft, when she moved her mouth to his neck and sucked gently on the salty skin there.

She was lost in sensation, and when Nick grabbed the hem of her tank top she lifted her arms to assist him in removing it quickly. With a smooth move, he rolled her onto her back, smiled down at her and bent his head to take a nipple into his mouth. One and then the other. And then again.

The rest of the world faded away. Shea no longer thought, she simply felt: the coolness of the sheet beneath her back, the warmth of Nick's mouth and his hands, the thrum of her blood and the gentle, throbbing ache in the center of her being. The softness of his skin beneath her hands, the hardness of the muscles beneath. She closed her eyes and surrendered to sensation.

He unfastened and unzipped her shorts, and she lifted her hips as he yanked them, and the underwear beneath, down and away. She was now naked beneath him, her legs slightly spread, her heart about to burst through her chest.

She slipped her fingers beneath the waistband of his boxers and slowly pushed them down. When she could reach no farther she slipped her foot between Nick's legs and pushed the boxers down and off.

Unable to be still, she shifted against him, bringing his body closer, touching him everywhere. Flesh on flesh was more arousing than she'd imagined, more beautiful than anything she'd ever known. And as they kissed, their bodies adjusted. A smooth sway here, a rhythmic lift there, until they were perfectly balanced and aligned.

Nick touched her, where she throbbed for him, and reached for a condom at the same time. When he stroked her intimately she lifted her hips and moaned low in her throat. When he covered himself she reached down to help, to feel the hard length of him in her hands.

Shea cradled Nick between her legs, wrapped her arms around his neck and arched her back to bring him closer. Surely her heart would explode if he didn't become a part of her, in body as well as in spirit.

He guided himself into her, slowly, gently, and her body stretched to accept him, as if she were unfolding to take him inside her. He rocked, so gently she trembled to her toes, and a whole new sensation invaded her body. A need so great it eclipsed everything else. He made love to her, with every thrust, every sigh, the rhythm increasing with each stroke.

She wrapped her legs around him, held him tight, and with one last, hard thrust he pushed her over the edge. She shattered, climaxed with a throaty cry and a thrust of her own. As the intense culmination of their joining rocked her and took her breath away, she felt Nick give over to his own release. Pounding into her, moaning her name, shuddering in her arms.

The light was gone and they lay, entwined and short of breath, in the dark. Nick rested his head on her shoulder, stretched his long, hard body over hers. Oh, she liked this. She liked this almost as much as what had just happened to them.

Surely this was what love felt like. She would die before she'd let Nick go. She would be lost without him.

"When we were on the mountain," she whispered, "would you really have shot me if I'd kept running?"

"I don't know," he breathed into her shoulder, answering without hesitation.

Shea threaded her fingers through the hair at the back of Nick's head, lazily trailing them down to his neck.

"Would you be horrified if I told you that…that I think this must be what love feels like?"

"Yes," he answered, just as quickly.

But he didn't move away, didn't let her go. And he didn't bother to tell her that what she felt couldn't possibly be love.

Chapter 11

Nick rolled over, opened his eyes slowly and reached out to brush the hair from Shea's face. *I think this must be what love feels like.*

Maybe she was right, but he wasn't ready to accept such a possibility. Not yet. As soon as she got back to her reality, back to the television station and her friends and a normal life, she'd know better. She'd know this was just a casual fling in an intense situation, sex to ease the tension. Their own heat wave that would burn itself out as soon as the predicament was resolved.

If what they had felt like more it was because they both needed, and wanted, it to feel like more. It wouldn't last.

Her eyes drifted open and she smiled at him. "Good morning," she whispered.

"Good morning."

"You're not usually up so early." She scooted across the short space between them to brush her bare body against his. His response was immediate.

"I'm not usually sleeping with a beautiful, naked woman beside me."

Shea closed her eyes against the sunlight that broke through white curtains and lit her face, but she didn't go back to sleep. Her hands explored, a palm lazily trailing down his chest, fingers at his neck. She sighed, as if what she felt was deeply satisfying.

Last night there had been very little light, and then none. By morning's sunshine he could see, with heartbreaking clarity, how fragile she looked against him, how delicate and precious she was.

And every inch a woman. Creamy smooth and curved in all the right places; a face so perfectly pretty he could find no flaw. The eyes were enchanting, the lashes long and ideally curved, the lips...her lips drove him to distraction.

He kissed her, gently at first, a little harder when she parted her lips and silently demanded more. Her hand trailed down from his chest to boldly touch his erection, to stroke with gentle, curious fingers until he almost forgot about the condoms on the bedside table. Almost.

No woman had ever captured him this way, made him feel so much a part of her that she crept inside him long before he pushed inside her. He had never needed anyone this way, with his body and something deeper. Something so deep inside he had never reached it before.

There was magic in the way Shea touched him. He had known a lot of women, he had even considered asking one to be his wife, but he had never felt magic before. He hadn't known he was capable of feeling magic. *Casual fling my ass.*

He made love to her again, eyes open to watch their bodies come together, to watch the amazing joining of his hard rough body to her smooth, delicate one. To savor the smile and the contentment on her face. To savor, even

more, the moment when her smile faded and she was over-
come with a passion so wild, so fierce, that it swept her
away and she carried him along.

They came together, hard and fast, with a deep kiss and
a shared moan. *This must be what love feels like.*

Impossible. No matter how good this felt, no matter that
she had worked her way inside him, he would have to let
her go. The sooner the better.

Satisfied, she wrapped her arms around him and closed
her eyes again. When he rolled over, she followed, smiling,
resting her head against his shoulder, threading one leg
around his.

Letting her go was going to be pure hell.

When Shea woke again it was almost ten. She glanced
at the bedside clock, and then at a sleeping Nick. She was
a little sore, her knees were still weak…and she was so
glad she'd waited for him. He was her first lover. Her last?
Her only?

His bare body was long, hard, dusted with a sprinkling
of dark hair. It was amazing to her how different they were
physically, how perfectly they fit together. Her body trembled at the memory of just how perfect it had been.

"Rise and shine," she whispered, leaning over to kiss
Nick awake. "We have work to do today."

His arms snaked around her and he held her fast. "We
do?"

"We have a murder to solve."

His eyes came open. How could such an icy blue be so
warm? Somehow he managed. "We can't do anything
more from here."

"I know," she breathed.

"We're going to have to go back to Huntsville."

"Today?" she asked, eyes wide.

Nick smiled at her. Oh, when he smiled he was beautiful. Young and carefree and happy. She wanted to see him smile more often.

"Maybe tomorrow." He kissed her, barely slipping the tip of his tongue in her mouth.

Sore or not, she wanted him again. And he, she could see quite clearly, wanted her.

The crunch of gravel yanked her from her tender thoughts. Nick heard the same noise, and he left the bed quickly to stand to the side of the window and look down. "It's a black Oldsmobile sedan."

Shea cursed, biting out a word that made Nick turn his head and raise his eyebrows. "Dean has a black Oldsmobile sedan," she explained as she looked down on the car that was coming to a stop outside the kitchen door.

She tossed Nick's jeans in his direction and stepped into her cutoff shorts as she ran to her bedroom to grab her purse off the bed, quickly gathering the contents she'd scattered there the night before and tossing them inside. She grabbed up the purse and her notebook, and ran back into Nick's room. She handed him her stuff and grabbed for her tank top, yanking it over her head.

"We can hide in the old servants' stairway. The boys didn't spend as much time here as I did. I don't think they even know it's there."

"Shea," Nick began in a ridiculously calm voice. "Maybe it's for the best. I can't hide forever."

"You don't understand," she said, reaching for the one remaining condom and stuffing it into her pocket, gathering up everything in the room that reminded her of Nick. His shirts, his underwear, his socks. Her arms were full when she led him to the hallway closet. "They'll kill you."

Nick, who was right behind her with her purse and notebook, raised his eyebrows again. "You mean they'll turn me in."

"No, I mean they'll *kill* you."

She opened the closet door, shoved aside the coats and dresses hanging there and revealed the hidden door. It opened on a dank, musty stairwell. She dropped Nick's things, grabbed his wrist and pulled him in after her, and rearranged the coats and dresses before closing the door.

They were lost in complete darkness, so she held on to Nick's hand as she carefully sat and urged him to lower himself to sit beside her.

"The key's not still under the pot," Nick whispered. "Maybe they won't be able to get in."

"Ha!" she whispered. "Boone never let anything like a locked door get in his way."

Nick sat beside her, very still, his fingers threaded through hers. Their belongings, hopefully anything that might be used to identify them, were scattered along the stairway.

Sure enough, it wasn't long before she heard the sound of booted footsteps in the kitchen.

"Shea Lyn!" Dean shouted.

Shea cringed. No one called her Shea Lyn anymore!

"Get your butt down here right this minute!"

She didn't move. She heard the boys spread out, each of them taking a room or two as they searched for her.

"She's been here!" Clint shouted from the kitchen. "That godawful tuna casserole she makes is in the fridge."

Shea withheld an outraged gasp. Godawful! She'd always thought Clint liked her tuna casserole!

Booted footsteps pounded up the stairs. Shea held her breath. She listened as doors were opened, as one brother—Boone, by the sound of the step—searched the bedroom. When he reached Carol's room he let loose a snort of disgust, then a string of foul language. Prominent in his monologue was the forbidden word he had learned at age eleven and used regularly ever since, much to the dismay of their very straitlaced parents.

Boone ran down the stairs, Clint left the kitchen and Dean's more civilized step echoed softly from the parlor. Judging by the sounds below, they met in the dining room.

Clint spoke first, his voice low and ominous. "Martha Reeves is in the cassette player. She's been doo-wopping for this guy."

"Big deal," Boone spat. "Only one bed has been slept in, and I found *these* in the garbage can."

Shea closed her eyes.

"Condom wrappers," Dean said in a deceptively low voice.

"Damn bed's still warm," Boone growled. "The place reeks of—of…" He grunted instead of finishing his sentence.

"Taggert's a dead man," Clint drawled in a low voice.

For a second all was quiet, then Dean took command, as he always did. "We're going to look in every closet, under every bed, in the garage, the attic…and if we don't find anything we wait."

Shea had the urge to borrow Boone's favorite word, but she knew if the boys' voices carried so well through the old house, so would hers.

"If Mom had told us sooner that Aunt Irene and Uncle Henry were in California, we could've been here days ago," Clint drawled. "No wonder no one else has heard from her!"

Shea squeezed Nick's hand as the boys began their search. Doors were thrown open, furniture moved roughly aside, curses muttered at every turn. When the upstairs hallway closet was thrown open, Shea held her breath, waiting for whoever was searching there to shove the dresses aside and find the hidden door.

And would any one of them think to move aside the

huge tapestry that hung on the wall in the dining room? That wall hanging hid the ground floor entrance to the old servants' stairwell.

Finally, a voice shouted from the dining room. Clint. "Dean?"

"What?"

It was Dean at the closet, dammit. If any of the brothers would think to shove the clothes aside and check for a hidden door, it would be her oldest brother.

"There's an old lady here, and she has a gun," Clint said. "She's pointing it at my...well, I'd like to have children, one day."

Maude!

Dean closed the closet door and ran down the stairs, his step lighter than Boone's had been.

"Ma'am," he said in his most polite voice. "I'm Deputy U.S. Marshal Dean Sinclair and this is my brother. Would you kindly lower that weapon?"

"Show me some ID," Maude demanded.

All was silent as Dean apparently complied.

"The man in the garage, the one with the long hair like a girl, is he your brother, too?" Maude asked brightly. "All three of the Sinclair boys? My goodness. If you three would visit your aunt and uncle more often, I wouldn't be likely to mistake you for burglars."

About that time, Boone reentered the house. "Nothing!" he shouted. "No sign of the truck, just Uncle Henry's Caddy."

"You boys probably don't remember me. I'm Irene and Henry's neighbor, Maude Wilton. Would you like some pie? I have blueberry pie at the house."

"No thank you, ma'am," Dean said calmly. "We're looking for our sister, Shea. Have you seen her?"

"Of course!" Maude said cheerfully. "Such a sweet girl."

Shea closed her eyes and sighed. Beside her she heard Nick sigh, as well, and he squeezed her hand.

"Let's see, it was three summers ago...or was it four? Susan was home and so was—"

"This week," Boone snapped impatiently. "Have you seen her this week."

"I saw her on the news," Maude said innocently. "I do hope she's all right. I imagine she will be. That girl always had gumption."

"Someone's been here," Clint said accusingly. "Someone's been...sleeping here."

Even from her dark hiding place Shea heard the foil crinkle as someone, Boone most likely, offered the condom wrappers for Maude's inspection.

Maude sighed deeply. "You boys have found me out. I have a gentleman friend, and my sister, Abigail, does not approve. Irene asked me to water her plants and keep an eye on the place, so I decided..." there was a meaningful pause. "Well, you see, my gentleman friend has these new blue pills, quite the wonder, and we were rather anxious to give them a whirl."

One of the boys cleared his throat.

Maude was not deterred. "Oh, I have no need of birth control, but in this day and age a girl can't be too careful. Why, for all I know my gentleman friend is using those blue pills all over town."

"Thank you, Mrs. Wilton, that'll be all," Dean said, dismissal in his crisp voice.

"How about some lemon squares?" Maude asked, still undeterred. "I've been cooking for my gentleman friend, you see, but I'm afraid I made too much!"

"You didn't by chance make a tuna casserole, did you?"

"Yes," she practically squealed. "Would you like a plate?"

"No," all three boys answered quickly.

Shea felt another rush of indignation. See if she ever cooked for them again!

Maude finally left, unwillingly escorted, from the sound of it. Shea could hear her brothers sigh and groan as the kitchen door closed behind her.

"Maybe they weren't here, after all," Dean said, sounding defeated.

"And maybe we missed them," Boone snapped. "Dammit, I don't like this."

"Let's go," Clint said, "before the old lady comes back and tells us more about her love life. Yikes!"

Shea held her breath as the boys left the house, one after another, and the kitchen door closed again. With a bang this time. She exhaled slowly, and Nick rose to his feet.

"Just a minute," she whispered, not trusting her brothers to leave right away.

Sure enough, the kitchen door opened and a booted step sounded on the linoleum floor. Boone or Clint, then.

"I must've dropped it in here somewhere," Clint called loudly. "Hang on, I'll be right out."

He walked slowly into the dining room and came to a dead stop. All was silent for a few long seconds, and then he began to speak.

"Shea Lyn, I know you're in here somewhere," he said, his voice warm and kind and inviting. "Don't you know better than to hide from me? Your favorite brother?"

He shuffled his feet. Ha! She'd seen him use this tactic on women a hundred times. The only thing missing was the "aw shucks."

"Dean is pretty mad right now and so is Boone, but you know I would never let them hurt you. Come on out and we'll take them on together. You and me, just like the old days when our big brothers ran us ragged."

She squeezed Nick's hand. Clint was too good at this. She was tempted, really, truly tempted.

"Please," he said. "We've been worried sick."

In the silence that followed, Shea felt tears burn her eyes. For all their faults, she loved her brothers and they loved her. She had never intended to hurt them.

And then Clint muttered a vile curse word and stomped into the kitchen. "It didn't work," he yelled as he stepped outside. "I guess she's really not here."

The engine of Dean's Oldsmobile fired up, and a few seconds later gravel churned noisily again.

And Nick tugged her to her feet.

"Now I'm certain I should be more afraid of your brothers than of the authorities." He pulled her against his chest. "How did you turn out to be so sweet, growing up with that?"

"I'm not always sweet," she whispered.

"You coulda fooled me."

His life was still a royal mess he might never get straightened out. So why did he feel so much better than he had yesterday? Not just better physically but deep down, in places he'd rather not explore. More whole. More content.

He packed what little he had into a duffel bag Shea had borrowed from her aunt's closet, tossing his belongings in carelessly. What he had didn't come close to filling the small bag. Shea had half filled a duffel bag of her own, with what she'd borrowed from Lenny's late wife's closet and a few things from her cousins' drawers.

Somewhere in there was that third condom. He had to let Shea go, had to make certain she was not a part of this when it fell apart. But he surely would like to get the chance to use that last condom.

As he walked down the stairs for the last time he heard

her voice, soft and low, sweet and arousing as if every breath washed over his skin. When he stepped into the kitchen doorway he saw her, standing against the counter with her back to him. For the trip she'd confiscated something a little more proper from her cousin's closet. A pair of navy blue pants and a white knit top with a touch of lace around the neckline. She'd even found a pair of strappy white sandals in her aunt's closet.

The pants hugged her hips, and the knit top accentuated her fine curves.

"No," she whispered loudly into the borrowed cell phone. "Mark, I'm fine, I swear."

She tapped her toes nervously as she listened to Mark's response.

"This is the story of a lifetime. I'm not about to let it get away from me, no matter what you have to say about the matter."

Nick's smile faded. *The story of a lifetime.* He'd heard that from Shea before, but he'd begun to think he meant more to her than a story. He'd been sure of it, for a while.

"Mark," she said, exasperated. "I'll see you in a few days. For now I'm sticking to Taggert like glue."

Nick got a sick feeling in his stomach, low and acute. All of a sudden what had happened last night made perfect sense. He starts to talk about leaving, and she comes to him with three condoms and a come-hither smile that would do in any man.

Did she think that if she slept with him he'd be reluctant to let her go? Was this her way of making sure she saw her damned story through to the end?

She turned around, saw him there and smiled. As if nothing had changed, as if she wasn't every bit as manipulative as her brothers.

"I gotta go, Mark," she said, cutting her cameraman off

and hitting the end button while the sounds of the young man's voice still echoed desperately from the phone.

She placed the cell phone on the counter. "Nothing new," she said. "Boone hasn't done anything but look for me, and Grace has kinda hit a wall."

"It was nice of her to do what she did," Nick said as Shea walked toward him with that damned smile on her face. "Thank her for me."

"You can thank her yourself," Shea said as she placed her arms around his neck. "When this is all over and you meet Grace and her husband."

He couldn't believe her gall. She acted as if nothing had changed. He had made an absolute fool of himself, and she was smiling like the cat who ate the canary. He could almost see the yellow feathers sticking from her mouth.

But she didn't have to know he was a complete idiot. He could keep that information to himself.

He gave her a quick, passionless kiss. "Give me the keys to the truck and I'll pull it around." He offered his hand, palm up, for the keys. Shea wouldn't know for a few minutes that she'd just gotten herself a goodbye kiss.

She wasn't at all suspicious as she headed for the purse on the counter, removing the keys to Lenny's truck. Confident, wasn't she?

Before she could hand the keys to him, a sharp knock sounded on the kitchen door. A gray head appeared; eyes lively and laughing peered in. Shea admitted the very pleased Maude, who cast them each a bright smile.

"Were you in the servants' stairwell?" she asked.

"Yes," Shea said. "You were brilliant."

And a little scary. Nick decided to keep that opinion to himself. He approached Shea, bag in hand. "We have to get out of here. Give me those keys and I'll pull the truck around."

Shea was in the process of obeying when Maude

snatched the keys from her hand. "Are you daft?" she snapped, bringing the keys to her chest. "The coppers will be looking for that truck." She reached into her handbag. "That's why I'm here. You can take my car!" She seemed delighted with the plan.

Shea glanced up at him. "It might be a good idea," she said softly. "Everyone is looking for Lenny's truck, and it won't do either of us any good to steal a car at this point."

He couldn't argue with her, because she was right.

They gathered their bags, made sure all the lights were off, and locked the door behind them. Shea returned the spare key to its hiding place beneath the flower pot.

They walked toward Maude's house, the old lady in front, Nick bringing up the rear. What on earth would he be traveling in? A pink Cadillac? A powder blue Lincoln? Some thirty-year-old monstrosity?

A brown paper bag sat on the driveway outside the garage. "I packed you two a snack." The bag Maude lifted looked heavy enough to contain a snack for a regiment of starving soldiers. She had to hold it with both hands. Shea took the brown paper bag and Maude opened the garage door.

Sure enough, the vehicle before him was a whale of a car, and, heaven forbid, it was the most awful shade of green....

And then he noticed that Maude was pointing to the car beside and slightly behind her own green one. "My brother Louis passed away a few years back, and he left me his car. Bless his soul, he loved that car and I didn't have the heart to sell it. I have it serviced regularly, so you shouldn't have any problem with it."

Nick's eyes were riveted to his getaway car, a 1969, midnight-blue Z28 Camaro.

"I think it's older than Lenny's truck," Shea whispered as Maude walked toward the car.

"Bite your tongue," Nick said with the proper respect. "This is a fine car."

"If you say so," she said skeptically.

They threw their bags and the huge snack into the back seat, Maude gave them each a hug and then they climbed into the Camaro.

Maude leaned into the car through Shea's rolled-down window. "I'll expect to be invited to the wedding," she said with a prim smile.

"Wedding?" Shea asked, casting Nick a quick and terrified glance.

Maude shook her finger at Nick. "There had better be a wedding." She nodded her head in finality. "I'll have Abigail paint you some fruit as a wedding present."

Nick started the loud engine and carefully pulled the car out of the garage. Maude followed, waving enthusiastically, and Shea put on her seat belt.

As soon as the opportunity arose, he'd dump her. It didn't matter where or when, but it was time. Shea Sinclair, weathergirl, had all the story she was going to get out of him.

Chapter 12

Nick was too quiet, his attention on the road ahead, his mind elsewhere. He was probably nervous about what would happen once they reached Huntsville. Hiding in Marion had been nice, but they'd both known it wouldn't last.

But Shea did wish he would turn his head now and then and give her an encouraging smile, that he would take her hand and acknowledge, in some small way, that what had happened last night and this morning had been extraordinary. Spectacular and life-altering.

Loving Nick was going to change her life in so many ways, she couldn't begin to count them.

She hoped he hadn't been frightened by Maude's comment about a wedding. Maude was a sweetheart, but she was also very old-fashioned. She knew, thanks to Shea's interfering brothers and the telltale condom wrappers, that she and Nick had slept together. In Maude's mind that was probably grounds for an immediate wedding.

Shea lifted her chin defiantly. She was more modern than Maude, more worldly wise. Times had changed.

But a small chapel would be nice, she thought warmly. Just close friends and family, of course. Tulips instead of roses, if the season was right. Candles, of course, and lots of greenery. They could play Martha Reeves at the reception and she could wake up next to Nick every day for the rest of her life.

And he thought she would make a great mother! The kids she'd never really wanted seemed real to her now, necessary and inevitable. Nick's babies, dark-haired children who would fulfill his dreams and hers. Dreams she'd never known she had. Maybe, if she played everything right, she *could* have it all.

Shea shook off the thoughts, wondering where on earth they'd come from. Nick had never said anything to her about a permanent relationship. He had never even mentioned the word *married*, except in relation to that femme fatale Lauren.

They'd been traveling all morning, and the tension in the car was so thick she could almost reach out and touch it. Of course the tension was thick! They were driving into battle, and the rest of their lives depended on the outcome.

"Where will we go first?" she asked.

Nick didn't even turn his head in her direction as he answered. "I'm going to drop you off near the I-65 interchange," he said in an apathetic voice. "After that, it's best you don't know where I go."

He was trying to keep her from the battle that was still to come, even though she'd told him she didn't need any man to protect her. "You'll need my help," she insisted softly.

Nick turned to look at her then, planting icy blue eyes on her face. "No," he said coldly. "I don't need you. I used you to get safely away and you cared for me while my leg was healing. Other than that…'' He returned his eyes to the road.

She couldn't believe what she was hearing. Nick had just basically told her that he was finished with her. That he didn't need or want her around.

''What about that state trooper?'' she asked, a hint of panic welling up inside her. ''He saw me. I can't just show up at work tomorrow morning as if nothing happened.''

''Deny everything,'' Nick said succinctly. ''There are no pictures and he didn't get the license plate number off the truck.'' He picked up speed and changed lanes sharply. ''I have no doubt that you can make a complete fool of any man who dares to disagree with you.''

This time she heard it. There was anger in his voice, a sharp, biting fury.

''What's wrong?''

''My life is in a shambles and you ask me what's wrong?''

''No, what's wrong with *us?*''

He looked at her again and gave her a cold, cynical smile. ''Honey, there is no us. If you think last night changed things, you really are a virgin.''

She felt like he'd stomped on her chest, knocked the breath from her lungs and ripped out her heart.

''Did you think that because we had sex I'd let you tag along to the end of the story?'' he asked, returning his eyes to the road. ''Hell, weathergirl, if you wave condoms in any man's face and tell him you've got an itch that needs to be scratched, it'll get scratched. You don't really have to have the condoms, but it does show a man that your intentions are serious and you're safety conscious. Men appreciate that in a woman.''

''Last night wasn't…like that.''

''Of course it was,'' he said calmly. ''But last night is over and I've got things to do.''

''I could help,'' she began, her heart sinking.

''I don't want your help, weathergirl.''

Too soon they reached the Huntsville-Decatur exit. Nick took the exit too fast, speeding down the ramp and taking the road to Huntsville. He hadn't gone far before he turned off the pavement, guiding the car onto the shoulder.

Shea didn't move. He couldn't be serious. This was some kind of sick joke.

''I'm not leaving,'' she said softly, her eyes on a car that sped past.

Nick reached past her, grabbed the door handle and threw the passenger door open. He reached into the back seat and grabbed the duffel bag that had her borrowed clothes in it, and he tossed it in front of her and out the open door. The bag landed on a patch of soft grass.

''The last time I tried to let you go I didn't have the physical strength to force you from the car,'' he said softly. ''Today I do. Don't make me drag you out of your seat and dump you in that ditch over there.''

With a sinking heart she realized he was serious. She wanted to believe that his intentions were noble, that he loved her and didn't want her involved any further...but Nick was a terrible liar, and there was no love or nobility in his voice or his eyes. He was done with her, and there was nothing she could do but walk away with what little dignity she had left intact.

''What do you want me to tell the police?''

''I don't care what you tell them.''

Shea took a deep breath and left the car. She would not cry in front of Nick. She would not beg him to take her along.

''Be careful,'' she said, slamming the door and leaning in through the open window.

''You, too.''

"You know where to find me, if you need me," she said, feeling pathetic as the words left her mouth.

"Thanks, but I won't be needing you." He put the car in gear and turned his attention to the highway, so Shea stepped away from the car and picked up her bag. She watched as Nick pulled the Camaro onto the highway and sped away, and then she started walking.

He'd love to go to his house, sit in the upstairs window and watch the neighbors and see what was going on there. But he didn't dare. The Feds or the local cops were probably watching the house, as well as his old office and the homes of anyone he'd called friend during his years in Huntsville.

Like it or not, he missed Shea already. He hadn't had any choice but to turn her loose, but still he missed her. No one would ever know he was so foolish.

Wearing the baseball cap low to disguise his face, he drove to a deserted warehouse at the south end of town. He'd once bought plumbing fixtures here, before the place went out of business. He parked Maude's Camaro out back, where it was hidden from the street, and walked around the building until he found an unlocked window. Like Shea's brother Boone, he wasn't about to let a locked door keep him out.

His investigating would have to wait until dark, when he would be less recognizable driving around town in the Camaro. There wasn't a soul in Huntsville who hadn't seen his face a thousand times. He could get busted sitting at a red light, if he wasn't careful.

He found a chair, abandoned because it didn't sit steady on the ground, and sat, extending his leg to rest on an empty crate. His leg was better, but it wasn't completely healed by any means. The ache went deep, and he wondered if it would ever go away.

He wondered if he'd live long enough to completely recover.

Shea's head buzzed, her stomach churned and she'd been asked so many questions nothing made sense anymore. She was tired, she was hungry and she wanted a long, hot bath and a nap, if she could manage to sleep ever again.

She sat in a padded blue chair in the detective's office, but it was a group of FBI agents who continuously asked the questions. They leaned over her, they paced, they asked the same questions again and again. Where had she been for the past week? Why had Taggert dropped her off so close to home? Had she been acquainted with Taggert before the alleged kidnapping?

The "alleged" made her head swim again. Some of the eyes that bored into her were not friendly. They were accusing. Suspicious.

Tired beyond tired, hurting deep inside and afraid to show it, Shea lifted her head and saw a familiar face on the other side of the room.

She raised her hand to quiet the herd, steeled her heart against the tears that constantly threatened and said, "You guys are making me sick. I'll answer questions, but only if he asks them. I'll only talk to *him*."

The FBI agents turned their heads in unison, and Luther lifted a hand to his chest. "Me?"

She nodded.

The FBI agent who had been asking most of the questions tried to dissuade her with a smile, then stern disapproval, then thinly veiled threats. She would not be dissuaded.

Finally they relented.

Luther took her arm and led her into a cool, quiet office. As he closed the door on the unhappy FBI agents, Shea glanced around, searching for a two-way mirror. She didn't see anything to make her think she and Luther weren't completely alone.

He leaned against the door and sighed, weary and disapproving. His white dress shirt was slightly rumpled, his navy blue tie loosened and the jacket of his dark gray suit swung open to show off the badge on his belt and the shoulder holster and smallish gun. He was the picture-perfect homicide detective, skeptical and hard and basically good.

"Are you all right?" he asked.

She nodded and took the chair before a wide desk piled high with manila folders and office memos. A huge jar of jelly beans added the only color to the messy desk.

Luther crossed the room and propped his leg against the desk, placing himself just a little bit too close to her. He wasn't as broad as Nick, but he was definitely as tall. He knew how to use his size to intimidate.

In his best cop voice he asked, "Why don't you just tell me what happened?"

In the quiet of the cool office, looking up at a familiar face, Shea felt the buzzing in her head finally start to fade. Her stomach quit churning. "He's innocent."

Luther emitted a sound that was somewhere between a groan and a snarl.

"He panicked after the trial and ran. Surely you can understand that."

It was clear that Luther did not understand. "If he was innocent he could've gone through the proper channels to prove it. His lawyer could've filed an appeal—"

"His lawyer is currently engaged to the woman who was his girlfriend at the time of the murder," Shea snapped.

"So I understand," Luther said with a sigh.

"Besides, why would a man who's spent ten months in

jail and then gets convicted of a crime he didn't commit trust the system?'' She gave Luther her most determined glare.

"Because the system is all we've got."

Shea sighed in turn. Maybe talking to Luther wasn't such a good idea, after all. He was too darn stubborn.

"Where have you two been?" he asked.

"I don't know," she said, staring at the jar of jelly beans.

"You don't know?"

"I was blindfolded."

Luther reached into the jar of jelly beans and drew out a handful. She declined when he offered the colorful palmful to her. "I talked to Lenny," he said as he popped one into his mouth.

Her heart leaped. "Lenny who?"

Luther smiled. "He told me everything."

Shea sighed. "Why would you believe the ramblings of a half-blind old man—"

"How did you know he was a half-blind old man if you never met him?"

Shea bit back a curse and refused to answer.

"Okay," Luther said casually. "Let's change the subject. Where is Taggert now?"

"I don't know."

"Which direction did he head in after he dropped you off?"

She didn't hesitate, since she'd anticipated this question. "He got back on the interstate and headed north. He mentioned an old army buddy who has a ranch in Montana. He might be headed there."

"Montana," Luther said lifelessly. "I don't suppose he mentioned this army buddy's name."

"No."

"What was he driving?"

"The truck he...he borrowed from Lenny. He painted the blue part white, though, so it would look different." Ha! Let them try to stop every old white truck on the highway! That would keep them all busy for a while.

Luther popped a red jelly bean into his mouth. "Have you been reading the papers? Surely you have. Surely you read that a state trooper saw you very willingly traveling with Taggert just hours after the kidnapping. He said that the two of you were *very* friendly. Shea, you're in a world of trouble."

She turned her most innocent gaze to him. "He's mistaken."

Luther did not believe her, but somehow she had to *make* him believe. If the cops stayed all over her, if she was subjected to days of questioning, how could she investigate the murder? "Taggert stole a truck, blindfolded me and took me to goodness knows where. He never threatened me, he never hurt me and I believe he's innocent of the crime he was convicted of."

"Shea, everyone in the country who owns a television has seen him threaten you," Luther said impatiently. "Have you forgotten that he dragged you off the courthouse steps at gunpoint?"

"No, I haven't forgotten," she whispered.

"Well, you'd better clear your head and start telling the truth."

No one would ever know the truth. Not all of it, anyway. "I am telling the truth."

Luther leaned in close, too close. He narrowed his dark, calculating eyes. "Why do I have the feeling that if you say he went north, he went south? That if you say he's driving a white truck he's driving a black car? Why is that, Shea?" He locked his dark eyes to hers. "Why do I have a feeling Taggert's around here somewhere, trying to find the evidence to prove himself innocent?"

Shea looked Luther in the eye, unflinching and brave. "He doesn't need to and he knows it. I'm going to prove Nick innocent myself."

"It's Nick now," Luther said softly.

Shea licked her lips. "Do you have any other questions? I'm tired and I'm hungry and I just want to go home."

Luther stepped back, away from her. "I'll drive you home. You can expect to see your brothers there in a couple of hours. I called Dean on his cell phone as soon as I found out you were here. They were talking to some old friends of yours in Mobile."

"How very thoughtful of you," she said, her heart in her throat. She was not looking forward to the coming confrontation!

"I'd like to be around when they start asking *their* questions," Luther said softly. He popped another jelly bean into his mouth and offered his candy-free hand to help her from the chair.

Like it or not, she needed the support.

Chapter 13

He didn't dare drive the Camaro into his own cul-de-sac, but from the street directly to the east he had a fairly good view of his old backyard. And Norman's. All appeared to be quiet there, but appearances could be deceptive. He knew that.

The car radio was tuned to a local rock station, the music turned low, but when the news came on he turned the volume up.

"Kidnap victim Shea Sinclair was released earlier today." The announcer had a down-home drawl and sounded as if he were talking casually to a group of friends. "You'll recall that one week ago today she was seized outside the Madison County Courthouse by fugitive Nicholas Taggert, a convicted murderer."

Convicted murderer. The newscaster said the words as if he relished the taste of them on his tongue, and Nick felt slightly ill. That label would follow him forever, even if he proved his innocence.

Pushing his sick self-pity aside, he turned his thoughts to the weathergirl. Lucky Shea, she was the number one story. Had he really known her only a week? It seemed like a lifetime ago that he had locked his eyes on her face, grabbed her in desperation and dragged her off the courthouse steps.

He pulled his car to a stop at the curb outside a neat little colonial house that had a For Sale sign in the front yard. The uncurtained windows marked it as empty.

"So far Miss Sinclair has refused all requests for interviews," the newscaster continued, "but a spokesman for the FBI says she has been cooperative."

Of course Shea was cooperative, but why was she turning down requests for interviews? Wasn't this what she wanted? The spotlight, her moment of glory. Ah, maybe she was waiting for something big. The network, CNN, her own show.

"Authorities have now shifted their search out of Alabama. Roads in Tennessee and north are being combed for any sign of the white truck Taggert is now driving. It's the same vehicle that was stolen hours after his escape, but it has recently been painted white. Taggert is apparently heading to Montana, where an old acquaintance resides."

Montana? Nick leaned closer to the radio. A white truck? What the hell was she doing? When the FBI and the local cops found out he was here in town—and they would eventually find out—Shea would be in deeper than before.

But if what he heard was true, the coverage in Huntsville had been cut in half. Agents were heading north, searching for a truck that was presently parked in a dilapidated barn in Marion, Alabama. Looking for a man who was right here in town.

Nick turned off the radio as the newscaster reminded his

listeners that Nicholas Taggert was armed and dangerous and to "be on the lookout, you hear?"

What was Shea up to? After the way he'd dumped her this morning she should be angry, should be telling the cops everything she knew. Well, everything that wouldn't incriminate *her*.

Nick turned off the engine and left the car parked at the curb. It was late, but if anyone was watching they'd probably assume he was interested in the house for sale. He pulled the cap low over his eyes and took a flyer from the box near the sign, and pretended to study the stats by the light of the streetlamp. He approached the house, peering into the uncovered living room window.

When he walked around the house, his eyes shifted to the rear of Norman's residence.

Lights burned warmly, visible through the slats of the wooden fence that surrounded the backyard. He wondered if Lauren was there. If she'd moved in with her fiancé.

Nick vaulted over the fence, noting and cursing the pain and weakness in his injured leg when he hit the ground on both feet.

Shea thought Lauren might've killed Winkler. To keep him from talking about what had happened that night? Seemed extreme, especially since Nick had been the one to discover them. What did it matter if anyone else knew?

Unless she and Norman had been involved even then. Unless she didn't want her married lover to know what she'd done. Norman was a snake, but he was an unforgiving reptile and would not have been happy to know the woman he was cheating on his wife with was as unfaithful as he.

Nick dropped down low and watched as Norman, dressed in a salmon-colored golf shirt, walked past the kitchen window. Sure enough, Lauren wasn't far behind, a smile on her face, her blond hair piled in an artfully careless way atop her head.

Had a woman he'd considered spending the rest of his life with killed a man to protect herself and then pinned the crime on him? Maybe so. Nick couldn't look at her right now and swear she wouldn't do it, much as he wanted to. His taste in women was worse than he'd imagined. First Lauren and then Shea.

After watching the house for a while, searching what he could see of the rest of the neighborhood for people and vehicles he didn't know, Nick spotted a car drive by slowly. He dropped to his haunches and watched as the police cruiser crept past, stopping in front of his house, which was also for sale, and shining a bright, wide-beamed flashlight across the front of the house and into the side yard. Seeing nothing suspicious, the officers drove on.

Nick left Norman's yard the way he'd entered, vaulting over the fence. His leg burned when he landed, and he limped back to the car. If there ever had been constant surveillance on his house it had been pulled, downgraded to a drive-by every now and then. He'd be back, when the residents of the cul-de-sac were fast asleep, to see how often the police car drove by, if there was a pattern he could work with.

And as he drove away he wondered again why Shea was not granting any interviews.

"I made your favorite," Shea said with a wide smile. "My tuna casserole."

Clint was good. He didn't so much as blink. "Great!"

Boone paced in her living room, as angry as she'd ever seen him as he took long strides across her beige carpet. "I'm not hungry."

Dean lowered himself to her sofa, leaned back in a falsely casual pose and gave her the eye. "I'd really rather talk about this situation some more before we even think about eating.''

Shea rolled her eyes. "I've done nothing but talk all day. To the FBI, the local cops, my boss." Who wanted her to return to work immediately. He had been stunned when she'd told him she wasn't ready to go back to work. "I'm tired, I'm hungry, all I want is to eat and fall into my own bed for a good night's sleep. I might sleep for the rest of the week.''

Shea pretended not to notice as the boys exchanged a cryptic glance that did not include her.

She knew getting rid of her brothers would not be easy. It might even be impossible. How could she do what needed to be done when they were dogging her all the time?

"Boone," she said sweetly as she piled Clint's plate high with tuna casserole, "didn't Mark ask you to investigate the Winkler murder for me?"

He gave her a murderous glare. "I didn't have time," he said in a low voice.

"Well, you have time now." She gave him a wide-eyed, innocent smile. "The only reason Taggert escaped was to prove himself innocent. I believe him...."

"He kidnapped you!" Boone said through gritted teeth.

"Only because he was desperate.''

Dean rose from the couch. "Why do you insist on defending Taggert?" he asked calmly. "Is there something you're not telling us?"

Three brothers who were so protective they wouldn't even risk hurting her feelings by telling her they didn't like her casserole wouldn't understand that she cared about Nick, that she believed in him. That maybe she even loved him. But they all understood ambition.

"Think of what a great story it'll make," she said, putting a trace of excitement into her voice and her smile.

"The station manager won't let the weatherman send me out to pose in front of a tornado if I can make a name for myself as a real reporter."

Boone took a threatening step toward her. "He put you in front of a tornado?"

Shea scooped up another healthy serving of tuna casserole. "Yes. I can't tell you how many times last spring I had to go out in storms actually searching for funnel clouds. The station meteorologist was always quite disappointed when I didn't find one."

"And what's his name?" Clint asked as he shoveled in a mouthful of tuna and noodles.

Shea smiled. "Never you mind. If I can find out who really killed Gary Winkler, I won't ever have to do it again."

She spooned another serving of tuna casserole onto a plate and held it high for Dean. "Here you go. If you're going to help Boone you'll need your strength."

With a sigh, Dean stood and walked toward her. "Who said I was going to help Boone? I plan to stay right here and keep a close eye on you, in case Taggert decides to come back."

She lowered her eyes and fixed her own, smaller serving. "He won't."

"How can you be so sure?" Clint asked.

Shea sat down and stared at her plate. "I didn't escape, he let me go." Forced her to go would be more like it, but she couldn't tell them that. "He's long gone."

Where was he sleeping tonight? How was his leg? She felt like a complete sap for worrying about him, even now. How could she have been so wrong about Nick and the way he felt?

"I had Grace give Luther all the information she gathered for me, but I'm sure he wouldn't mind sharing it with you three."

"Two," Clint said. "I'm no lawman. Never have been, never will be."

Shea smiled wanly. "I'm sure they miss you at the rodeo. When are you going back?"

His gaze was penetrating. "When Taggert is captured."

"That's very sweet, but it's not—"

"Oh yes it is," he interrupted.

She adored her brothers, even when she was annoyed with them. Their parents had always been distant, not uncaring but living in another world at times. The four of them had compensated for that distance by being there for one another. The boys had come to Shea's school plays when her father had a golf tournament and her mother was busy with one women's club or another. Her brothers had been the ones to bandage her scraped knees and take care of her when she got up in the night, sick.

Even now... Shea had talked to her mother on the phone earlier this evening, and Patsy Sinclair had been relieved to hear that her daughter was safe and well, but didn't even ask about coming down to stay for a while. Apparently there was a fund-raiser coming up this weekend, and she was swamped.

How many times had Shea wished for a mother and father like Irene and Henry? Caring, warm people who loved their children to distraction and smiled a lot and didn't mind making fools of themselves now and then, in the name of fun or love.

But it didn't matter. She had Dean and Boone and Clint. She loved them dearly, and now she had to get rid of them.

"Where are you boys staying tonight?"

"Right here," Dean said, in a voice that held no room for argument.

"I only have the one bed," she protested.

"You have a couch and a whole lot of floor," Boone said. "That'll do us just fine."

If she tried to kick them out, it would only raise their suspicions. Getting past them was going to be difficult enough. "Well, I hope I have enough pillows and blankets to go around."

"We'll do fine," Dean said in his most matter-of-fact voice.

They all ate every bite of their tuna casserole.

It was after two in the morning before she felt confident enough to slip out of bed, place her note on the pillow and grab her duffel bag. It was the same bag she'd carried as Nick sped away in Maude's Camaro, only now it was full with not only the borrowed clothes, but a number of her own things. She wasn't sure how long she'd be gone.

She opened the sliding glass door slowly, noiselessly, hoping the boys were as exhausted as they'd seemed to be after dinner. They should all three be sound asleep by now.

Her steps onto the balcony were carefully measured, since it had a tendency to squeak in certain spots. She knew those spots well, though, and avoided them as she made her way to the railing.

Tossing the bag to the ground would make too much noise, so she placed the strap over her shoulder and carried it with her as she held on to the railing and lowered herself carefully over and down. Since her apartment building was built on a slope, there was an easy three-foot drop.

She glanced back twice, but saw no one burst onto the balcony, heard no one call her name.

Oh, the boys were going to be so angry when they found that note! She silently and fervently apologized to them in advance. But what choice did she have?

It was just over a mile to Mark's apartment. All was quiet, the apartments dark and the street deserted, but for one car. She stepped off the sidewalk and into the cover of brush as it passed. Couldn't be too careful.

He wasn't expecting her, so she had to knock several times before she heard his sleepy "just a minute" and the shuffle of feet. A light came on, and a shadow passed in front of the peephole in his door.

The door flew open to reveal a just-from-the-bed Mark, complete with stand-up red hair and baggy pajama bottoms and faded T-shirt. "Shea!" He grabbed her arm and pulled her inside, closing the door behind her. He gave her a big hug and grinned as he set her back to look at her. "I was so worried."

"I told you I was fine," she said with a smile.

"Yeah, but..." He ran his hand through unruly hair. "It's good to see you." His smile faded. "What's wrong? Why are you here so late?" He glanced at her bag. "And why are you carrying that duffel bag?"

She didn't want to tell him more than he needed to know. The boys would do their best to get it out of him, and it might not take long. Mark was a sweetheart, but bravery wasn't high on his list of attributes. Still, who else could she trust?

"I need a ride."

She waited patiently in the living room while Mark dressed. This was what she had to do. For the story, for herself. Most of all for Nick.

For Nick. What would he do when his name was cleared and he was a free man? Call her for a date. Tell her to get lost. Disappear. She had been so sure, twenty-four hours ago, that what they had would last. Right now she couldn't be sure of anything.

Mark was quick, and he grabbed his keys from the bookcase as he walked by, properly dressed and hair neatly combed.

"Where are we going?"

"First of all, you have to swear you won't tell anyone."

"I swear," he whispered as they stepped outside and he closed and locked his apartment door.

Shea bounded down the steps and headed for Mark's familiar beat-up car. When they were inside, Mark slipped the keys into the ignition and turned to her. "Where to?"

"You'll be hearing from my brothers," Shea said softly.

Mark's eyes narrowed. "Again?"

"Whatever they say or do, don't tell them you saw me tonight. Especially don't tell them where you're taking me."

"All right," he said skeptically.

"They bark a lot, but I promise you they don't bite. Usually."

Mark flinched, but agreed, and Shea gave him the name of the street.

After he'd started the engine and was pulling out of the apartment parking lot, she continued, "I'm going to lie low for a couple of days, but stay close to your phone in the evenings. In a day or two I'm going to need you again."

"You got it," he said without hesitation.

She nodded her head and watched the dark, quiet houses go past, then they pulled onto the well lit and surprisingly active Parkway. Where they were headed was not far away, but walking had been out of the question. A lone woman, this time of night, with a packed bag and a well-known face? It just wouldn't do.

In a few minutes Mark pulled off the Parkway and took a side road that led them east into a residential neighborhood. He took the twists and turns at an easy pace, unhurried. And still, with every second that passed, her heart thudded harder.

"Here," she said, deciding at the last minute that it wouldn't be wise for Mark to pull into the cul-de-sac. She had him stop on the small leg of a street that led to the neighborhood where Winkler had been killed. As she threw open the car door, Mark reached across and grabbed her wrist.

"Be careful."

Her heart was really pounding now. "I will."

"And Shea, when you make it to the top, will you take me with you?" He cast her a surprising grin. "I want only to ride your coattails."

"I wouldn't have it any other way."

The only problem was, she didn't know what she wanted anymore. Making it to the top of her profession no longer seemed all that important. She still loved her job, she still wanted to work, but she no longer thought a career in television would be enough to keep her happy for the rest of her life. Loving Nick had turned her careful, safe plans upside down and inside out. He had put her aside with a cold glare and a careless goodbye, and still...she couldn't go back.

The cul-de-sac was quiet. Dark, but for the streetlamps that shone onto perfectly manicured lawns and a narrow street. Nick's house, toward the end of the circle, was the only one for sale.

There were a few toys here and there, on the lawns she passed, and a fair number of porch swings, of wooden forts in fenced backyards. She couldn't help but remember what Nick had said about his dream. The house, the kids, the safe life. He'd tried to build it here and the dream had blown up in his face, turning into a full-fledged nightmare.

For a few wonderful, delusional hours, she had made Nick's dream her dream. It had hit her with blinding force, coming out of the blue and surprising her with its clarity. The white house, the swings, the babies. They were such simple desires, and yet...they had power, a power she had not expected to feel.

She tried to see him in the neat house that was for sale,

but couldn't. The Nick she knew was hard, desperate, passionate. None of that echoed in the red brick or neatly trimmed boxwoods. In the drawn blinds or the empty window boxes. There was no porch swing, she noticed. Not yet.

Nothing stirred in this deceptively peaceful neighborhood, so she felt confident as she walked through the grass to the empty driveway. Someone here, someone who had been at the barbecue that night, was a killer. A killer who had pinned the crime on Nick and had, until now, gotten away with it. She heard a car and hurried to the side of the house. Someone was coming home quite late, or else someone was lost. You didn't come to Teakwood Court unless you were heading for Teakwood Court. No one passed through here en route to another street.

She hid in the shadows and pressed her shoulder to the brick wall of Nick's house, watching the street to see who passed. The car came closer, humming slowly, advancing without haste or purpose.

Perhaps it really was someone who was lost.

She didn't hear a sound, but suddenly a strong hand clamped over her mouth and an arm circled her waist, so quickly her breath left her. She swung back an elbow that had no effect on her attacker as he pulled her quickly backward. She scraped her feet across the ground and kicked as he dragged her into the backyard and behind the cover of a low bush.

She continued to kick until he whispered in her ear, "Be still."

Knowing that voice, she obeyed, and the arm that held her loosened, the silencing hand fell from her mouth. A split second later a bright beam raked across the side yard where she'd been standing just a moment ago.

"Coppers," Nick whispered, and against all reason Shea smiled.

Chapter 14

Nick kept a stilling arm around Shea until the police car had turned off Teakwood Court, gone down the short road that led to the next street over, and passed by to the rear. He watched the flash of headlights pass houses and trees, the light flitting in and out and finally disappearing.

Then he spun Shea around and grabbed her chin, forcing her to look up at him. "What the hell are you doing here?" he whispered harshly.

"The same thing you are, I imagine," she said, her voice as low as his and much calmer.

He hated to admit it to himself, and would never admit it to *her,* but he was glad to see Shea again. Most of all he was glad to hold her, even in this less than romantic way. She felt good, soft and warm and right in a way he could not begin to explain.

"Isn't this going a bit far for a story?"

She didn't answer, but in the moonlight her eyes accused him. Branded him.

"But then," he added, lowering his head so his lips almost touched her ear as he whispered, "we both know how far the weathergirl will go to further her career."

She was too close to resist. He kissed her earlobe, then the sensitive neck beneath. His mouth lingered on her skin, lips parted as he breathed deep. Like it or not, he was lost in her scent and the taste of her. Everything else faded, until there was nothing but the easy way he leaned into her, the way she responded, with a sigh and a supple yielding.

And then it hit him. When he'd run from Huntsville and the unfair conviction, Shea at first an unwilling hostage and then a partner, he had hidden inside her. Not literally, at first, but...yes, he had definitely done his best to hide inside her. To slip beneath her skin, to shroud himself in something that didn't exist.

She lifted a tender hand to the back of his head, and he took his mouth from her neck. He couldn't hide in her, or with her. It was a foolish notion that could get them both killed.

"Go home," he said coldly, dropping his arms, freeing her to run.

"No."

"This is not a damned story, it's my life," he protested.

"I know that," she whispered, bringing her hand to his face and resting her palm on his cheek. "That's why I'm here."

She dropped her hand and slipped from the cover of the bushes, staying low while she made her way to the back door. He followed her.

This spot, directly before the kitchen door, was shielded on the right by the wooden fence that hid the unsightly garbage can from the neighbors' view, to the left by a thick hedge and to the rear by a densely wooded portion of his backyard. Someone would have to be standing in just the right place to see them here.

Shea dropped down on her haunches, unzipped her bag and reached inside. Quickly finding what she was searching for, she withdrew a credit card.

"What are you doing?" he whispered.

"Breaking into your house."

Much too expertly, she slipped the credit card between the door and the frame and worked it up. He heard the lock jiggle, Shea's muffled curse when the door didn't open as quickly and easily as she'd expected. Then finally, no more than two minutes later, the lock slipped and she opened the door.

She entered the house and he followed, silently closing and relocking the kitchen door behind them. Shea dropped her bag onto the linoleum floor and sat, her back to the counter so she was out of the moonlight that streamed through the window above the sink. He heard her breathing heavily—from the excitement of almost being caught, he imagined. From the excitement of breaking and entering.

He sat across from her, his back to another set of cabinets. Oddly enough, he felt safe here. Maybe because Shea was here and he wasn't alone anymore. One more thing he didn't dare admit to anyone.

"Where on earth did you learn to do that?"

"Boone taught me," she answered softly. "He thought I should know, in case I ever locked myself out of my apartment."

Nick shifted uncomfortably, his heartbeat ratcheting down as they sat in the quiet darkness. He heard Shea take a deep breath and let it out slowly, heard the shift of her body, the slow zip of her bag as she returned the mangled credit card to its place.

"Do you really think I'm only here for the story?" she asked softly.

"You never lied to me. I knew all along what you wanted." He stared at her tempting profile, tried to see her more clearly as his eyes adjusted to the darkness. "The story and your Lone Ranger justice," he added lowly.

She dropped her head back to rest against the counter. "In the beginning that was true. But that was before I got to know you, before I..." She hesitated, shifted uncomfortably on the floor. "Before I started to like you."

"So what does that make me? Tonto?" he snapped. The night, the silence, the emptiness of the house made him keep his voice at a whisper.

He could've sworn he heard her laugh, lightly and reluctantly. "Why is it so hard for you to believe that I just want to help you?"

"Everyone has their own agenda, weathergirl."

She grabbed her bag and shot to her feet, turning her back on him to stalk from the kitchen. She no longer bothered to keep her body low. "Fine," she said as she headed for the front of the house. "If it makes you feel better I'm only here for the story. But the story is to prove you innocent, so what difference does it make?"

"None," he said, following her.

She stood in the foyer, the light breaking through the blinds just bright enough to illuminate her and his living room in shades of gray. His furnishings were still here— most of them, anyway. A long, chocolate leather sofa and matching chairs, a television and stereo, a wildlife picture and an assortment of tables. Lauren had complained that his home was too masculine, and he'd been perfectly willing to let her make the changes she wanted. They'd never gotten that far.

"The cops drive by every hour to an hour and a half," he said to Shea's back. "So far they haven't done anything but shine a light on the property and drive on. Apparently they think I'm heading for Montana,'' he added sardonically.

Shea twirled and smiled at him. "I thought that was rather brilliant."

"Yeah, until they figure out you were lying."

She shrugged her shoulders. "I'll handle that problem when I have to. Where's the Camaro?"

"I parked it at a grocery store and walked."

"There's not a grocery store for at least three miles."

"That's it," he whispered.

"What if the police show up?" she asked sharply. "What if you have to run?"

He had planned to walk back to the car well before sunup and return to his warehouse hideout during the daylight hours, but now that Shea was here, apparently for the duration, his plans had changed. If she wasn't careful, the weathergirl was gonna find herself in a helluva lot of trouble. She was already in way over her pretty little head.

With a calculating eye he looked her up and down, amazed, still, that she was here. "I'm not running anymore."

She'd been concerned about Realtors showing the house to potential customers, but Nick informed her that even before the trial they'd had so much trouble with sightseers that they'd removed the lock box from the front door, and only one Realtor was allowed to show the house—the woman who'd listed it for sale. She was an old friend of Norman's and had done her best to keep the curious at bay. Initial interest had died down, and there was little activity. Still, they'd have to keep a lookout for that Realtor friend of Norman's.

Norman and the Realtor had handled everything. They'd left the furnishings and stored Nick's personal belongings, so the house had an odd model-home feel, as if no one had ever lived here. The pictures on the wall were impersonal, the drawers and the medicine cabinet empty.

Shea had slept well, once she'd fallen asleep all alone in the master bedroom. Nick had slept on the floor in the spare bedroom that had been converted into a now sterile office, not once suggesting that they share the only bed in the house, even though it was a king-size monster in a room large enough to accommodate such a piece.

To be safe, she kept her duffel bag packed and made the bed neatly after she left it. If the Realtor came in to show the house, she and Nick would have to get out if they could. Hide if they couldn't.

Unfortunately, she suspected there was no secret servants' stairway in the house Nick had built.

Teeth brushed and hair pulled back into a ponytail, bed made and bag packed, Shea sat on the floor near the bedroom window that overlooked Teakwood Court. She parted the blinds very slightly and looked down on the cul-de-sac as it came to life.

She knew, from the map Nick had drawn her while they'd been hiding in Marion, who lived where. Norman lived next door, in the house just past Nick's. To the left was the smaller, but still quite nice, home of Carter Able and his wife. Beside Norman, at the end of the cul-de-sac, was where Tom Blackstone and his family lived. He and Able had been two of the neighbors to stop by the morning after the murder, making them automatic suspects in Shea's mind. Either of them could've planted the evidence that helped to convict Nick.

Next to the Blackstones' house was the neat and colorful home of Lillian and Vernon Casson, a retired couple. There were flowers everywhere, and the shutters on their white house were painted a welcoming and cheerful yellow.

Then there was the Winkler house, where Polly Winkler

still lived. Her husband, Gary, had been killed, bludgeoned and painted green, in the backyard. Why did she stay? Sentimental reasons? From what Shea had learned of Gary Winkler, she couldn't imagine him sparking warm, fond memories of any kind.

Just past the Winklers' was another ranch-style house. The residents of that house had been out of town the night of the ill-fated barbecue, so Shea mentally crossed them off her list.

Neighbors from the other end of the double cul-de-sac had attended the barbecue, but those who had stopped by the next morning, giving them the opportunity to plant the evidence against Nick, all lived on this end. These were her suspects.

She heard Nick come up behind her, but did not take her eyes off the street below. Especially not when a woman stepped out of the house next door. Norman's house. The woman had to be Lauren.

Shea's heart sank. Lauren was gorgeous. Blond and stacked, she had a face that might've been ripped off the statue of a Greek goddess. She could've been a model. Or an anchorwoman.

"Yes, that's her," Nick said softly. "Apparently she's moved in."

"Cozy," Shea muttered as Lauren turned to wave good-bye to someone in the house. Norman, of course.

Across the street an elderly woman exited the Casson house, wide straw hat in place, long baggy pants in spite of the heat that was coming, gardening gloves on her hands. Lauren waved. Mrs. Casson did not wave back. Even from this distance Shea could see the distinct expression of distaste that flitted across the older woman's face.

"I think you can strike her off your list," Nick said, lowering himself to sit behind Shea.

"Lauren?" she snapped.

"Mrs. Casson."

Shea relaxed.

One by one the residents of the cul-de-sac left their homes on this workday. Some of them waved and even said hello to one another. Others obviously needed another cup of coffee or two to get themselves going.

Norman, she noticed, did not leave.

"Is your lawyer playing hooky or does he sometimes work at home?"

"He has an office there. He usually works at home a couple mornings a week, if he can. Says he gets more done there than at the office."

She nodded, alternately watching Mrs. Casson work in her garden and checking the Burgess house for activity. All was quiet there.

"I'm going to go talk to him," Nick said, rising slowly to his feet.

Shea snapped her head around, noticing that Nick was limping still. "It's too dangerous."

He laughed without turning to look at her. "I'll circle around, so if he by chance sees me coming it won't be from this direction. And when I leave I'll walk back to the grocery store and move the car. If it sits too long someone will call the police to have it towed. They'll trace it to Maude and that will be all she wrote."

"In broad daylight?" Shea shot to her feet.

"I'll be careful, *kemo sabe.*" Again he didn't turn to look at her. As if he didn't want to see her face, as if he was afraid to look at her.

She followed him down the stairs, wincing at the way he limped. What he really needed was a week in bed. He needed to get the weight off that leg, not to be walking three miles to move his car, and then walking who knows how far back.

"Let me move the car," she said.

"Won't the Sinclair wild bunch be out looking for you?" he asked sarcastically.

"Well, yes, but…"

"Then you'd better stay put."

He stopped in the foyer, just before entering the kitchen. "You don't have to be here when I get back."

Shea caught up with him and laid her hand on his back. "Yes, I do."

"You already have enough for a major story." The back beneath her hand went rigid as his muscles tensed. His hands flexed into fists. "Weathergirl kidnapped by convicted killer and held hostage for seven days should be good for a lot of airtime."

"Probably."

Nick had no intention of turning to look at her, so she slipped around him and glanced up, into his face. Her heart skipped a beat. Last night she'd told him she liked him. She was afraid of how he'd react if she confessed that what she felt for him was much, much more.

"Until we know who killed Winkler, I'm not going anywhere," she said, softly but insistently.

"All right," he agreed in a lifeless voice.

"I'm a part of this, to the end."

"That was never my intention."

"Well, it looks like you're stuck with me."

Something glittered in his eyes. A memory, a spark of hope. Whatever it was, what she saw there gave *her* hope.

"A kiss for luck," she said, rising up on her toes as he willingly listed down toward her. Their mouths met, briefly, securely, and with a comfort that comes only from practice.

He went the long way around, sticking to the wooded area of his backyard and Norman's, and out of Lillian Casson's range of sight, until he slipped from the woods and crept up the stairs to the multitiered deck. Norman usually had coffee here in the morning, so with any luck…yep, the door was unlocked.

The deck had been built off a large kitchen. Norman's house was bigger than Nick's, grander, with larger rooms and the amenities Nick had not cared about. A fireplace, vaulted ceilings, a fourth bedroom upstairs.

And an office on the ground floor. That was where Norman holed up, most mornings when he could work at home. Nick slipped quietly down the hall, his back to the wall, his heart pounding too fast. What if Shea was right? His lawyer and his ex-girlfriend. Shea suspected Lauren, but what if Lauren and Norman had been in this together? Maybe Norman had discovered his fiancée's crime and covered it by allowing Nick to be convicted. There was only one way to find out.

Before he stepped into Norman's office, his heartbeat slowed, his panic disappeared. He gritted his teeth and prepared himself for anything.

Norman had his head down as he thumbed through a sheaf of papers. He didn't hear Nick come into the room to stand behind him, he was so engrossed in his work.

"Hello, Norman," Nick said in a low voice.

Norman dropped his papers and spun in his swivel chair, coming to his feet in a burst of energy and leaving the chair twirling.

"Nick," he said, his eyes raking up and down and a small smile coming to his face. "Good God, I can't believe it." He laid his hands on Nick's shoulders and the smile grew. "How are you? How's your leg? Where the hell have you been?"

Given his suspicions, it was not the reception Nick had expected. "One question at a time, and I get to start."

Norman's smile faded, and he lowered his hands. "Sure."

He took his chair, leaned back and gestured to the single visitor's chair in the room, a fat, padded armchair just a few feet away. Nick sat.

"When did Lauren move in?"

Norman's face turned to stone. "I should've told you, but you had enough on your—"

"When?" Nick whispered.

"Two and a half months ago."

"When's the wedding?"

"October."

Nick leaned back in his chair, trying for a casual pose. "How very nice for you both."

"I wanted to tell you, and so did Lauren, but Nick..." Norman leaned forward in his chair. "You have more important problems at the present time."

The truth was, Nick didn't care about Lauren. Not anymore. He thought of telling Norman, here and now, how he'd found Lauren and Winkler that night. He decided against it. Norman would discover, soon enough, what kind of woman she was.

He did care that his lawyer and friend had lied to him, that if Norman would hide this fact, he would hide others.

"My turn," Norman said. "How's your leg?"

"Better. I was lucky. It was just a scratch."

"Where have you..." Norman lifted a hand and silenced himself. "Never mind. I don't want to know where you've been or where you're staying now. If I know I'll have to tell the police. But Nick, you have to turn yourself in. If you keep running they *will* find you, and next time they might do a lot worse than scratch you."

"I'm not turning myself in until I find out who killed Gary Winkler."

The expression that flitted across Norman's face was

one of surprise, but it faded quickly and was replaced by the look Nick had come to recognize. His professional face, the one that gave nothing away.

"You think I did it, don't you?" Nick asked, the pieces coming together easily. No wonder there had been no thorough investigation by his lawyer. No wonder Norman hadn't pushed the police to look into other suspects.

"Now, Nick…"

"Save the condescending voice, Norman," Nick snapped. "All this time, while you defended me, you thought I was guilty."

Amazingly, Norman blushed. "Lauren told me about…about what happened that night."

Now it was Nick's turn to look surprised. So much for Shea's theory. "She did?"

Norman nodded and dropped his head down to stare into his lap. "That night was a turning point for her."

"I can imagine," Nick muttered.

When Norman lifted his head, he no longer wore his cold, unreadable lawyer's face. He looked vulnerable. Older. "She quit drinking after that night and joined AA."

"Lauren's not an alcoholic."

"Yes, she is," Norman insisted. "You never saw it because…because she didn't want you to know and because you have a bad habit of only seeing what you want to see."

Nick didn't appreciate being analyzed by his lawyer at a time like this, but, dammit, it made sense, in retrospect. The erratic behavior he'd thought was a part of Lauren's eccentrically charming personality, the sharp mood swings he'd believed to be a normal part of womanhood, the way she flitted from one undemanding job to another…

"That night, when she realized what she'd almost done, she decided to quit. And she did."

"I notice she didn't offer to testify," Nick said bitterly.

"Telling all in court would've damaged her reputation, such as it is."

Norman's face hardened. "And it would've given the jury another piece of evidence against you. She was thinking of you when she kept her mouth shut, Nick. She deliberately stayed away from the courtroom, and when the police interviewed her she said she had been drinking too much to remember clearly what happened that night. It wasn't like they needed another witness against you."

Nick didn't want to feel grateful, he wanted to hate Lauren. And Norman. And Shea. It was easier that way.

But he couldn't do this alone. "I've been convicted. I'll probably get caught long before I can prove that someone else killed Winkler. I have nothing to lose." He leaned forward in his chair, catching and holding Norman's eye. "I have nothing to lose by telling you the truth."

Norman sat stone still, hands in his lap, waiting for Nick's confession.

"I didn't do it. Someone else killed Winkler and planted the evidence against me. Someone who was there that night set me up."

"Oh my God," Norman whispered. "You're telling the truth."

"One of your neighbors is a murderer."

Chapter 15

Shea wanted to observe before she questioned. The more she knew about the suspects, the more prepared she'd be. Her eyes shifted again and again to Norman Burgess's house, but she saw no sign of Nick or the lawyer. All seemed to be quiet, perfectly normal, there.

Appearances aside, nothing in this neighborhood was perfectly normal.

The Ables and the Blackstones had small children who played on their lawns and in the circle, enjoying the last days of summer. Tricycles, inline skates and basketballs were popular, she noticed. Mrs. Casson worked in her garden until the children were out in force, then with a puckering of her mouth she gathered up her gardening tools and retreated into her own cool house.

At the Realtor's insistence, the electricity in Nick's home was still on and running. Thank goodness. This house wasn't built for a summer day with no air-conditioning, like the house in Marion.

Eventually Burgess left, his car pulling slowly and carefully out of the garage. The kids in the cul-de-sac moved out of his way, and he smiled and waved at them...as if nothing unusual had happened this morning.

Her imagination got the best of her, as it often did. Nick had lied to her. He hadn't gone to talk to Norman, he'd dumped her again. He'd walked away and by now he was in Maude's car driving away from Huntsville, laughing at her for being so trusting, so naive.

A worse possibility occurred to her. What if Norman was the murderer, or he was covering for Lauren, and he'd killed Nick? Right now Nick could be lying in that man's house, dead or bleeding, or stuffed into the trunk of that fancy car that had driven so cautiously down the street. Her imagination ran wild, until she could see the horrific possibilities in her mind. The what-ifs plagued her, until she was certain something had gone terribly wrong.

There was only one way to be sure.

She gathered up her duffel bag and Nick's, in case the Realtor should come by, and left by the back door. She circled around, keeping to the cover of the trees at the back of the lot, and with her heart pounding fiercely in her chest, she crept onto the deck. With credit card in hand, she easily slipped the lock on Burgess's door.

All was quiet, cool and clean and well ordered. Here she could see the woman's touch that had been missing in Nick's house. The lace curtains in the kitchen, the yellow-and-white-checked dish towels, the fresh flowers.

There was no sign of foul play. Yet.

Confident that neither Norman nor Lauren would return anytime soon, she dropped her bag and Nick's onto the living room sofa and continued her search. Up until now she'd been careful not to do anything too blatantly illegal, but this was definitely against the rules. This was breaking and entering. Dean would be furious, if he ever found out.

But her crime was justified, she reasoned. What if Nick was hurt?

"Nick?" she whispered as she walked down the hallway. "Are you here?" She poked her head into a small office, searching for a clue. Nothing. No blood, no signs of a struggle.

After searching the ground floor, she climbed the stairway to the second floor. Unlike Nick, Burgess had furnished all his bedrooms. Four bedrooms, each with a bed and a dresser. Three of them looked like impersonal guest rooms. Winter clothes were stored in one closet, but the others were almost empty. A roll of wrapping paper, a box of Christmas decorations. Nothing sinister.

And no Nick.

There was only one room left to check, and that was the bathroom at the end of the hall. She stepped inside, pulled back the shower curtain and stared into an empty, gleaming white bathtub.

And next door she heard a car door slam.

Peering through the narrow window, she had a clear view of the street. A long gray sedan had parked at the curb, and five people walked toward Nick's front door.

In the lead was a stout woman in a navy blue power suit, and even from here Shea could see she was not happy. She carried a ring of keys in her hand.

Luther Malone, his handsome face set in a mask of pure annoyance, followed her. He seemed to be grumbling to himself as they approached the porch.

And behind Luther, Dean, Boone and Clint stalked, side by side and looking for blood. Hers this time, she imagined.

Luther sat in the living room while the poor Realtor, the harried Ms. Tilton, tried to keep up with all three Sinclair brothers as they searched the house. Luther leaned back on the soft leather couch and tried to relax.

The brothers hadn't listened when he'd told them Shea would not be stupid enough to come to Nick Taggert's house. She'd have to know they would search for her here. Taggert sure as hell wouldn't take the chance of returning to the scene of the crime.

Maybe Shea was right and Taggert was heading for Montana. Maybe she was heading for Montana herself.

In the past couple of days, he'd spent most of his spare time looking into the Winkler murder and the Taggert investigation. What he'd found had been skimpy, to say the least. Everything about this case had fallen into Daniels's lap, and he'd happily accepted the gift.

Daniels had never investigated the wife, who was usually suspect number one. He'd never investigated the neighbors, who all apparently had a motive of one kind or another. Daniels was lazy, but Luther had to wonder if he himself would've looked any further, given the preponderance of evidence. Usually what came too easily was the truth.

But after Luther spent a couple of days looking into the other possible suspects, at Grace's request, an uneasy feeling had grown steadily in his gut. Something here was not right. He felt it, deep down and he had learned to never ignore his instincts.

"Nothing," Clint said as he marched into the living room.

Luther withheld the urge to say "I told you so" as Clint dropped into a fat leather chair that sank slowly under his weight.

Dean, a scowl on his face, was right behind Clint. "She's not here."

Boone entered shortly after Dean, the persimmon-faced Ms. Tilton directly behind him. "What next?" he barked.

"We got nowhere with her friend Grace, and her cameraman swears she hasn't called him this time."

"We'll find her," Dean said.

They had tried to interrogate Grace this morning, but hadn't gotten far. Luther still wanted to know exactly how Ray had gotten rid of the Sinclair brothers so quickly. God knows he wouldn't allow them to berate or upset his pregnant wife! Ray had been overprotective before, but he was now safeguarding Grace with everything he had.

Ms. Tilton stood in the foyer, nervously fiddling with her keys.

"I hate to break it to you boys," Luther said. "But Shea is all grown up."

In unison, they gave him a warning glare he ignored.

"She doesn't have to tell you where she is at all times, she doesn't have to report in like she's twelve years old." Given the looks he was already getting, he decided not to share his theory that they were likely to find Shea wherever they found Nick Taggert. They wouldn't like it and besides…they were smart guys. They'd figure it out on their own soon enough, if they hadn't already.

"Cut her some slack," he said as he rose to his feet.

Boone cursed, Clint stood up in turn and they headed for the door, much to the Realtor's relief.

"I was sure she'd be here," Dean said as Ms. Tilton closed and locked the door behind them. "She thinks Taggert is innocent, and if I know her she's trying to prove it. This is the logical place to start."

Boone made a snorting noise of disgust. "There's your problem right there. Shea has never been logical! I can't believe she let that bastard Taggert sucker her in like that. I can't believe she actually thinks he didn't do it!"

Luther let them all pile into his car before he took the driver's seat. The poor Realtor was once again squeezed into the back between Clint and Boone.

He looked at the houses on the peaceful cul-de-sac, at the playing children, at the homes of the people who had been at the barbecue that night.

As he started the car, Luther stared at Dean, who was the most reasonable of the three, he had discovered. "I don't know if it will make you feel any better or not," he said. "But I'm beginning to think she might be right."

She was relieved when Nick came home. So relieved that she almost ran to him and threw her arms around his neck. She refrained, though, not wanting to do anything to make him send her away...or to make him want to stay gone the next time. He was still wary of her, for some reason, suspicious of her motives and uncertain about her loyalties.

He brought food. Sandwiches, juice, two sodas and what remained of the bag Maude had packed. Cookies, mostly.

"Where'd you get the money for the food?" she asked as they laid out their feast in the upstairs bedroom, where they could watch the comings and goings on the street below and still be shielded from view by the partially closed miniblinds.

"Norman gave me the money," he said, his eyes on the street. "You can strike him and Lauren off your list of suspects."

Nick was not as suspicious as she was, and she had a feeling he'd wanted all along to believe that his friend and ex-girlfriend were innocent. "Does he know you're staying here?"

"No."

"Good."

Nick turned his eyes to her then, accusing and intense. "He explained everything. More than I wanted to know, to tell the truth."

"And you believed him."

"Yes."

When they had eaten and Shea cleared the garbage away, Nick sat on the floor by the bed and stared out the window. He couldn't see much from there, she imagined. Sitting beside him, she discovered she was right: she could see only a small segment of the street in front of his house.

"Lauren's an alcoholic," he said softly, and without looking at her. "I never saw it, but Norman did. That night, she realized she had fallen too far, and she quit. Norman helped her. He's been good for her, I think."

"What about his wife?" Shea snapped.

"They'd been having trouble for years, he said. There wasn't another woman or another man, they simply fell out of love. Decided they didn't want the same things anymore. It happens." He shifted uncomfortably on the floor. "I didn't see that, either."

"It's the sort of thing people hide very well," Shea said. "We never know…"

"I should've known. About Lauren, about Norman." Nick shook his head. "I've been going through the past few years with blinders on. I was so determined to start over, to make sure I left the crap of my childhood behind me, that I…I painted a pretty picture. My eyes were wide-open but I saw only what I wanted to see."

"We all do that, to a certain extent."

Nick turned his head and looked down at her, his blue eyes piercing. "You do that when you look at me—I know it. You dismiss what you should see and get caught up in something that isn't entirely true."

"I see quite clearly," she whispered. "And what I see is very, very real."

She got up on her knees, leaned over and kissed him. It was an easy kiss, and she was relieved that Nick didn't jump to his feet or turn his head away from her. He kissed her back.

Their entire relationship, short and intense as it was, had been colored by the knowledge that they didn't have much time. A day more, maybe. A night, if they were lucky. But it didn't make what she felt any less real.

She caught sight of the police car out of the corner of her eye, as it passed slowly by. Instinctively she grabbed on to Nick's T-shirt and pulled him to the floor, where he landed out of sight from the street and heavily atop her.

She licked her lips, shifted slightly until he rested between her legs, and wrapped her arms around his neck. "Coppers," she whispered.

There was a moment of quiet stillness, and then Nick lowered his head slowly, taking his time as he latched his mouth to hers, cupped her head in his hands and kissed her. This was no quick kiss, but continued on unrelenting, growing gradually deeper, until her knees were weak and her heart pounded against his chest.

She had wanted, more than anything, for Nick to kiss her, but she had never expected the kiss would grow so fierce. Quickly, surely, it burned out of control. For her and for Nick. She felt his passion as if it were hers. She breathed it in and absorbed it through her pores and her tongue.

He lowered his mouth to her neck and nuzzled there, slowing down as he slipped his hand beneath her T-shirt and settled it possessively at her side. His movements were undemanding, gentle, slow as molasses.

"I don't know what's real anymore," he whispered.

"This is real," she said, threading her fingers through his hair and holding on tight. "What we feel right now is very real."

Sun slanted through the partially open blinds, striping the floor and their bodies. The noises of summer—children playing and laughing, the distinct sound of a water hose running, the water splashing—were distant and comforting.

And Shea didn't want to let Nick go. Heaven help her, she couldn't.

"You make me crazy," he whispered.

"Good."

Nick kissed her again, barely sliding his tongue into her mouth, his hand climbing higher to cup her breast. He found his way impeded by a bra, but quickly located the front closure and flicked it open.

A feminine instinct that had gone unexplored before she met Nick seized her. She'd never felt such power in her own body, such a strong and spontaneous need that her insides quivered. She parted her lips and her tongue met Nick's. Her back arched so she was closer against him, tighter and surer, and it was not enough.

She untucked his T-shirt from his jeans, snaked her hand beneath to feel his hot, hard skin. To feel his chest rise and fall with every breath, to find and delight in the thud of his heartbeat beneath her hand.

Beneath strained denim his erection pressed insistently against her bare thigh. Her body moistened in response as her thighs parted farther and she latched her mouth to his neck, holding on and pressing her body tight against his. He rocked against her, teasing and arousing her, promising her everything he had to give. While she suckled at his neck he rode her higher, and if there had been no clothing between them, keeping them apart, he would be inside her now. Her body throbbed, ached and yearned and pleaded for release.

She lifted her hips when he began to slide her shorts down, and before he had them off she was working the snap and the zipper of his jeans. She couldn't wait a moment longer, but she didn't have the words to tell him so. Her breath wouldn't come; words would be impossible.

While he kissed her she thrust her hands beneath his waistband and pushed his jeans over his hips. His skin, hard and warm, glided beneath her hands, and she held on, her fingers caressing his hips as he guided himself inside her.

There was nothing gentle about the way they came together, not today. This lovemaking was hot and hard, relentless and furious. Nick's hips, still caught in her grasp, rocked in a powerful rhythm, growing faster with each thrust.

Shea slid her hands up, over Nick's thrusting hips, up his back to his neck, and wrapped her legs around him. Drawing him close, she urged him deeper, thrust against him, and shattered. She cried out as he held himself deep inside her and came with her. Their linked bodies shuddered, their heat and the sounds of their throaty cries filled the air around them.

When it was over, when the longing that had brought them together so quickly and pleasurably had faded, she took Nick's face in her hands and kissed him. Softly this time, without demand. It was a kiss that said "I love you" much more clearly than she could ever say the words.

"In my entire life, I've never known anything more real than that," she whispered.

He didn't try to leave, and she didn't drop her legs from his hips to let him go. She liked it here, with Nick a part of her, her heart beating too fast, her legs trembling still.

Nick kissed her back, and while he might not realize it yet, his kiss said "I love you," too.

Chapter 16

His instinct was to drag each and every suspect into the street and force the truth from the guilty party. While that method might momentarily satisfy his rage, it wouldn't be successful. Whoever the real killer was had played it cool so far. That wasn't likely to change just because he demanded it.

He sat on the floor before the window, watching as the sun went down and the lights came on. Seated behind him and slightly to the side, Shea leaned into his back and arm and watched with him.

"It looks like everything you wanted," she whispered.

"What?"

"The nice houses, the kids." She lifted a shapely arm and pointed. "Mrs. Casson even has a porch swing."

Nick grabbed her arm and kissed the sensitive skin at her inner elbow, and she answered with a soft laugh and a contented sigh.

He'd never lost control with a woman before, not the

way he had this afternoon with Shea. It was the situation, he reasoned, that made every moment with her seem so precious. It was knowing he might not have much time left that made him so damned impatient to touch her, to be inside her.

He wouldn't fight it anymore. Until this was over, Shea was his. He would sleep with her in the bed in this room; he would take and give whatever he could. *This* was his dream, but he hadn't known it until he met Shea, because he had never dreamed he could feel this way about anyone. It didn't matter where they were, what they had...only that she was here.

If he had the luxury, he might call it love.

Shea draped her arms around his neck and peered over his shoulder to the street below. "I have an idea," she whispered.

In spite of himself, he smiled.

"If Norman and Lauren are really on the up and up, then they can help."

Not the kind of idea he had in mind, at the moment. "We can trust them."

"Then I think they should throw a neighborhood barbecue tomorrow night, and invite everyone at this end of the cul-de-sac. Everyone who was at your party that night."

A warning shiver snaked through his body. "And I show up as a surprise guest?"

"No," she said quickly. "We find you a safe place to watch." She kissed his neck. "I'll be the surprise guest. Tomorrow, during the day, I'll visit everyone in the neighborhood and interview them. I can tell them it's a preinterview for a show I'm planning."

"No," he said lowly.

"Then I'll show up at Norman's barbecue and tell them all I know who really killed Gary Winkler."

"No," Nick said, more forcefully this time, taking her arm and pulling her into his lap. "You're talking about trapping a murderer, Shea. Someone who has killed and will likely kill again to cover what they did."

"I know." She kissed him briefly on the lips.

"I can't allow you—"

She grinned and interrupted. "Allow me?"

God, she was stubborn! He took her chin in his hand and glared at her. "I don't want you hurt."

"I won't be hurt," she whispered.

She would be, and so would he. They couldn't stay together when this was over, couldn't pretend that what they felt was anything lasting. But right now he wanted this to last. He wanted Shea in his life permanently.

He had a feeling that as soon as this crime was solved and the excitement was over, she'd be bored with him and move on to another story. Another injustice.

"If you go inside these people's houses to interrogate them—"

"Interview," she corrected, raising her eyebrows.

"Interview," he repeated. "I'll be there. You go in the front door and I'll go in the back. You interview them and I'll listen and make sure everything's okay. Maybe I'll even poke around a little while I listen."

"That sounds risky."

"Interrogating a murderer isn't?"

She rested her head on his shoulder. "All right. I'll lend you my credit card, in case you run into a locked door here and there."

He held her tight, and when he caught sight of the police car driving by he dropped to the floor with her in his arms.

Shea laid her head against his chest. "We'll start first thing in the morning," she said.

That meant they had tonight.

* * *

The blinds were closed tight, the house was cool and dark and Shea couldn't sleep. Her mind was spinning. Tomorrow. Everything would happen tomorrow. One of Nick's neighbors was a killer, and come tomorrow she was going to find herself face-to-face with him. Or her.

Her plan had been put into motion. She'd called Mark, as promised, knowing that if her brothers bothered to check with the cell phone company they'd only be able to tell that the call came from this area. And it was a very *big* area. Dean might have access to equipment that could trace her to a specific location if she stayed on her phone long enough, but he was too straight-arrow to use it to track his sister when he knew she'd left his "protection" on her own. It wasn't like she'd been kidnapped again.

Come tomorrow morning, Mark would call Boone with the news that he'd heard from Shea, who was heading to Montana by bus to find and interview Nick Taggert. They'd believe it, too, and while she was interviewing the residents of Teakwood Court, she wouldn't have to keep looking over her shoulder for those three familiar heads of dark hair.

Mostly she thought about Nick. He had become so important to her so quickly that her newfound feelings scared her. She loved him. What else could make her heart beat this way? Why else would she be so incensed over every injustice he'd ever suffered? She wanted to fix his life, and then she wanted to be a part of it. She wanted to make all his dreams come true.

She listened as he came in the back door, locked it behind him and stepped carefully through the kitchen to the foyer and the stairs. At the foot of the steps he hesitated, and she held her breath. What if he didn't come to her? What if he decided he should sleep on the couch or keep watch all night? No matter what happened tomorrow, this might very well be their last night together.

Finally he began to climb the stairs, and when he reached the second floor he turned toward the room where she waited. Her eyes were trained on the doorway when he appeared there.

"What did he say?" she whispered.

"He said yes. They're going to contact everyone tomorrow and say they're throwing an impromptu engagement party."

"Do you think everyone will come?"

Nick shrugged his shoulders and walked into the room. The blinds were closed, but they couldn't risk a lamp or even a candle. She was getting accustomed to watching Nick in nothing but dark shadows.

He barely limped anymore, and as he undressed she felt a rush of relief that the bullet had only creased his flesh. That wound, and the resulting blood loss, had been bad enough. If the bullet had gone through muscle he would have dropped right there in the courthouse and wouldn't have been able to walk for weeks.

Everything would've turned out differently if that had happened, if the deputy's aim had been a little better. Nick would've been taken immediately into custody, he would've been sentenced a few days later and no one would ever know that he was innocent.

Naked, as she was, he climbed into bed with her, slipping beneath the comforter and taking her in his arms. Their bodies came together easily, beautifully, and neither of them said a word as they settled into and against one another. Nick knew, as well as she did, that tomorrow everything would change.

So they held one another tightly, bodies close, legs entangled, hearts pressed together and beating fast and hard. Shea buried her nose in his neck and took a deep breath. Heavens, she loved the way he smelled. The scent of his

skin was comforting and arousing, and she was terrified
that after tonight she'd never have this luxury again.

They hadn't used any kind of protection this afternoon.
Things had spun out of control so quickly that by the time
she'd thought about the single remaining condom in her
duffel bag it had been too late. She had no regrets. She
loved Nick and she wanted all of him.

There was a touch of desperation between them, but
neither of them mentioned that this might be their last
night together. That come tomorrow, if their plan was un-
successful, Nick might have to go on the run again. The
thought made Shea panic, until she made a momentous
and calming decision. She was *not* giving him up. This
was *not* their last night together.

That decision made, she relaxed and melted in his arms.

Nick kissed her, softly and sweetly. He touched her and
trailed his mouth down her body. Licking and kissing and
nibbling, he made his way to her breasts and took a nipple
deep into his mouth. Shea pushed the comforter down. In
spite of the air-conditioning and the cool night air, she was
hot, her skin and Nick's generating their own heat. She
kicked the comforter to the foot of the bed, and a moment
later Nick kicked it onto the floor.

They spread across the big bed, arms and legs together
and then apart, mouths tasting and exploring.

This afternoon they'd come together impatiently, but tonight was different. They had all night, and some things
should not be rushed.

"Nick?" she whispered.

He hummed a disinterested response.

"Up there on the mountain, when you fired that shot at
me…" She wrapped her arms around his neck. "Would
you really have shot me if I'd kept running?"

"No," he said quickly, without hesitating. "I could
never hurt you."

"I knew it," she whispered with a smile as he turned his attention to her neck.

Shea tried not to think about tomorrow, tried not to think about what would happen when this was over, but tomorrow was on her mind. The only way to remedy that problem was to make the confession that would change everything.

She rolled over, pushing Nick onto his back and holding her face close to his. She kissed him, softly, then again with the fierce hunger she felt.

Holding his face in her hands, she barely touched her nose to his. "I love you," she whispered.

"Don't." The single word was harsh, but the hand that settled in her hair was tender. Gentle and loving.

And she didn't let that word deter her. "If we find the murderer tomorrow and you're cleared, then everything will be fine. If we don't and you have to run again, I want to run with you."

"No," he whispered.

"I would rather live my life on the run with you than live it anywhere else without you." Heaven help her, it was the truth. She would give up everything to be with this man forever. Living without him would be sheer misery.

Nick didn't bother to argue with her again. He rolled her onto her back, spread her thighs and continued his most thorough exploration.

Her confession made, Shea's mind cleared, and for now—for now there was only this. Nick's wide bed and her love for him and the way they touched.

And touched. Nick kissed her in places she'd never been kissed before. He trailed his fingers over every inch of her body. She touched him, as well, following his lead and being bold. Fearless. Smiling softly when he shivered or took a sudden deep breath. Glad to know that she could arouse him with something so simple as a well-placed kiss or a gentle caress.

Her body was alive, her mind was foggy, her heart was full. And they all belonged to Nick.

He trailed kisses from the valley of her breasts down her torso, his hands beneath her hips, his mouth moving unerringly downward. He paused at her belly button, circling his tongue around it, then below it.

When he placed his mouth on her intimately, she gasped in shock at the sensation. His fingers caressed her inner thighs as he aroused her with his tongue. He found the nub at her entrance and teased her, hard and then gentle, fast and then slow. He tormented her, moving away when she was close to completion, returning a moment later to begin again.

When his fingers joined his tongue she climaxed quickly, coming off the mattress and crying out hoarsely as he brought her to an intense climax.

She was still breathless when he raised his head and kissed her inner thigh, the skin beneath her belly button. Then he wrapped his arms around her and slid slowly upward.

Shea trembled; he felt her response. Absorbed it. And did not stop. Her words, *I love you,* echoed in his ears. No matter how he tried to forget what she'd said, no matter how he tried to convince himself that what she felt wasn't real, still he heard the words.

"Nick," she whispered, threading her fingers through his hair, arching her back when he took a nipple into his mouth and gently suckled before resting his head on her shoulder.

She wasn't content to lie there for long, breathless and satisfied. Her hands skimmed down his sides, and she slithered beneath him, bringing her mouth to his neck, sucking and kissing and licking. Moaning and writhing beneath him.

She reached for him, and he grabbed her wrist. If she touched him he was lost. If she stroked those soft hands on his length once, he would lose control.

His erection, hard and long past ready, touched her. She wrapped her legs around him and pulled him close, into her slick wetness, and he closed his eyes as he plunged deep. She stretched and grasped him, took him inside her body and met him, stroke for stroke. He felt and savored her fiery response, which came as quickly and undeniably as his own. She held on, took quick, shallow breaths and arched into him.

She came again, moaning deeply. Her inner muscles caressed him, milked him as he gave over to his own release. And on the dying waves of their shared climax she said it again. She wrapped her arms around his neck and whispered in his ear. "I love you, Nick. No matter what happens, I love you."

Their bodies still joined, he raised up to look at her, what he could see in the dark. Not enough. Not nearly enough.

The sun rose, slowly but surely. It was a day Nick wasn't certain he wanted to see.

But it was here.

Shea slept with her head on his shoulder and her arm across his midsection. Even in sleep, she held on. And she looked so content by morning's light. She looked so happy.

She thought she loved him, and deep in his heart he wished it was true. He wished he could start over again, one more time, with Shea in his bed and his heart.

Maybe he loved her, too. Maybe he just wanted to so badly that it felt real. Last night he'd had to bite his tongue to keep from saying, "I love you, too." The truth was, he'd never told a woman he loved her. Not Lauren, not any of the women who'd come before her.

"Thank you," he whispered. "For believing in me when no one else did. For loving me." And then he knew it was true. He could deny it out loud, but not here. Not now. "For letting me love you back."

One thing was true: he loved Shea enough not to ask her to live with him if he had to run again. He wouldn't take her family and her career and her friends from her and ask her to live day to day, always wondering who was close to capturing him again.

He wouldn't make her a fugitive.

And if they did find the real murderer? It was what he wanted most of all, but he had his doubts. It had been almost a year since Winkler had been murdered. Any evidence was long gone, and what were the odds that Shea could wrest a confession from the real killer? Not good. And even if she could...she would have her own kind of notoriety once this was over, and so would he. How could they ever have a normal life?

He watched her until she came awake, cuddling against him, raking her fingers down his side. Her eyes opened a few minutes later and immediately landed on his face.

Her smile grabbed his heart. Her eyes were so warm and loving he could too easily take her up on her offer. He could love her. He could sweep her up and run from this place and not look back.

But he knew what he had to do. "Good morning," he said coolly. There was no smile to soften the emotionless words, no kiss. He couldn't afford either.

Shea's smile faded as she sat up. "Are you okay?"

"Fine and dandy." He turned his back on her and rolled from the bed. "A little tired. Damn, woman, you wore me out last night."

"Last night was…" she began.

"Fun," he snapped, turning to glance down at Shea as he interrupted. "That's all it was, sugar. One last night of diversion before it hits the fan."

She went pale. "Diversion." Shea was not the kind of woman to beg, plead or cry, thank God. She took the news stoically.

His back was to her as he dressed. "After ten months in jail I was pretty hard up, if you know what I mean. When I kidnapped you I really didn't intend for things to turn out this way, but I can't say I'm sorry they did."

"Really?" she said softly, and with just a hint of anger.

"You're hot stuff, sugar. Those brothers of yours are gonna have a tough time keeping you virtuous now that you know what good sex is like."

The bed creaked, and he wondered if she'd come up behind him and hit him. He almost wished she would.

"Well," she said, her voice in complete control. She recovered fast, his Shea. "It was a way to pass the time, since we couldn't very well risk turning on the television or a single light. There aren't many diversions to enjoy in the dark."

"Only the one," he said softly.

"I hope you didn't take any of my…my confessions seriously."

He glanced over his shoulder. Shea was still pale, but she was strong. She'd do fine without him, no matter what happened.

"Of course not," he said, forcing a small smile that hurt his face and his heart. "Part of the game, that's all."

"Part of the game," she said, turning her back on him and heading for the bathroom and a long, hot shower.

Chapter 17

Okay, maybe she was an idiot, but she could be a *professional* idiot. The story was all that counted. Finding the truth was all that mattered.

Shea told herself this on Saturday morning as she knocked on Carter Able's door. There had been no suit in her duffel bag, but she had thought to pack a pair of dressy black trousers, a lightweight, red knit blouse and a comfortable pair of black sandals that suited the occasion. She would start here at the Ables' house and work her way around the circle, ending with Polly Winkler's. The Able kids were playing down the street, and Carter and his wife, Amanda, were at home alone. Nick waited out back, watching and listening for his chance to slip through the back door.

She'd tried to convince Nick that she didn't need him along, that she was perfectly safe without him, but he didn't agree. Stubborn, obstinate, pigheaded, insensitive *man*.

The door swung open and she smiled widely. "Hi," she said in her peppiest voice. "I'm Shea—"

"I know who you are," Carter said, obviously stunned to see her. "Nick kidnapped you. It was all over the news." He looked over her shoulder. "Where's your car?"

Shea was unflustered. "I had my cameraman drop me off. This is just a preliminary investigation for a special show I'm going to put together. I didn't want the camera to scare people off."

Carter nodded and opened the door wide. "Come on in."

"I'd really like to talk to you and Mrs. Able together, if that's okay."

"Sure."

Carter went to fetch his wife, and Shea took a moment to gather her thoughts and study the living room. It was well kept, considering the Ables had three children. No toys scattered about, no crumbs, no snack cake wrappers. Her own living room wasn't this clean. If there had ever been any evidence in this house, it was long gone.

Carter returned with Amanda, a pretty, dark-haired woman dressed in shorts and a Soccer Mom T-shirt. She was as openly interested as her husband in Shea's investigation. They sat together on the sofa, and Shea perched on the end of a matching chair with her notebook in her lap.

They spoke eagerly about the barbecue the night of Winkler's death, but added nothing Nick hadn't already told her. They talked about Gary and how he'd flirted with Lauren, about Nick and his temper, about the fabulous casserole Mrs. Casson had brought. Gary held his wife's hand while he told Shea what he'd seen the next morning, after Gary's body was found. The entire time they both remained wide-eyed and anxious. If these people had anything to hide, they were fabulous actors.

As Shea listened to the Ables, she also listened for Nick. The faint sound of a slipping lock, a footstep in the kitchen. She heard nothing, and eventually began to wonder if he was in the house at all.

It didn't matter if he was here or not. It didn't matter if he did run to Montana or Canada or Mexico. She was going to see this through to the end, no matter how he felt. No matter what a jerk he was.

She smiled as Carter and Amanda told her about what had happened after the police arrived on the scene, but she was already set to move on. As far as she could tell they were being completely honest.

Unlike *some* people she knew.

She said her goodbyes, and when Amanda asked if they were going to be on television, Shea winked and assured them they would.

Head high, she walked past Nick's house, not even glancing up at the bedroom window. She walked past the Burgess house. To anyone watching it might seem odd that she skipped that house, but she wasn't ready to face Lauren. Especially not right now.

If Nick was keeping pace in the woods that ran behind the houses, she never saw him. Again, she told herself she didn't care if he was there or not.

The snake.

The Blackstones' back door was unlocked, so the mangled credit card stayed in his pocket. Shea had already begun, questioning Tom and Natalie in her most professional voice.

The Blackstone kitchen was set up much like his own, but was much warmer. There were flowers in the breakfast nook, a cake cooling on the counter. The kids had left their mark here, with juice boxes, Kool-Aid stains, and crumbs in every corner. Somehow the mess made the place seem more homey, lived in and welcoming.

Nick had told Shea he would look around the houses while she interviewed his neighbors, but he didn't even try. No one here was stupid enough to leave a clue sitting around for more than ten months. He got as close as he dared and listened. He listened to what his neighbors and friends had to say, but more than that he listened for signs of trouble. If Shea pushed the wrong buttons and got herself in too deep, he would be there to step in.

If Shea was in danger, it didn't matter who saw him, didn't matter if the police caught up with him or not. He wouldn't allow anyone to hurt her.

And it was entirely possible that someone would try. She was tenacious, pushed too hard at times. If he was guilty, Shea Sinclair would scare the bejesus out of him.

So he listened. The Ables had been boring and a little too interested, as usual. Tom was more reserved, but his wife, Natalie, was eager to tell Shea everything she knew. Including the fact that she thought Nick, bless his heart, was guilty as sin.

Nick flattened his back against the wall, close enough to listen and respond if necessary, not so close that anyone would know he was there.

"I never could quite figure out why," Natalie said. "I mean, no one liked that godawful green Gary was painting his house, but I don't think anyone would kill him over it. Except maybe Vernon Casson. He can be such a grump." She paused to take a deep breath. "But maybe Gary gave Nick that same awful stock tip he gave us—remember, honey?"

"I'm sure Miss Sinclair doesn't care about a year-old bad stock tip," Tom muttered.

But of course, Miss Sinclair did.

"What kind of stock tip?"

"We lost a bundle," Natalie said, unnatural cheer in her voice. "Gary said later he was sorry, but I wouldn't be surprised if it turned out he knew all along the company would tank. It was one of those Internet stocks? Gary said it would go up twenty, a hundred times what we paid for it, but…well, it didn't."

"No big deal," Tom said, in a low voice that told Nick it *was* a big deal.

The interview didn't last long. When Shea said her goodbyes and promised to be back at a later date with her cameraman, Nick scooted toward the kitchen door and the wooded area beyond.

"Poor Nick," Natalie said as she opened the front door for Shea. "I always knew he had a temper, but bless his heart, I didn't think he'd actually kill anyone."

As he opened the back door he heard Shea say, confident as ever, "He didn't."

They were far from Marion, but the profusion of flowers in front of the Casson house reminded Shea a little of the small town where she and Nick had hidden for a while.

That half-wit.

Like the others, Mrs. Casson recognized Shea immediately. Unlike the others, she was initially reluctant to talk.

Lillian Casson had the look of a strong woman, taller than average, solidly built. Her gray hair was done up in a soft, easy style, and she wore a minimum of makeup.

"I assure you," Shea said as Mrs. Casson finally opened the door and invited her in. "Nothing you say will go on the air unless you approve it beforehand."

"I'll be allowed to view the videotape and veto any part of my segment I don't approve of?"

No self-respecting newsman would ever agree to such a request, but Shea smiled and said, "Of course."

In her honeyed Southern accent, Mrs. Casson called her

husband in to join them. He'd been taking a nap in his den, and yawned as he entered the living room. Vernon Casson wasn't much taller than his wife, and she probably outweighed him by about twenty pounds. He came instantly awake when he spotted Shea.

"The weathergirl Taggert kidnapped," he said with a grin and a twinkling of his eyes. "Hot damn."

"Vernon," Mrs. Casson said tersely. "Behave yourself. We have company."

When she turned her head away from her husband, Lillian rolled her eyes.

Shea opened her notebook, poised her pen to take a few notes, and set her calculating eyes on the Cassons. There was certainly nothing sinister here!

"I don't believe Mr. Taggert is guilty," she said straight-out. "But someone in this neighborhood is. Who on this cul-de-sac might have had cause to murder Gary Winkler?"

Lillian Casson lifted her chin, placed her nose in the air and sniffed. "Who didn't? Gary Winkler was a mannerless Yankee who managed to offend everyone, isn't that right, Vernon?"

"You're absolutely right, dear," Vernon agreed halfheartedly.

"Why, that horrid green paint he chose for his house was atrocious, and clashed horribly with my azaleas." Mrs. Casson had been reluctant to talk, but once she started she got on a roll and didn't want to stop. "He used to allow his grass to get nearly a foot high, and then mow at the crack of dawn on a Sunday morning, when Vernon was trying to sleep, isn't that right, Vernon?"

"Yep," the old man said. "Winkler was a nuisance."

"He was a dreadful neighbor," Lillian finished.

"Mr. Casson," Shea began, "did you spend any time

with Gary? Do you know of anyone besides Mr. Taggert who might've wanted him dead?''

Mr. Casson opened his mouth, but it was Mrs. Casson who spoke. "Vernon and Gary were not close. They played golf a few times, but Gary cheated, so of course Vernon never played with him again."

"So you didn't socialize with your neighbors on a regular basis." Again, Shea's eyes were on Mr. Casson, but Mrs. Casson answered.

"Oh, no," she said, pursing her lips.

Shea made a few notes. Apparently Vernon was not allowed to talk. "What about Mrs. Winkler?"

Mrs. Casson smiled. "Polly is a sweet girl. Her people are from Georgia, I believe. How she ever hooked up with that Yankee, I'll never know."

Nick had been right. No one here had liked Winkler. They'd tolerated him, they might even have occasionally played golf with him, but no one liked him. He was definitely not missed.

"Would you like some tea?" Mrs. Casson asked, rising from her seat. "I have a special herbal blend I make myself. Polly loves it."

Since Mr. Casson had a hard time getting a word in edgewise when his wife was in the room, Shea was tempted to accept, though herbal tea was not on her list of favorite beverages. But Nick was probably hiding in the kitchen, listening. She didn't dare.

"No, thank you."

She tried to turn her attention to Mr. Casson. He was a little bit older than her father, she imagined. Retired but still kicking.

"So you think he didn't do it, huh?" he asked.

Shea shook her head. "That's right."

"So who did?"

Shea had to shake her head. "I don't know."

Lillian started to speak, but Vernon raised a hand to silence his wife. She closed her mouth, alerting Shea to the fact that the balance of power in this marriage was not completely one-sided.

"Let me give you a little advice, Miss Sinclair," he said, dipping his chin and looking her square in the eye. "I liked Nick, I really did. He kept his yard nice and neat and he never made much noise and he kept to himself, most of the time. But don't let yourself be fooled by a purty face. I was there that night, and Nick was sure as shootin' mad enough to kill."

Shea felt her face flush hot. Heavens, she was blushing! A real no-no in her profession. "I assure you, Mr. Casson, I was not fooled by a pretty face. In researching the case I discovered that the investigation was tainted in several areas—"

"Tainted my foot," he interrupted. "I saw them drag the bat out of the sewer drain. I heard all about the blood and paint they found in his kitchen. I saw Winkler trifling with Nick's girlfriend."

Mrs. Casson wrinkled her nose and sniffed.

"Let it go, Miss Sinclair," Vernon Casson advised. "You're only going to get hurt if you keep on dredging up the past."

She wasn't about to let an old man scare her. "Hurt? In what way?" she asked calmly.

He hesitated, but only for a moment. "I have a feeling you're going to be real disappointed when you find out your pretty boy is a cold-blooded killer."

Shea again declined Mrs. Casson's offer of tea, and left the house with a sigh of relief. Mr. Casson, a murderer? Over green paint and Sunday morning mowing? Would that nice old Southern man who spent his days napping and playing golf kill a "mannerless Yankee" over such trivialities?

There was only one house left, the most important interview of all. Polly Winkler.

The woman who answered the door was just as Nick had described her. Mousy, drab. She looked like she'd jump if Shea said boo.

But like the others, she asked Shea in. And as with the others, when Shea told the widow that she thought Nick was innocent, she had the woman's attention.

Polly's kitchen door was locked, but using Shea's credit card, Nick opened it easily. Already Polly and Shea were discussing the murder. In this case, Shea was being more sedate, gentler than in the other interviews. This was, after all, the widow she was speaking to. Polly might not take kindly to the idea that someone was trying to clear the man who had been convicted of murdering her husband.

The house had been completely repainted. It was white now, with a tasteful slate-blue trim. Polly didn't do her own yardwork; she hired a service. They had watched the team of young men tackle the yard yesterday, finishing up in no time and leaving behind an orderly lawn.

Nick glanced around the kitchen as he listened. There was no sign of Gary Winkler in this room, and perhaps there never had been. It was all Polly. There were cookies on the counter, a collection of herb teas to the side, an artful arrangement of mismatched china cups and saucers. Above the sink, on a small shelf, was a small collection of medicine bottles. Aspirin, allergy medications, a prescription. Nick sidled closer to the sink to get a better look. Sleeping pills.

Maybe Polly had had trouble sleeping at night, after Gary's murder. Then again, maybe she had always needed help to sleep. Marriage to Gary couldn't have been pleasant.

Polly seemed surprisingly receptive to the theory that

someone else had murdered her husband. The others Shea had spoken to had expressed open skepticism, but not Polly. Nick listened as she told Shea how surprised she had been to hear that Nick was the one. As she said, sounding sincere, what a nice young man he was.

Like Lillian Casson, Polly offered Shea tea and cookies, an overture Shea declined.

Nick leaned against the wall and relaxed his guard for the moment. God, he was on edge! When Vernon had told Shea she'd be sorry if she kept sticking her nose into the past, he'd almost rushed into the living room to protect her from the old man. And then Vernon had explained why.

Shea had hesitated before responding. Was she beginning to doubt him, the way everyone else did? Nick wouldn't blame her. He wouldn't blame her if she walked out of here right now and called the police and told them where to find their escaped murderer.

If the plan worked tonight, they'd soon know the truth. Everyone would know the truth.

If it didn't work he'd run again. Alone, this time.

Chapter 18

Shea wanted to hate Lauren, but she couldn't. The woman was anxious to prove Nick innocent, and she threw herself wholeheartedly into putting together a quick barbecue for the neighborhood suspects.

Lauren was beautiful—blond and tallish and long legged. And she obviously loved Norman very much.

She even insisted on loaning Shea a white sleeveless sundress for the occasion, and with the white sandals Shea took from the duffel bag she'd been storing at Nick's house, she was set.

Nick would be watching from the dark wooded area behind the house. Shea had hoped he'd be satisfied to watch from a window, but he had rejected that option because it would limit his field of vision. She was terrified that he would step on a fallen branch or move into a ray of light that reached into the woods from Norman's deck. But so far, so good.

Everyone was here—even Lillian Casson, who so obviously disliked Lauren. Maybe Lillian was afraid she would be the subject of neighborhood gossip if she weren't here to defend herself.

Shea stood alone at the far end of the deck, watching. People were spread across the sprawling deck and a small portion of the backyard. The kids appeared now and then, but for the most part they played in the driveway and the cul-de-sac. Norman flipped burgers like a pro, the ladies had their heads together and the men talked golf and fishing. All in all, it was a very normal neighborhood party.

But from the way they kept glancing her way, Shea had a feeling she and Nick were the most interesting topic of conversation tonight. Of course, no one knew the extent of their relationship. Well, of the relationship she'd thought they had. To them, Nick was the fugitive and she was the nosy reporter who'd had the misfortune to be in the wrong place at the wrong time and was now making the best of a bad situation.

Lauren, wearing a cool blue sundress, sidled up to Shea, a glass of iced tea in her hand. "What do you want me to do?" she whispered.

Lauren and Norman, in particular, didn't know what had happened between Shea and Nick. They saw only the face she wanted them to see, the reporter who had her hooks in a good story. They didn't know that if she failed she'd never forgive herself, that no matter what happened between her and Nick—which would be nothing at all, if she bought the story he'd told this morning—she would never forgive herself if he went back to jail. She couldn't bear it.

"In a few minutes," Shea said, "I want you to join the neighborhood women and tell them that I know who killed Gary Winkler."

Lauren started to walk away, but Shea called her back, placing a hand on the woman's bare arm. "Not so fast.

We should talk for more than thirty seconds before you run off to share the news. We don't want this to look like a setup.'' She raked her eyes over the crowd, noting the glances that were often cast her way. ''How about a glass of that iced tea?''

Together, she and Lauren walked into the kitchen, where paper plates, napkins, plastic cups and an ice chest had been set up. Lauren filled a blue plastic cup with ice, poured sweet tea from the pitcher on the counter and handed it to her. Grateful to be away from the melee for a moment, Shea leaned against the counter and took a long sip.

''So,'' she said casually, her eyes on Lauren. ''When this is over and Nick is free again, will you two take up where you left off?''

Lauren shook her head vigorously. ''No. It was never serious between us, and I'm with Norman now. I love him. We really are going to get married.''

Shea wondered if she should tell Lauren that Nick had been *very* serious.

''Norman is just the kind of man I need,'' Lauren said, the soft smile blooming on her face and making her even more beautiful, darn her hide. Her eyes glowed; her cheeks flushed pink. ''And I think I'm what he needs. We click, you know? Some of the women in the neighborhood hate me because they think I broke up Norman's marriage, but that's not true. Norman and Margaret hadn't been good for one another for a very long time.''

Margaret! Darn, Shea had thought she'd covered all her bases, but she'd forgotten about Norman's first wife. Margaret Burgess had been at Nick's barbecue last year, too.

This was all Nick's fault. Shea never forgot a detail like that, but he had her mind going in too many different directions.

''Nick and I were temporary,'' Lauren said with a sigh.

''I had too many problems, and he was too closed off. I like a man who can tell me how he feels, and who makes me feel like there's no other woman in the world. Even if this hadn't happened, we wouldn't have lasted much longer.''

''You never loved him?''

Lauren flashed a sad smile. ''I liked Nick a lot, but I never loved him and he never loved me.''

Nick had been planning to marry Lauren, to spend his life with her. If that wasn't love, what was? Lauren didn't know about Nick's plans, of course, and it wouldn't do anyone any good to tell her now.

Shea was surprised Lauren didn't know how much she'd meant to Nick. After all, he was so transparent! His emotions were raw, his eyes telling. All you had to do was look at him to know what he was feeling, what he was thinking.

She and Lauren stepped onto the deck, into the muggy night air. Lauren went one way, toward the cluster of women, and Shea, the outsider, moved to her solitary post on the deck. She allowed her eyes to flicker to the woods only briefly.

If she didn't mean anything to Nick, why hadn't he looked her in the eye when he'd told her to get lost? Why had he kept his back to her through most of that hellish conversation, when he'd told her she was nothing more than a bit of fun for a man who'd been in jail for almost a year?

Lauren said Nick was closed off. That statement was proof to Shea that the blonde had never known Nick the way she did. He was the most passionate man she'd ever known, the most openhearted. And he was *such* a terrible liar.

It was like watching a play from a darkened theater. When he moved he did so silently, taking care with each step. His jeans and black T-shirt blended into the shadows, even when he shifted positions. Most of the time he stood very still and watched.

He should be watching his old friends as the rumor worked its way through the crowd, but his eyes constantly found and held Shea.

She was beautiful. What he wouldn't give for one more night with her. One more night before he had to let her go. They hadn't had enough time together. Of all the terrible things that had happened to him in the past year, that seemed the most unfair.

Nick searched for a guilty face in the crowd, but saw none. After today he at least knew the truth: all his neighbors thought he was capable of murder. Polly, the widow, had been the only one to agree with Shea that he wasn't.

But Nick knew that anyone was capable of murder, in the right circumstances.

He stood there, silent and still, while Norman took the burgers off the grill. The crowd moved in and out of the house, filling their plates from the side dishes in the kitchen, camping out here and there to eat. Natalie and Amanda sat together at a table on the deck, the youngest of their children with them. The men stood in a knot, laughing and eating too fast. Lillian and Vernon stayed together, as usual, and they joined Polly at the well-lit kitchen table. Nick could see them clearly through the bay window.

He didn't see Lauren, though. She was probably off somewhere fixing her face. If he remembered correctly, she usually didn't go a full hour without checking her makeup.

Shea didn't eat. She stood on the deck and sipped at something in a plastic cup. Her eyes watched and catalogued everything. She listened, taking notes as surely as if she had her notebook in her hands. Her stomach was probably in knots, and she didn't ever eat much when she was excited. She had to be excited now.

While everyone else ate and visited, Nick moved closer. It was a risk, he knew, but he wanted to be close enough to hear what was said. He didn't make a sound as he stepped carefully through the shadows, ending up behind an old oak tree that shielded him from view. He couldn't see everything from here, but he could listen.

Sure enough, it wasn't long before the discussion took the turn he'd been waiting for.

"Can you believe that Sinclair woman?" Tom asked. "I thought this was finally over, and she comes around stirring things up again."

"Yeah," Carter said. "But what if she's right?"

Tom scoffed. "Please. What more do you want? A videotape? A signed confession?"

Norman remained silent. Since he was usually outspoken about any subject, he was probably biting his tongue right about now. Still, he had to allow the conversation to continue. Eventually he excused himself and stepped away. Good idea. The others would speak more clearly without the lawyer present, of that Nick was certain.

He heard soft, tentative footsteps through the grass, as more of the party joined the men. Ah, he was a subject that could bring the husbands and wives together at one of these shindigs. Murder crossed all gender lines.

"Are y'all talking about Nick?" Amanda asked. "Can you believe it? You know, that reporter says she knows who really killed Gary, and it wasn't Nick."

A voice he rarely heard at these get-togethers joined in. "Her heart's in the right place I'm sure," Polly said sweetly. "But we all know Nick is guilty."

A different tune from the one she'd been singing this

afternoon. Everyone let Polly talk. After all, her husband was the victim.

"I hate to admit it, because I liked Nick very much, but there's too much evidence to ignore."

There was a murmur of agreement.

"The bat with his fingerprints, the T-shirt." She sniffled, and did not mention her husband's blood on that incriminating piece of clothing. "We all heard them argue that night, and if that's not enough there was that blood and paint the police found on the underside of his kitchen table."

It was damning; Nick had known that all along. If Shea didn't scare up a confession, if he didn't remember something that would lead them to the real killer...this was it. He'd light out of here tonight. Saying goodbye would take too long and hurt too hard, so he'd just go. Where, he had no idea, but he had to go alone.

Luther sat at his desk and frowned down at Grace's file of hodgepodge information on the residents of Teakwood Court. He picked up the phone and dialed from memory.

"Daniels," he snapped. "The Winkler woman."

"What are you doing working so late?" Daniels asked. "And on a weekend?" He sounded like he'd been asleep, napping on the couch.

Luther ignored the question, as well as the heated response he bit back. "Polly Winkler. You didn't find anything odd in her background?"

Daniels hemmed and hawed and finally admitted, "I didn't really check into her background."

"You always check the spouse's background, Daniels," Luther snapped. Hell, he had a headache coming on. "Always."

"We had so much evidence," Daniels whined. "Fred was about to retire and he was no help, and I was swamped. Most criminals are not geniuses, Malone, and Taggert is no different. He left a trail of evidence a rookie could've followed.''

With that, Daniels hung up.

Luther stared down at the file. Grace hadn't been able to find anything on Polly Winkler more than six years old, and he was having no better luck. It made the hair on the back of his neck stand up.

Shea had wondered who would come to her, once the rumor had circulated. She hadn't really expected Polly, who was shy and had been silent through most of the evening.

''Hi,'' Polly said, leaning against the rail beside Shea. ''You're not eating.''

Of course not. Her stomach churned unpleasantly. Anything solid that went down was likely to come back up. ''I'm not hungry.''

Polly nodded as if she understood. ''I hear you know who killed Gary,'' she said, her voice soft and her eyes wide.

''Yes,'' Shea said confidently. ''I do.''

''You've been very persistent in your investigation. Very thorough. How clever of you to succeed where the police failed.'' Her voice remained calm, but her eyes were bright. ''Tell me who it is. Gary was my husband, and I have a right to know who killed him.''

''Not until I've shared what I found with the police.''

''You haven't done that yet?'' Polly asked softly. ''I'm sure they'd like to know what you've uncovered.''

Shea nodded. ''Soon enough. I don't want every other reporter in town on this story until I have it wrapped up.''

Polly leaned slightly closer. ''I understand. But how can you make me wait for this kind of news? Tell me, was it Margaret?''

Shea's heart skipped a beat. Norman's ex-wife! "Why do you say that?"

"She and Gary were…" Polly looked away and shrugged her shoulders slightly. "I guess there's no use pretending Gary was a saint. Everyone knows he wasn't. After he died I found these terrible pictures."

"Pictures?" Shea said, unable to hide the excitement in her voice.

"I should've burned them, I know," Polly said contritely. "They were proof that Gary was not a faithful husband. They were tangible evidence that I failed miserably as a wife."

"You still have the pictures?" Shea grabbed Polly's arm in her excitement. "Can I see them?"

Polly seemed reluctant. She looked down at her feet and pursed her mouth. "They're quite scandalous."

"Please," Shea whispered.

Polly lifted her head and looked at Shea as if she were still trying to make up her mind. "Well," she finally sighed. "I suppose."

They didn't walk across the deck and through the crowd, but took the most direct route—through the house, out the front door and across the street. They had to step past kids on their tricycles and bigger kids throwing a baseball by the light cast from the tall streetlamps.

Polly's front door was unlocked, and they went in. Walking through the door took them into a small foyer, and Shea followed Polly into the living room.

"Have a seat," Polly said, gesturing to a chair by the window. "I'll be right back."

Shea sat in the same comfortable wing chair she had occupied during her interview earlier that day. Polly was not all that old, but her living room had an old-fashioned feel to it, like an elderly lady's visiting parlor. The furnishings were deep green and shades of red, and there were knickknacks everywhere. Ceramic figurines of animals of every kind decorated the room.

On the table beside Shea sat a good-size philodendron in a ceramic pot, a small reading lamp, a doily and a sandstone coaster.

"I'm going to put on water for tea," Polly called from the kitchen, "while I round up those pictures. I'm not sure exactly where I put them."

"No tea for me, thanks," Shea called out.

"Don't be silly," Polly said from the kitchen. "I have a microwave. We'll have hot water in no time."

Shea tapped her foot nervously on the floor. Margaret! If she hadn't been so distracted, she would have thought of her this afternoon. No other man or woman in the world could distract her, but Nick turned everything upside down. Even her brain. Norman couldn't very well invite his ex-wife to an engagement party, but something could have been worked out.

Gary and Margaret. Gary and Lauren. Norman and Lauren. Sheesh, they should've named this cul-de-sac Peyton Place Court. What went on here was more interesting than any soap opera. Murder, adultery. Pictures! It was true what they said, about a picture being worth a thousand words.

"Here we go," Polly said, carrying in two cups of steaming tea. One cup was tall and decorated with violets, and that was the one Polly placed in Shea's hands. The other was a more traditional shape and was adorned with hand-painted red roses. Polly placed that cup and saucer on the table by the couch. "I'll be right back."

Shea held the warm teacup in both hands, sipped at the bitter brew and then set it aside, using the sandstone coaster. While Polly left the room Shea made a face at her back. Herbal tea.

The party had begun to die down. Amanda and Natalie made excuses about getting the children inside before it got too late, and Lillian and Vernon said good-night.

So far, Nick was still the only suspect. The case against him was too great. The weapon, the shirt, the evidence in his kitchen.

The blood and paint that had been planted there. Something niggled at his brain, an idea, something that wasn't quite right. He turned, taking a small chance of being seen as he looked around the backyard for Shea. In her white sundress she should be easy to find, but he saw no sign of her.

No sign of Polly, either.

He had nothing left to lose, anyway, he thought as he ran from the woods and straight to Norman, who was nervously scraping off the grill.

Those still in attendance, Carter, Tom and Lauren, turned their eyes to him. Carter and Tom each took a wary step back.

Nick ignored them and gave all his attention to Norman. "Was the exact location of the evidence that was found in my kitchen ever on the news or in the paper?"

"No," Norman said, looking around to see if anyone present was running for a telephone. "It was the one bit of crucial information the police managed to keep out of the papers."

"Then how did she know?" he hissed, grabbing Norman's shoulders. "How did Polly know the blood and paint were found under my kitchen table?"

"She did?" Norman asked, setting his grill brush aside.

Tom took a step forward. "Yes, she did."

Nick looked toward the house, hoping for a glimpse of Shea through one of the big windows. "Where's Shea?" he asked hoarsely.

Lauren licked her lips nervously. "I saw her and Polly go into the house awhile back. They didn't come back out, so I figured they went over to Polly's for a while."

Nick took off running.

Chapter 19

Shea's feet went numb and her eyelids grew heavy. Her arms tingled strangely and it seemed, for a moment, that her body was not her own. Suddenly, she wanted a nap more than anything in the world.

Polly continued to rummage through the drawers in the kitchen, making lots of noise as she searched for those pictures of Gary and Margaret. Shea had a sinking feeling there were no pictures.

The noise in the kitchen stopped, and a minute later Polly appeared with a short stack of Polaroids in one hand. She smiled sweetly and sat primly on the couch, took a sip of her own tea and fanned the pictures out so she could see them all. She tilted her head as she studied one particular photograph.

"How was your tea?"

"Lovely," Shea said, her lips feeling thick and somehow wrong. Ack, the stuff had been awful.

Polly took another sip, set her cup aside and rose slowly to her feet. "Would you care for more?"

"No, thank you," Shea said, trying to shake her head and finding that she couldn't. More than her toes were numb.

Polly glanced down into Shea's empty teacup and smiled. "Good girl, you drank every drop."

Shea knew what had happened. She couldn't move; keeping her eyes open was an effort. But for now, her mind continued to work. "What was in the tea?"

"Sleeping pills," Polly said with a smile. "And since you were a good girl and drank it all down, I'll let you see the pictures."

Polly held out the fanned Polaroids for Shea's inspection. They were of Gary, but Margaret was nowhere to be seen. Just Gary. On his knees in the backyard, on his belly with his head bashed in, rolled onto his back, before and after he'd been painted green.

"He was a vile excuse for a human being," Polly said tersely. "No one will ever miss Gary. That's one of the reasons I married him. I knew the right time would come, that there would be someone convenient to blame his death on."

"But what about Nick?" Shea whispered. He wasn't a vile human being, he hadn't done anything wrong...but Polly had no misgivings about using him as her scapegoat. Shea's eyes drifted closed. She tried, but could no longer keep them open. "Not fair."

"Poor Nick, he will be quite distraught when you're dead, I imagine."

Nick. He'd been watching from the woods. Did he know that something was terribly wrong? Or was he still waiting for the murderer to make his move? Shea felt herself slipping into darkness, but she didn't want to go. Not yet.

"They'll know," she said softly. "You won't get away with murder twice."

Polly was not concerned. "You came over here to discuss the case, distressed that your amateur sleuthing turned up no other suspects. You decided that Nick was guilty after all, and were so upset I suggested that you stay and rest until you'd composed yourself. While I was across the street, collecting my casserole dish and saying a long and leisurely good-night to my hosts, you found my sleeping pills and took them." She tsked. "What a silly, silly girl."

Polly lifted Shea's uncooperative arm and wrapped her fingers around a small plastic prescription bottle. Fingerprints. That chore accomplished, she carefully placed the empty bottle on the table by Shea's empty teacup.

If Shea could open her eyes, maybe she could force herself to stay awake a little longer. But she couldn't open them, and no matter how hard she tried, the darkness crept steadily onward.

"And besides," Polly whispered, "I've already gotten away with murder twice. My first husband was as wretched and expendable as Gary, only I didn't know it when I married him. I had to find out the hard way. No one will miss either of my dearly departed husbands," she hissed. "But I have a feeling Nick will miss you. So sad. You should have minded your own business."

A shudder worked its way through Shea's body, and everything went black.

"Call the police!" Nick shouted as he ran across Norman's side yard. "Tell them I'm here. That'll get them here quick enough."

God, he prayed it would be quick enough. Polly!

He no longer thought about hiding, but ran directly across the street and into Polly's front yard. He leaped to the porch and tried the door. Locked. There was no time to dig around for Shea's mutilated credit card, so he kicked the door in. It gave on the first kick and swung in with a bang.

"Shea!"

He managed to startle Polly, who jumped away from the chair where Shea slumped, her eyes closed and her limbs slack.

"What did you do to her?" he whispered hoarsely.

Polly, not so mousy this evening, regained her composure quickly. Her eyes flashed; her jaw clenched. "I gave her enough sleeping pills to kill a man twice her size," she said calmly. "You're too late."

He dropped down in front of Shea's slack body, reaching out to touch her throat. Her skin felt warm, and he found her pulse without difficulty. It was weak, thready and irregular, but she was alive. If he could get her to a hospital in time…

"Why didn't you just run?" Polly asked, sounding annoyed. "You could have ruined everything by coming back here and raising all your pesky questions. All you had to do was keep running."

He ignored Polly and very gently picked Shea up, easing her out of the chair and into his arms. He waited for her to squirm, to place her arms around his neck and hold on to him, the way she did when she rested in his arms. She didn't.

His heart sank, and he couldn't breathe. The world closed in until there was nothing but the two of them. He willed Shea to open her eyes, but she remained too still. Unresponsive and slack in his arms.

Polly might've administered the sleeping pills, but he had killed Shea. If he had never panicked and escaped, if he had controlled himself and let Norman handle the case through appeals and private investigators…he'd be in jail for the rest of his life, but Shea would be alive.

Polly made an attempt to stop him, but he easily pushed her back and carried Shea out the open front door. Norman, Tom and Carter waited in the cul-de-sac, and the

Cassons stood on their front porch, watching. As Nick walked down the front steps, three police cars, lights flashing and sirens blaring, pulled onto the street.

He could put Shea down and run, through the woods and into another neighborhood, where he'd disappear, or he could stand here and hold her awhile longer. In truth, it was no choice at all.

He walked slowly toward the curb, dipping his head toward Shea's. "I love you," he whispered. "You have to know that."

The uniformed police officers left their cars, weapons in hand and trained on him.

"Call an ambulance," he said hoarsely. "Shea…" On the chance that she made it, that Polly was wrong about the dosage being lethal, he had to make sure she was never implicated in this. "The hostage needs to get to the hospital."

The police did not respond. Three eager armed officers, two of them appearing to be younger than Shea, were poised to fire.

A strident voice cried from behind him. "He killed her!" Polly shouted from the porch. "Shoot him. Shoot him!"

A couple of the officers, standing spread-legged by their cars, looked as if they were considering the suggestion.

"Wait just a minute," Norman said with authority, bursting forward to intervene. "My client is unarmed, and he's willing to come along peacefully. Isn't that right, Nick?"

"After they radio for an ambulance."

"Done," Tom said, holding his cell phone aloft. "They're on their way."

In the middle of the Winkler yard, Nick dropped to his knees. After the run from Norman's to Polly's his leg was weak, unable to hold him and Shea up any longer.

One of the officers, the more senior one, moved forward. "Put the girl down and very slowly lie down on your stomach with your arms outstretched."

"I'm not putting her down," Nick said, glaring up at the officer. "When the ambulance gets here and she's on the way to the hospital, then I'll do whatever you say. Until then leave me the hell alone."

Nick looked down at Shea. Her face was pale, her lips parted. To keep himself from falling apart he focused on those small, pale freckles sprinkled across her nose.

"I can't do that," the officer said.

"Then shoot me," Nick growled.

"My client is naturally upset, but he's not presenting a danger to anyone," Norman said, stepping forward. "If we all stay calm and wait for the ambulance, we can get out of here tonight without anyone else getting hurt."

Nick raised his arm to bring Shea's face close to his. The cops and Norman stayed clear, so no one else was close enough to hear, if he kept his voice low. "More than anything, I wish we could start over," he whispered. "I can thank you for that, too. After everything that happened, I was ready to give up. I didn't think there was any way I could bear to start over with nothing again, but if I could start over with you I would. You gave me my life back." And he would just as soon die if he ended up taking hers.

"Open your eyes, Shea," he commanded softly. "Look at me."

Another car, unmarked but with a throbbing red light on the dash, swerved in behind the police cars. More police cars followed. Nick glanced up as a man in a black suit, white shirt and loosened dark tie jumped from the car, badge in hand as he walked past the stalled police officers.

The man's appearance got Polly stirred up again. "Taggert poisoned her! He killed her! Shoot him!"

The detective approached slowly, but Nick barely noticed. Shea stirred in his arms, very subtly, and barely opened her eyes. "Nick didn't try to poison me," she rasped. "She did." With that, she lifted her arm and pointed at Polly. She turned her attention to the detective who hovered over them. "And Luther, she killed her husband. She even has *pictures*."

Polly ran into the house and Luther took off after her. Nick didn't watch, but lowered his head until it was so close to Shea's his cheek brushed hers. "You're awake. Thank God you're awake. Polly said she gave you enough sleeping pills to—to…" He couldn't say it.

"I knew something was wrong," she said, her words slow and careful. "The tea was so bitter, even for herbal tea. I dumped most of it in the philadem…the philonem…the plant," she finished, letting her eyes close again. "But I drank some of it, and I am so tired. Nick, I've never been so tired."

"You'll be okay," he said, smiling. Believing it.

She snuggled against his chest. "Do sleeping pills make you hallucinate?" she whispered.

"I don't know."

"I could've sworn you said you loved me," she breathed into his ear. "But that can't be right. Can it? I'm just…we just…"

"You're not hallucinating," he said softly. "I do love you." He heard the ambulance siren approaching. It didn't matter what happened to him now. Shea was going to be all right.

With a great amount of effort, Shea lifted one arm to drape around his neck. She smiled and raked her cheek against his shoulder, nuzzling him like a cat. "Oh, that's good. That's *very* good."

Norman held the police back, and Luther led a handcuffed Polly Winkler from her house. The street and the yards were filled with onlookers. All eyes were on him.

Nick sat on the ground and held Shea close, not caring who watched. Not caring what anyone thought.

"How about I call you when I get out of jail?" he asked.

"You're not going to jail," Shea said, snuggling against him, warm and alive. "You're innocent. They have Polly now."

He was innocent of murder, but not of assaulting two deputies, escaping from the courthouse and taking Shea hostage on camera. At least if he ended up doing time for those crimes, his penance would be for offenses he'd actually committed.

A few of the police cars pulled out of the way, making room for the ambulance that turned onto the street. His time was almost up.

"I do love you," he said again.

Shea smiled, closed her eyes and passed out once more.

She hated hospitals! It was bad enough to be a visitor in one, but to be forced to stay here was sheer torture.

Her brothers had still not forgiven her for sneaking out or for sending them on a wild-goose chase, but since she had been wounded in the line of duty, so to speak, they were behaving tolerably.

Boone had fetched her a pair of her own pajamas from her apartment, and Clint had brought her a milkshake when she complained about the hospital food. And she hadn't been here a full day.

Nick was back in jail, an injustice that made her blood boil. If he hadn't escaped, no one would ever know that he was innocent of murder, and no one would ever know that Polly Winkler had taken out a big insurance policy on Gary and then killed him, or that it was the second time she'd committed the crime. Polly wasn't even her real name. She'd changed her identity after being suspected of the first murder she'd committed, years ago.

With her fingerprints, the whispered confession to Shea, the juicy information Grace had managed to dig up with the help of her hacker friends, and Luther's dogged determination to discover all the facts, everything was coming together nicely.

So why was Nick still in jail? Why wasn't he *here?* Dean told her the wheels of justice turned slowly, and she had borrowed a few of Boone's choice words to respond to *that* bit of brotherly wisdom.

She had never been patient and she didn't intend to start now.

Looking up at her brothers, she smiled. "I get out of here in a few hours."

"We'll take you home," Clint said. "And stay with you as long as you need us."

"I'm sorry I had to trick you, but..." The expression on Dean's face told her he did not want to be reminded that he'd wasted half a day chasing Greyhound buses. "You know I love you. And I know you love me. I know you would do anything for me."

Anything. Oh, she hoped that was true.

Nick was surprised to see Detective Luther Malone arrive to escort him from the Madison County Jail for the last time. Almost as surprised as he was to be released after spending just under three days in jail.

The detective offered Nick a lemon drop, and when Nick declined, Malone popped the candy into his own mouth. "Just thought I'd bring you up to date on your case. The detective who was in charge has taken an early retirement. It was that or be fired, since he screwed up so bad." Malone cast a weary glance in Nick's direction. "Though I can't say I wouldn't have made some of the same mistakes. The woman you knew as Polly Winkler set things up pretty solid."

"Yes, she did."

"She's done this before, you know—taken out a second insurance policy on her husband and then made sure she collected." He cast a wary glance at Nick. "You know Ray and Grace?"

"Not really."

"They found the second insurance policy. The company had never questioned paying, because we had you, and the case was so solid. I was headed to the Winkler woman's house to question her about it before I got the call that you were there." Malone shook his head. "She looked so normal, right up until the end. Your everyday, average housewife. It's enough to make any man think twice about getting married," he added with a shake of his head.

Married.

"Anyway," Malone continued, "Daniels is gone, and since we had to bring in another detective, a damned rookie, I've ended up with a partner again. He's this young, enthusiastic whippersnapper who will probably never take anything at face value. So, we're all being punished, if that makes you feel any better."

It didn't make Nick feel any better. In truth, he didn't care. "How's Shea?" he asked.

The detective nodded. "She's fine. Smart girl to pour that tea into the plant. If Polly had known she didn't finish it, there's no telling what she might have done."

The thought gave Nick chills.

Malone led Nick into the underground garage.

"So why am I getting out of here? This seems too easy."

"Oh, it is," Malone agreed with a nod of his head. "You had a little help. A lot of help, to be honest."

"What kind of help?"

"Shea Sinclair, weathergirl extraordinaire, promised to make a national issue of your case if you weren't released, and she also claimed that the kidnapping was a planned media stunt. Norman Burgess, annoying twit of a lawyer, threatened to sue, listing a heap of civil rights that were violated. Boone Sinclair managed to convince a state trooper that when he'd thought he'd spotted Shea in a country gas station, he was mistaken. Deputy U.S. Marshal Dean Sinclair called in every favor he was owed to make sure there were no federal charges filed."

"So, I'm really free to go," Nick said, not quite believing it.

Detective Malone broke into what had to pass as a grin, for him. "I wouldn't say that," he said, glancing to his right.

Nick's head turned in that direction, and he saw them. Three men—a cowboy, a thug and a man in a blue suit and burgundy tie—stood before a black sedan with scowls on their faces and their arms folded across their chests.

"Let me guess," he said. "The Sinclair brothers."

Malone slapped Nick on the back. "Good luck, buddy."

Chapter 20

Nick sat, as directed, in the back seat with Clint, who in truth seemed to be the least threatening of the three. Dean was stony faced, and Boone kept glancing over his shoulder and…growling.

"Where are we going?" Nick asked, for the fifth time in the past ten minutes. He had yet to get an answer delivered in recognizable syllables.

Boone glared at him again. "Let me shoot him," he said to no one in particular.

"No," Dean said without so much as blinking an eye. "That's why you had to ride in the *front* seat, remember?"

Boone growled again.

"Just let me out at the next corner," Nick said, not caring for the direction of this conversation. He wanted to call Shea, ask her… Hell, he didn't have her phone number. He didn't know her address! He thought about asking her brothers for the information, but decided it would be safer to get in touch with the station where she worked.

The car didn't so much as slow down.

"Come on, guys, give me a break. This is…" Nick stopped speaking suddenly.

"Kidnapping?" Clint suggested with a grin. "Is that the word you're looking for?"

Nick slunk down in his seat and decided to go along for the ride. What choice did he have?

She hadn't been this nervous since she'd gone on camera for the first time, stuttered twice and mispronounced the name of the anchorman. *Back to you, Blob.*

This was actually worse than that horrifying moment. The outcome was so much more important. Everything she had and everything she wanted was wrapped up in her plan. It was extreme, perhaps, but she didn't want her first meeting with Nick after he was released to be in front of cameras. Her place was too well known; there would be media everywhere. His place was out of the question. What did that leave? A hotel? No. Somehow that wasn't quite right.

They wouldn't have to worry about media here, at least not for a while. Besides, she'd had to return Maude's Camaro, so coming here made perfect sense.

"Better than sex," Maude said, jolting Shea out of her nervous reflection.

"What?"

Maude held her dark and beautiful cake aloft. "Your dessert. Better than Sex Chocolate Layer Cake."

Shea smiled at the older woman as Maude walked into the dining room and carefully placed the cake in the center of the round table.

"The way to a man's heart is through his stomach," Maude insisted as she returned to the kitchen. Her eyebrows lifted and she attempted to appear properly scandalized. A soft smile gave her away, though. "I don't think you're aiming for the stomach with that dress, young lady.''

''Thanks for all your help,'' Shea said, growing more apprehensive with each second that passed.

Maude waved off Shea's thanks and headed for the back door. ''I hope you like yellow. Abigail is painting an eighteen-by-twenty-four oil of bananas for your wedding gift.''

''Bananas?''

''For some reason she thought that was an appropriate choice.'' Maude stopped in the open doorway and turned to face her.

''He hasn't asked me to marry him,'' Shea said softly.

''Between your dress and my cake, what chance does the boy have?'' Maude teased.

That observation didn't make Shea feel any better.

Her reservations must've shown on her face, because Maude's wide smile faded. ''Oh, honey. It's Nick's heart that will bring him to you. The dress and the cake are just gravy.'' With a knowing wink, Maude closed the door and left Shea alone.

And still she had doubts. Until now, every moment she and Nick had shared had been colored by an intense situation. He'd kidnapped her; they'd become fugitives running from everyone, hiding from the world. Every sound had made her heart race; every day had been precious because they knew they didn't have many. She'd been doped and Nick had found himself at the wrong end of a number of guns. Their feelings, their love for one another, hadn't grown slowly, but had hit with the force of a hurricane. It had blindsided them and taken them both by surprise.

So what would happen when there was no tense situation to get their blood boiling? No reason to run, no adrenaline pumping. Would Nick find her tedious? Would she look at him and feel nothing?

There was only one way to find out.

Had she forgotten anything? The table was set for two, dinner was warming in the oven and Maude's best chocolate cake, Better than Sex, sat smack dab in the middle of the dining room table. Shea wore her most seductive dress—a black slinky slip of a thing Dean would definitely not approve of.

When she'd had to pick a place to hide, for a while longer, she had been able to think of no other place but this house. She had fallen in love with Nick here. She had watched him heal, and become his partner and fallen head over heels in love. She walked through the house, drifting slowly through the dining room and the parlor, sitting on the bottom step for a few minutes, tapping her fingers nervously against her thigh.

When she heard the car turn onto the gravel drive, her heart skipped a beat and she jumped to her feet. This was it, the moment she'd been looking forward to and dreading all day. She checked her hair and the little bit of makeup she wore in the dining room mirror, straightened her dress and went to the kitchen to wait.

Nick's heart.

Nick was caught in the middle, herded into the house like a prisoner, but when he saw her he grinned and pushed past Dean. "God, you look good," he said softly, taking her in his arms and lifting her off her feet.

The moment she saw him she knew this was right. What had she been worried about? Here, in Nick's arms, this was her place in the world. She felt comfort and love and passion, all at the same time.

"Hey, *hey*," Boone snapped. "Put her down."

Nick smiled at her and gave her a quick kiss. "I don't think so."

"The man doesn't know what's good for him," Clint murmured.

"What the hell are you wearing?" Dean asked tersely.

Nick placed Shea on her feet, kissed her quickly again and turned to bravely face her brothers. Shea expected fireworks, maybe even bloodshed.

But instead of shouting or raising his fists, Nick stepped forward and reached out to take Dean's unoffered hand and shake it. "I want to thank you boys," he said, smiling all the while, even as he stepped to the side and lifted Boone's uncooperative hand. "For watching after Shea all these years." He dropped Boone's hand and moved on to Clint, who had the grace to extend his hand, even if he did look suspicious. "I appreciate it, I really do." He stepped back to stand beside her. "But I'll take it from here. You can go."

Dean shook his head, Boone blustered and Clint looked Nick up and down like he was crazy.

"She said she wanted to see you," her youngest brother drawled. "She didn't say *nothin'* about us leaving you here."

"Well, of course you're going to leave him here," Shea said impatiently. "Did you think I'd ask you to drive three and a half hours for a fifteen-minute visit?"

"Your plans don't always make perfect sense, Shea Lyn," Dean said wearily. "But we have been trying to humor you since you've been—"

"Humor me?" she interrupted.

"I smell dinner," Clint said, trying to change the subject.

"Well, you don't smell *your* dinner," Shea said, crossing her arms and striking a pose much like their own.

Things were getting tense, but Nick raised a hand to silence them all. "Fellas," he said with a sigh. "I love your sister. I don't know what else I can say to you. I love her, and you're not going to scare me off. Not by threatening to shoot me, not by threatening to leave my body parts scattered by the side of the road—"

"Boone!" Shea snapped.

Nick ignored her. "If I have to fight all three of you for her, I will."

Boone looked like he was prepared to do battle, as always, but Dean held him back. Shea was ready to throw herself into the middle of the fray, since one-to-three odds were not at all fair. Surprisingly, no fists were raised, no accusations made. Tensions were high, though. They practically crackled through the room.

Dean was, uncharacteristically, the one to surrender first. "Is that pizza place still down by the courthouse?"

"I think so," Shea said calmly.

"We'll have dinner there and be back in a couple of hours."

Nick put his arm around Shea. "How about you have dinner there and hit the road. Shea doesn't need a trio of bodyguards anymore."

She slipped her arm around his waist. "I just need the one."

Those words spoken, she expected a fight, but the boys seemed oddly docile.

"I guess I really should get back to work," Dean said lowly.

Shea left Nick's side and went to her eldest brother to kiss him on the cheek. "Thanks for everything," she said softly. "Love you."

Boone wrinkled his nose and shifted on his booted feet. "I do have a case I need to get to, myself."

"You're a doll," she said, kissing him on the cheek as well. "What would I do without you?"

He growled.

"Love you," she said, giving him a quick and tender hug.

Clint was grinning widely by the time she got to him.

"Well, Shea Lyn, it looks like you finally found yourself a real man."

"Looks that way."

"About time."

She gave him a kiss on the cheek. "Love you."

"Love you, too."

It was amazing. They all left peacefully, and she and Nick were finally alone.

He swept her up again, and this time there was no one to tell him to put her down. No one to interrupt their reunion. He held her tight and buried one hand in her hair while he breathed deep. He laughed and sighed and whirled her around until her head spun. She held on and kissed his rough cheek and his neck, and as he slowed the dizzying twirl, she placed her head on his shoulder.

"Everything with us has been moving so fast," he said softly.

Her heart sank. Did he want to slow things down? Was he having second thoughts? She didn't have to worry for long.

"I don't see any reason to change that just because you aren't a hostage anymore."

She hid her smile against his shoulder. "Neither do I."

He placed her on her feet and tipped her head back so she had to look him in the eye. Had she ever thought those eyes were cold? Had she ever believed that he didn't love her?

"I want to start over, with you," he whispered. "I don't care where, as long as it's not in Huntsville. I want someplace new for us, someplace..." He looked around the kitchen. "Like this."

She took a deep breath, gathering her courage. Time to lay it all on the line. "How about someplace near—say, Atlanta?"

Nick raised his eyebrows, but in truth he didn't look at all surprised. "Why Atlanta?"

"I got a job offer yesterday, a pretty good one."

"The Weather Channel?"

He was kidding her, she could tell, so she grinned and rose up to kiss him briefly on the mouth. "No. CNN."

She searched for a growing wariness on his face, but saw none. She waited for the storm to come but saw only peace and love. He'd known all along that she was ambitious, that she would sacrifice anything for her career. Maybe he already knew, as she did, that she was no longer willing to give up *anything*.

"Sounds like just what you always wanted," he said in a low voice.

"Well, it's not a sure thing. And I did give them a few conditions."

"You gave CNN conditions."

She nodded. "I won't talk about my personal life, not ever, and that includes you."

"And they're still interested?"

She nodded. "I also told them I wouldn't work sixty and seventy hours a week. A woman has to have time for a personal life."

"Is that a fact?"

"And Nick—" she draped her arms around his neck "—they have great maternity benefits."

He tried not to smile, but didn't do a very good job of it. The corners of his wonderful mouth twitched. "So you gave them conditions and asked about maternity benefits, and they *still* want you?"

There had been a time when she would have been so excited about such an offer that nothing else would've mattered. Those days were gone, but it *was* an awfully good deal. "Yes. They want me to do a series of specials on criminals who claim they've been wrongly convicted.

I'll have a team, including my cameraman Mark, and we'll investigate these cases and put together a show on each one.''

''When do you start?''

''I haven't accepted yet.''

''Why not?''

She leaned against him, into him. ''I was kinda waiting for another offer to come along. If I can make both work, fine. If I can't, choosing will not be a problem.''

''What other offer?'' he whispered.

''One that comes with a porch swing, and a fort in the backyard, and three or four kids.'' She wrapped her arms around his waist. ''I love you, Nick. I want a lot out of life, that's true. I want everything and I want it right now. But most of all, I want you.''

He grinned at her, a warm, confident grin that told her he would be with her all the way. Always. She saw that promise, felt it, loved him all the more for it.

''Marry me,'' he said.

''Anywhere, anytime,'' she whispered.

''I think we should elope at the first opportunity.''

''Fine by me.''

Nick swept Shea off her feet and headed for the stairs. Almost at once his leg hitched, but he recovered.

''Put me down,'' she insisted. ''You'll hurt your leg.''

''Gee, that would be too bad,'' he said as he continued on, limping just slightly and showing no intention of slowing down, much less stopping. ''I'd probably have to stay in bed for at least a week while I heal up.''

She swung her feet lazily and relaxed against him, one arm stretched languidly around his neck. ''Oh,'' she muttered. ''Never mind.''

As Nick lifted his foot onto the first step she reached for the foil packet she had tucked into her bra.

"We still have this," she said, holding the condom between two fingers and waving it gently.

He looked at her, his eyes piercing and warm at the same time. "Are we going to need it?"

She really did want it all, and she really did want it *now*. For all she knew she was already carrying Nick's baby, and if she wasn't...well, if their relationship continued to move as quickly as it had so far, she didn't think it would be long.

"I don't think so." Shea nonchalantly tossed the foil-wrapped condom over her shoulder. It landed in the center of Maude's chocolate layer cake.

Better than Sex, indeed.

* * * * *

Will Luther ever realize that
marriage can be more than deadly?
Find out early in 2002—
only from Intimate Moments

Mystery and passion await as
heart-throbbing excitement
comes alive with

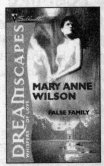

▼ *Silhouette*®
DREAMSCAPES...

Four dark and sensual
romances that invite
you to take a walk on
the dark side of love:

HEART OF THE BEAST
by Carla Cassidy

WHO IS DEBORAH?
by Elise Title

SHARING THE DARKNESS
by Marilyn Tracy

FALSE FAMILY
by Mary Anne Wilson

*Look for them in your
favorite retail outlet, starting
in September 2001.*

▼ *Silhouette*®
Where love comes alive™

Visit Silhouette at www.eHarlequin.com   RCDREAM3

SILHOUETTE® MAKES YOU A STAR!

Feel like a star with Silhouette.

We will fly you and a guest to New York City for an
exciting weekend stay at a glamorous 5-star hotel.
Experience a refreshing day at one of New York's
trendiest spas and have your photo taken by a
professional. Plus, receive $1,000 U.S. spending money!

Flowers…long walks…dinner for two… how does Silhouette Books make romance come alive for you?

Send us a script, with 500 words or less, along with visuals (only drawings,
magazine cutouts or photographs or combination thereof). Show us how
Silhouette Makes Your Love Come Alive. Be creative and have fun. No
purchase necessary. All entries must be clearly marked with your name,
address and telephone number. All entries will become property of
Silhouette and are not returnable. **Contest closes September 28, 2001.**

Please send your entry to: **Silhouette Makes You a Star!**

In U.S.A.	In Canada
P.O. Box 9069	P.O. Box 637
Buffalo, NY, 14269-9069	Fort Erie, ON, L2A 5X3

Look for contest details on the next page, by visiting www.eHarlequin.com or
request a copy by sending a self-addressed envelope to the applicable address
above. Contest open to Canadian and U.S. residents who are 18 or over.
Void where prohibited.

Silhouette®

Where love comes alive™

Our lucky winner's photo will appear in a Silhouette ad. Join the fun!

SRMYAS1

HARLEQUIN "SILHOUETTE MAKES YOU A STAR!" CONTEST 1308
OFFICIAL RULES
NO PURCHASE NECESSARY TO ENTER

1. To enter, follow directions published in the offer to which you are responding. Contest begins June 1, 2001, and ends on September 28, 2001. Entries must be postmarked by September 28, 2001, and received by October 5, 2001. Enter by hand-printing (or typing) on an 8 1/2" x 11" piece of paper your name, address (including zip code), contest number/name and attaching a script containing <u>500 words or less, along with drawings, photographs or magazine cutouts, or combinations thereof</u> (i.e. collage) on no larger than 9" x 12" piece of paper, describing how the <u>Silhouette books make romance come alive for you.</u> Mail via first-class mail to: Harlequin "Silhouette Makes You a Star!" Contest 1308, (in the U.S.) P.O. Box 9069, Buffalo, NY 14269-9069, (in Canada) P.O. Box 637, Fort Erie, Ontario, Canada L2A 5X3. Limit one entry per person.

2. Contests will be judged by a panel of members of the Harlequin editorial, marketing and public relations staff. Fifty percent of criteria will be judged against script and fifty percent will be judged against drawing, photographs and/or magazine cutouts. Judging criteria will be based on the following:

   - Sincerity—25%
   - Originality and Creativity—50%
   - Emotionally Compelling—25%

   In the event of a tie, duplicate prizes will be awarded. Decisions of the judges are final.

3. All entries become the property of Torstar Corp. and may be used for future promotional purposes. Entries will not be returned. No responsibility is assumed for lost, late, illegible, incomplete, inaccurate, nondelivered or misdirected mail.

4. Contest open only to residents of the U.S. <u>(except Puerto Rico)</u> and Canada who are 18 years of age or older, and is void wherever prohibited by law; all applicable laws and regulations apply. Any litigation within the Province of Quebec respecting the conduct or organization of a publicity contest may be submitted to the Régie des alcools, des courses et des jeux for a ruling. Any litigation respecting the awarding of a prize may be submitted to the Régie des alcools, des courses et des jeux only for the purpose of helping the parties reach a settlement. Employees and immediate family members of Torstar Corp. and D. L. Blair, Inc., their affiliates, subsidiaries and all other agencies, entities and persons connected with the use, marketing or conduct of this contest are not eligible to enter. Taxes on prizes are the sole responsibility of the winner. Acceptance of any prize offered constitutes permission to use winner's name, photograph or other likeness for the purposes of advertising, trade and promotion on behalf of Torstar Corp., its affiliates and subsidiaries without further compensation to the winner, unless prohibited by law.

5. Winner will be determined no later than November 30, 2001, and will be notified by mail. Winner will be required to sign and return an Affidavit of Eligibility/Release of Liability/Publicity Release form within 15 days after winner notification. Noncompliance within that time period may result in disqualification and an alternative winner may be selected. All travelers must execute a Release of Liability prior to ticketing and must possess required travel documents (e.g., passport, photo ID) where applicable. Trip must be booked by December 31, 2001, and completed within one year of notification. No substitution of prize permitted by winner. Torstar Corp. and D. L. Blair, Inc., their parents, affiliates and subsidiaries are not responsible for errors in printing of contest, entries and/or game pieces. In the event of printing or other errors that may result in unintended prize values or duplication of prizes, all affected game pieces or entries shall be null and void. **Purchase or acceptance of a product offer does not improve your chances of winning.**

6. Prizes: (1) Grand Prize—A 2-night/3-day trip for two (2) to New York City, including round-trip coach air transportation nearest winner's home and hotel accommodations (double occupancy) at The Plaza Hotel, a glamorous afternoon makeover at a trendy New York spa, $1,000 in U.S. spending money and an opportunity to have a professional photo taken and appear in a Silhouette advertisement (approximate retail value: $7,000). (10) Ten Runner-Up Prizes of gift packages (retail value $50 ea.). Prizes consist of only those items listed as part of the prize. Limit one prize per person. Prize is valued in U.S. currency.

7. For the name of the winner (available after December 31, 2001) send a self-addressed, stamped envelope to: Harlequin "Silhouette Makes You a Star!" Contest 1197 Winners, P.O. Box 4200 Blair, NE 68009-4200 or you may access the www.eHarlequin.com Web site through February 28, 2002.

Contest sponsored by Torstar Corp., P.O Box 9042, Buffalo, NY 14269-9042.

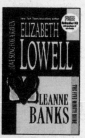

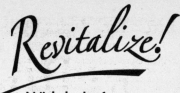